TWO MUST DIE

Novels by

COLIN ROBERTSON

Peter Gayleigh Stories

THE TEMPLE OF DAWN
THE AMAZING CORPSE
ZERO HOUR
ALIBI IN BLACK
EXPLOSION !
TWO MUST DIE
THE DARK KNIGHT
THE DEVIL'S LADY
KNAVES' CASTLE

Other Novels

WHITE MENACE
THE STALKING STRANGER
DEVIL OR SAINT?
NIGHT SHADOWS
SOHO SPY
THE YELLOW STRANGLER
HOUSE OF INTRIGUE
PAINTED FACES
THE MARBLE TOMB MYSTERY
GHOST FINGERS

TWO MUST DIE

A PETER GAYLEIGH STORY

by

COLIN ROBERTSON

WARD, LOCK & CO., LIMITED
LONDON AND MELBOURNE

First published...1946
Reprinted 1948

MADE IN ENGLAND

Printed in England by C. Tinling & Co., Ltd.
Liverpool, London, and Prescot

CONTENTS

CHAP.   PAGE

I   IN WHICH TREVOR MERSON ASKS FOR TROUBLE, AND
     PETER GAYLEIGH PROVIDES IT   .   .   .   7

II   IN WHICH HE INVADES NO MAN'S LAND, AND DAVE
     LYMAN IS A LITTLE DISCOURAGED   .   .   21

III IN WHICH HE ACQUIRES AN APPRENTICE, AND
     ENTERTAINS A LESS ATTRACTIVE ALLY .   .   34

IV   IN WHICH TREVOR MERSON MOVES ON, AND PETER
     IS UNAVOIDABLY DETAINED   .   .   .   53

V   IN WHICH HE VISITS PINEWOOD, AND HIS DEPARTURE
     IS ACCELERATED BY SPORTSMEN WITH UNKIND
     IDEAS   64

VI   IN WHICH HE INVITES HIMSELF TO A PARTY, AND
     TREVOR MERSON ISSUES ANOTHER INVITATION   85

VII IN WHICH MARCIA LAWSON SEEKS EXCITEMENT,
     AND GETS MORE THAN SHE ANTICIPATED   .   109

VIII IN WHICH JERVIS GRANT PRODUCES WHISKY, AND
     PETER GAYLEIGH SLEEPS IT OFF   .   .   132

IX   IN WHICH HE MAKES A STATEMENT, AND
     HERRINGTON HAS THE LAST WORD   .   .   150

X   IN WHICH LARRY BECKET BROADCASTS, AND PETER
     TUNES IN TO SONA BOYD   170

XI   IN WHICH MILES LAWSON SPRINGS A SURPRISE, AND
     DAVE LYMAN JOINS THE PARTY .   .   .   190

XII IN WHICH THE SUN SETS, AND JUSTICE IS DONE   . 203

     EPILOGUE   219

CHAPTER ONE

IN WHICH TREVOR MERSON ASKS FOR TROUBLE, AND PETER GAYLEIGH PROVIDES IT

I

THE girl with the hopeful eyes appeared unexpectedly at the top of the companion-way, and Peter Gayleigh stifled a groan. This time there could be no escape, he realised. The huntress had sighted her quarry.

"Oh, hullo!" she exclaimed, and with a diffidence that was as false as it was exasperating, for he knew she had worked very hard to bring about this conversational gambit.

"Hullo, yourself," he returned ungraciously.

There was amusement and quiet satisfaction in her gaze.

"Are you going somewhere?"

"I was!"

"You're Mr. Munroe, aren't you?"

He did not deny it, since he was travelling under that name, and for the very good reason that his own had frequently added sparkle to the newspaper headlines, and was apt to attract unwanted attention. He had dallied with the police of two continents, a quip on his lips, and mockery in his eyes, and though, nowadays, he rarely clashed with the law, he was not above burnishing the lance of adventure on the pate of officialdom. Had it become known that the notorious Peter Gayleigh was aboard *S.S. Cornelius* he would have had about as much privacy as an exhibit in an aquarium. Yet, even although he had avoided that, his lean, handsome face had attracted a ubiquitous manhunter, this very persistent girl, whom he had found it quite impossible to avoid.

She came down the companion-way towards him, her slim body rippling the satin of her evening gown. She was a natural blonde with intriguing dark blue eyes and a devastating smile, but Peter Gayleigh saw only a designing female

7

determined to plunge, and with as little delay as possible, into the emotional shallows of a shipboard romance.

"My name is Gordon—Marcia Gordon," she told him.

"Some other time, Miss Gordon."

He was turning away when she placed a hand on his arm.

"But I want to talk to you."

"That," he said wearily, "is very obvious."

"Is it? I rather hoped it would be." Impishness danced in those dark eyes as she flashed him a coquettish smile. "I'm lonely. I've been alone all night."

"Too bad! My heart bleeds for you."

"You're not very friendly, are you?"

"That's putting it mildly. I'd hoped I was being rude."

The mobile lips quivered into a little grimace.

"You are . . . extremely rude. But I can take it. When one has been alone all night . . ."

"Please!" he implored quickly. "Don't give me that again. We both know that you wouldn't have been alone if I hadn't sought temporary refuge in the smoking-room."

"You mean you made up that four at bridge just to escape me."

"Just to escape you," he echoed. "A forlorn hope! As a matter of interest, Miss Gordon, why are you making a dead set at me?"

"Oh I don't know." She was not in the least abashed. "Perhaps it's the sea air. It affects quite respectable girls in all sorts of ways, you know."

"Apparently! Ever since I came on board you've been following me around—stalking me would perhaps be more correct."

"And you've been taking evasive action."

"In self-defence. Frankly I haven't found it amusing. I'm not partial to childish games or girlish exuberance. To put it very bluntly—why don't you go away and leave me alone?"

But it was useless as he realised immediately. It seemed impossible to snub this girl.

"Of course I knew you'd be difficult. Handsome men usually are. I expected that."

"Now listen, my child," said Peter mordantly. "Despite this very modern approach, this apparent lack of all decent reserve, anyone with half an eye can see that you're what is known as a good girl . . ."

"How perfectly delicious! Go on."

". . . and girls of your sort should be in bed by this time, not prowling about in search of erotic distraction. It is after one o'clock. You must be tired. I hope to God you *are* tired! Now why not call it a day?"

Her mouth quivered again. She was enjoying his irritation. He looked at the smooth white skin of her throat and arms, and wondered where she hid the rhinoceros hide.

"Well it's an idea," she said presently. "After all we're only twelve hours out from New York. There's plenty of time."

"Good night, Miss Gordon," he said very firmly, and strode quickly past her and up the companion-way towards the promenade deck. The business on which he was very intent did not lie in that direction, but it must wait, he decided, until this incorrigible romanticist was safely in bed. He emerged on to the deck, glanced back over his shoulder, and heaved a sigh of thankfulness. For the time being it seemed that he had shaken her off.

Save for a couple of men smoking final cigars the deck was deserted, the flood of light from the main lounge extinguished. Peter lit a cigarette, inhaling deeply as he stared over the dark swell of the sea merging into a canopy of stars. Southampton—London in four more days! Once again he had added to his stock of memories. American hospitality, he reflected, was no half-hearted gesture. At times it was rather overwhelming, for it was only by exercising a great deal of tact that he was not returning with a variety of things—including a sports-car and a cocktail-cabinet—pressed upon him by American friends. Such generosity was embarrassing in its bigheartedness, but it was not something that was easily forgotten, or something he wanted to forget.

He finished his cigarette, and lighting another made his way up to the games-deck, where he turned facing the wind, breathing in its invigorating saltiness. So might a pirate have stood searching for floating plunder. For though he wore a tuxedo, the lines of the lean, determined face, the square almost truculent set of the muscular shoulders, gave strength to this comparison. On occasions, and despite all his lighthearted insolence, he had been called the dangerous Mr. Gayleigh. And it was necessary that a fellow-passenger, a half-caste Indian, with whom he had played cards that evening should be taught a lesson.

For Trevor Merson had taken him for a fool, and what rankled most was that he had actually fallen for that elegant gentleman's very elementary line of graft.

"Which just goes to prove," he reflected bitterly, "that the precepts of adolescence are pretty sound. One should never play cards with strangers—unless one has a stacked deck!"

There were few tricks employed by the professional card sharp with which he was not familiar, though usually he disdained to make easy money in that way. On this occasion he had played a strictly honest game. And there lay the rub. For though he would have detected any sharp practice during play, Merson had succeeded in duping him during the settling up. That misguided individual had lost fifty dollars, and had asked Peter if he could change a five hundred dollar bill. Peter had given him the difference in good money and had received, as he had discovered afterwards in his cabin, a beautiful example of the forger's art. A state of affairs which would be remedied just as soon as he could talk to this enterprising grafter without fear of interruption. He was not to know that once again Fate was cocking a beckoning finger, and that this comparative trivial incident was the climbing rope to further peaks of adventure.

He thought of the other two men who had made up the four at bridge. There was Larry Becket, the young American correspondent, travelling to Europe on behalf of one of the big American broadcasting networks. A likeable guy, if ever there was one, very intelligent, making pots of money—lecture tours, books, articles for well-known journals, all came his way—but doing his job for its own sake, for the excitement it offered. His name had been on the lips of the world during the War when the familiar phrase "This is Larry Becket speaking from SHAEF"—or from somewhere in north-west Europe, Italy, or the Pacific theatre—had thrilled millions of listeners. Everyone, of course, knew he was aboard, and he had been lionised as one would expect. But he was the same eager and unaffected Larry whom Peter had met in Washington some years before. Nothing hidden, nothing phoney about Larry Becket.

Then there was Lyman. "Call me Dave" seemed to be his signature tune, though in other respects he was somewhat reticent. A stockily built man of perhaps fifty with a heavy, jowled face, he might at one stage of his career have been a doorman at a honky tonk, a prizefighter, or a bootlegger. Even now he might be a racketeer, or the solidly aggressive brand of self-made business man that flourished in the States, or almost anything between these two extremes. He just didn't say. But there was no doubt that he was interested in Trevor Merson, although, it appeared, they had first met on board only a few hours before. Very little escaped Peter Gayleigh, and he had noticed the surreptitious way in which Lyman had eyed the Indian during the game.

He pondered this for some time, his cigarette glowing brightly in the wind, before he decided that he had waited long enough. The girl must surely have retired for the night. It was unlikely that he would run into her again. The promenade deck was completely deserted when he descended to C deck and made his way very purposefully towards Trevor Merson's cabin. He knew exactly where it was, for he had taken the trouble to acquire that information earlier. It was now after two a.m., and he saw no one until he was turning into the alleyway in which the cabin was actually situated.

There was no reason why he should have paused and darted back hurriedly at sight of a steward. That alone would not have deterred him. But although he caught only a glimpse of the man, it was enough to arouse his interest. For the other was approaching rather furtively, glancing back as he did so, as though afraid of being seen. Peter's interest was still further aroused when, peering into the alley-way again, he saw the man stop before Merson's cabin. He tapped gently on the door. It was opened almost immediately, and he vanished inside.

Peter remained where he was until, less than a couple of minutes later, the door opened again. The steward came out, walking backwards, and grasping one end of a large cabin-trunk. The other end was supported by Merson himself. He appeared in the alley-way, then lowered the trunk to the floor for a moment, locking the cabin door behind him. Very slowly, and as quietly as possible, the two men carried their burden from the direction from which the steward had come, edged it round a corner, and disappeared from sight.

Peter glided after them, moving with that soft-footed speed that had often served him in good stead. When he saw them again they were approaching a companion-way, which they ascended laboriously. It led to the promenade deck, and when Peter reached the top of the companion-way they had set the trunk down near one of the smaller lounges facing to starboard.

There was no sound, other than the deep, rhythmic breathing of the ship as it ploughed its way through the night, and when the steward spoke to Merson in a breathless whisper Gayleigh caught the words without much difficulty.

" I'd like to get this job finished with," he was saying anxiously. " I ain't a bit happy about it."

" For God's sake stop whining !" Merson snarled savagely. " Fifty dollars—just to dispose of some old junk. Isn't it worth it ?"

" I ain't grousing about the money, sir. But this cabin-trunk—it ain't natural to dump it overboard. I wish I hadn't got mixed up in this !"

" Oh shut up !" was the curt response. " All right. Come on."

The steward responded with scared alacrity. They edged towards the side of the ship, hoisted the trunk, and rested it for a moment on the rail. Then at a grunt from Merson it was thrust overboard. Peter heard the splash, and before the other two turned back towards the companion-way, darted round the side of the lounge.

What was in that trunk ? The macabre atmosphere had stimulated his imagination, but he refused to let it run rife. He could be sure of nothing beyond what he had actually seen, though he felt the trunk must contain something of an incriminating nature, otherwise Merson would not have disposed of it in that way and at such a time. Also he had good cause to know that Merson was a crook.

But what he did not realise was that someone else had witnessed this very unusual proceeding. A motionless figure was standing in the shadows only a few yards from Peter Gayleigh.

Dave Lyman's heavy face was quite expressionless, though his eyes were half-veiled. He was very interested in Trevor Merson.

"Quite," said Peter gaily. " . . . a little late. But better late than never. You're on your last council."
" . . . I've tried reading.

Gayleigh saw the two men disappear below deck and kindled a cigarette. It seemed this trip was not going to be so boring as he had imagined. Out over the water the moon had dipped behind a leaden cloud, so that his surroundings were as dark as his thoughts as he walked to the rail, leaning with his back towards it. And he was conscious of something deep down inside him, a premonition that he had often experienced before. This was the beginning of another adventure which would lead him once again through the dark labyrinths of crime. He knew it intuitively. The prologue was over. The play was about to begin. It was already written, and nothing he did would change it. It just had to be.

He had no intention of putting off his talk with Merson. What would happen after that he didn't know, but he had never been dissatisfied with the parts he had been given, and he felt he could leave that to fate. He contemplated the glowing tip of his cigarette, and crushing it under his heel decided that by now Merson must have paid off the steward. The time seemed propitious for a little plain speaking. Still unaware of the man who was watching him intently he returned to C deck, and this time met no one as he approached the cabin.

He had to knock twice before the door was opened. And evidently Merson had just slipped on his dressing-gown—an ornate silken garment which might have been worn by a Maharajah—for he was still fumbling with the belt as he frowned apprehensively.

" Hullo, Merson ! " Peter produced his most dangerous smile. " Mind if I come in ? "

" Sorry, Munroe. I'm just going to bed."

" I don't think so," said Peter. " I want to have a talk with you, Merson. If you're reasonable it won't take long."

The other stared very intently into those chilly blue eyes, then lowered his own quickly.

" I don't want to seem inhospitable, but it's after two o'clock."

" Quite," said Peter gently. " It is a little late. But better late than never. You're up pretty late yourself."

" I've been reading."

" You don't say! Improving your mind no doubt. It certainly needs it. I'm getting tired of standing out here, Merson."

He waited expectantly. The other avoided his gaze, but made no move to invite him inside.

" Well?" he pursued. " Are you going to remember your manners, or must I forget mine?"

Still no response. He placed the flat of his hand against the other's chest and pushed him very firmly back into the cabin.

" Now look here, Munroe . . . !"

Peter stepped smartly inside and shut the door.

" Apparently you haven't read ' What every gentleman should know,' " he remarked very softly. " I was afraid you hadn't. That's really why I've called. Before I leave I hope we shall both see eye to eye as regards the niceties of social conduct. I hate violence, if y'see what I mean."

Merson stared at him balefully. The dressing-gown accentuated his litheness and his sloping shoulders; the cream cuffs the dark tint of his finger nails. His hands, with long slender fingers, were almost white, as were the thin, sullen features. He was tolerably good looking, but the furtive chocolate-coloured eyes, and the tight set of his lips now reminded Gayleigh of a hawk.

He was in no hurry. He surveyed the cabin appreciatively, his gaze resting on a most unusual ornament on the wall. A bizarre and colourful object very much out of place amidst the other tasteful, but very sober furnishings. It was a sword, obviously of Eastern workmanship, and just as obviously it had been hung there by Merson himself. A strip of green leather attached to the hilt and the blade held it in position.

" You've made yourself quite at home, I see," said Peter.

He stepped towards it, inspecting it with interest. The handwrought blade was two edged and about two feet in length, dull and unpliable, and there was some writing in Eastern characters inscribed upon it. But it was the hilt, lacquered in a variety of vivid colours which had attracted his attention. For at first glance it seemed to sparkle with a fortune in precious stones—diamonds the uninitiated might have thought, incongruously out of place in that garish setting. But they were not diamonds, as he realised almost immediately, for he was a connoisseur in such matters. They had neither the purity nor the scintillating splendour of such gems. They were white sapphires, fairly large but inferior stones such as could be picked up in the East Indies for less than a tenth of the price of diamonds of similar size. Nevertheless the sword was not a trumpery object. As a curio it was something any collector would have been glad to possess, and it must have been of considerable value.

"H'm, very interesting. Where did you get this?"

"In Borneo," said Merson shortly.

"So you've been out there," Peter returned conversationally.

"Yes . . . trading."

"You must be very proud of this sword."

The other merely shrugged. Peter eyed him askance. He put his hand into his pocket, and produced the forged note.

"I daresay you're proud of this, too."

Merson hesitated for a fraction of a second.

"I don't know what you mean."

"Don't you?" A crooked smile formed about Peter Gayleigh's lips. Merson was going to be difficult. Very difficult he hoped. He had waited quite a long time for this show down. It would be disappointing if there was no opportunity for good clean fun. "Don't you?" he said again. "I rather think you do." He flicked the note with his finger nail. "Surely you remember this, Merson?"

"I remember I asked you to change me a five hundred dollar bill, if that's what you mean."

"Quite," said Peter patiently. "This is it."

"Well?"

"Perhaps you'd like to examine it."

He handed it to Merson, who took it with a puzzled frown, looked at it, and glanced up questioningly again.

"It's a forgery," said Peter. "Didn't you know?"

"A forgery!" He examined the note carefully, holding

it up to the light. He was good. He played the part beautifully. "Yes—yes, it is a forgery," he admitted presently.
"But, of course, this isn't the note I gave you."

Peter looked at him admiringly. Merson was more than
good. He was very good.

"So that's the way, it is! So you're going to deny that you
bit me for five hundred dollars."

The man stared at him in outraged astonishment. One
might have thought that he was mortally offended.

"Do I understand that you are seriously accusing me——"

"Yes, brother, I am," Peter cut in unequivocally. "I
wasn't born yesterday, Merson. You pulled a fast one on me.
I know it. You know it. The question is, what are you
going to do about it? You'd better do something pretty
quick, otherwise I might get really sore."

"You can do what the hell you like," was the harsh
rejoinder. "I didn't pass you that note. You'll not intimi-
date me."

"Bud," marvelled Peter, "you're really asking for it, aren't
you. Suppose I take this little bit of evidence to the captain?"

"Go ahead. It's your word against mine." The thin lips
twisted into a sneer. "And my word might carry a lot of
weight."

There was something in his voice which made Peter look
at him keenly.

"Oh?"

"So I shouldn't be too impulsive if I were you."

"And just what do you mean by that?"

"I mean you've been caught on the wrong foot, Mr.
Munroe, or should I say—Peter Gayleigh!"

Peter's brows came together, and a less misguided man than
Trevor Merson would not only have seen but thought twice
before challenging the cold gleam, like sunlight on arctic
wastes, which had now appeared in those steely eyes. Instead,
Merson produced an automatic from his dressing-gown,
levelling the barrel swiftly.

"Now get out," he snapped. "I've had just about enough
of you."

"So you won't play," said Peter. "Smart guy, eh?"

"You heard me. Get out. Scram."

"Well, of course, if that's the way you feel I don't have

much choice." He gave a disconsolate shrug, and turned towards the door. Then, as though two very powerful springs had been concealed in his shoes, he leapt backwards against Merson, hurling him across the cabin. Completely off his balance he staggered against the far wall. Peter swung round, kicked the gun from the feebly waving hand, and snatched the weapon up from the floor.

"As I was saying," he said easily. "I don't have much choice. Now why don't you be a *good* boy?"

He spun the gun between his fingers, looked at it depreciatingly, and tossed it on to the bed.

"Okay. Try and get it—if you've got the guts."

No one could have said that Merson didn't try. He came at Gayleigh like a wrestler bouncing off the ropes. And if Peter didn't hit him with the pail, the effect was just as catastrophic. He stopped very suddenly at the end of a beautifully timed right, and blinked foolishly. Then as Gayleigh whipped his left across, crashing it against the unprotected jaw, Trevor Merson found himself looking in an entirely unexpected direction. The musical comedy dressing-gown sank slowly to the floor with a very sick man inside it.

Peter massaged his knuckles, and gazed down at him speculatively.

"Someone ought to have told you," he said sadly. "Never lead with your chin, feller. Now do I get five hundred dollars, or do you want Lesson Two?"

He didn't feel very clever. It had been much too simple, almost like hitting a defenceless child. Mr. Merson might be an optimist and a third rate crook, but he had evidently neglected a very important part of his education. He just didn't know how to mix it.

Peter bent over him, and yanking him to his feet pushed him into a chair.

"Well, anyway, you did try," he said. "And as the other looked at him with lack-lustre eyes. " I believe the Yogis tell us that striving is attainment. You should know that in your part of the world. But it doesn't quite mean what you seem to think."

Ignoring the other's sullen gaze he went to the wardrobe. He found Merson's jacket on a hanger. There was a wallet in the inside pocket stuffed with paper money and he had begun to count the notes when Merson made another ill-considered dash for the gun. At the same time his legs got inextricably mixed up with Peter Gayleigh's foot, and once again his face made very forcible contact with the carpet. Peter moved towards the bed, and slipped the automatic into his pocket.

"There's nothing like perseverence. But don't carry it too far. Get up."

He waited tolerantly until the man got to his feet, then with a significant movement of his forefinger indicated the chair. Merson sat down again, glaring at him malignantly.

"Don't worry, I shan't keep you much longer."

He dropped his eyes to the notes, completed his arithmetic, pocketed five hundred dollars, and dropped the wallet fastidiously on to the bed.

"I guess that's all for now," he said. "Better mix yourself a drink. You look as though you could do with it. Or shall we call it quits and have a spot together?"

"Damn you, get out!" snarled Merson. "Get out! *Get out!*"

"Tch! Tch! Such temper. I suppose it must be the bastard in you."

He opened the door, and tapped the gun in his pocket.

"I'll keep this as a memento, bud. It would be just too bad if I let you have it, and it went off while my back was turned. Good morning—and next time consider your sucker before you bite it."

III

Alone in the cabin, Trevor Merson felt he was not above taking some of Gayleigh's advice. He mixed himself a strong whisky and soda, gulped it down, and having replenished the glass lifted his smouldering gaze to the sword on the wall. Death had fashioned that blade, and some day Gayleigh might learn its sinister secret. The thought afforded him grim satisfaction. It was true that he had suffered a minor setback. Very foolishly he had tried to make some quick money. But it would have flattered his pride if he had succeeded, for he had thought the notorious Peter Gayleigh was much overrated. He had had a contempt for him—the contempt of the weak for the strong. He knew now that he had made a mistake, though he was not unduly depressed, for this incident paled into insignificance when he thought of the Greater Plan, the spring of gold that sword could tap.

The blade with its vast potentialities carried him back to his childhood. He was the son of a woman of mixed European and Indian blood and a low caste Hindoo. His mother had been a servant in an English household, and like most women of her kind had hoped to marry a white man. Instead, and when very determined efforts had failed, she had accepted a native servant in the same ménage. Distrusted and despised by her husband's relations she had borne him a child, a son almost as white as his English grandfather. The man who now called himself Trevor Merson had been an object of scorn, despised, as long as he could remember, by natives and whites alike.

He thought of the *chawl,* the one-roomed apartment with the veranda, where he had spent his early childhood, and where he had taken a delight in mouthing the coarsest oaths to be found in Hindi. Always a rebel and ashamed of his half-caste blood, he had run away to a missionary school, where he had learned enough English to become a professional letter writer, squatting in the market places. From this he had graduated to a pedlar, selling cloth to low caste Indian women, and listening avidly to the gossip inseparable from his trade. He had picked up useful scraps of information which had enabled him to carry out several small robberies, some of which unfortunately had been detected.

At twenty his prison record was inclined to hamper further progress. So he had shipped as a seaman on the P. and O. boats, and as a lascar had travelled widely. Acquaintance with the east end of London, the doss houses and vice, had merely been experience on the road to easy money which perpetually eluded him. During this period he had pulled off several small coups, but nothing that fulfilled his ambitious aspirations. He was over thirty when he became a merchant once again, though on a higher plane than before. He had sold Indian cloths to the Straits Settlements. And it was while he was in Brunei in North Borneo that he had acquired the sword.

It had been given to him by a Dyak chief after a ritual staged to celebrate a deal. (He had traded gaudy cloth for white sapphires of infinitely greater value). He would never forget the festive dance inspired by the witch-doctor; the torchlight bronzing the bodies of the half-naked warriors as they advanced slowly, swaying and writhing to the native music; those spurting flares of light shimmering on their swords as they brandished them above their heads, their bodies protected by the oblong shields; the clash of steel as they sprang into the air leaping murderously at one another. Miraculously, all of them had managed to protect their heads which, it had seemed, might be severed at any moment.

The dance had finally subsided when a wretched captive from a neighbouring tribe had been flung into the circle cf light. The witch-doctor, clad in a skirt of gold tinsel, and liberally festooned in gold coins, had come forward, unrecognisable beneath a grotesque and bestial headdress. The length of his finger-nails had been increased to a horrifying extent with lions' claws. Resting on the tips of these was the sword.

After the inevitable posturing and writhing he paused before the captive, to whom he offered the weapon. At first the man had refused to take it, until his hands were forcibly raised by two of the warriors. The blade was laid across the upturned palms, and the dance was resumed again. Suddenly the witch-doctor snatched the sword, but to Merson's surprise, for he had seen these rituals before, it was not plunged into the breast of the captive. The music and the barbarous dance continued, the warriors swirling faster and faster round the terrified man.

Then fully half an hour after handling the sword he sank to the ground, to expire in horrible convulsions.

There was no real magic in his death as Merson learnt afterwards when the chief presented him with the sword. The blade was impregnated with a native poison which seeped through the skin of anyone who held it. A devilish weapon, and one that Merson hoped to put to further use. Already it had played its part in the Greater Plan, claiming its first victim, while in Merson's possession, aboard *S.S. Cornelius.*

The body was no longer on board. It had been a very heavy cabin-trunk.

CHAPTER TWO

IN WHICH HE INVADES NO MAN'S LAND, AND DAVE LYMAN IS A LITTLE DISCOURAGED

I

PETER GAYLEIGH paced the promenade deck at eight o'clock that morning with all the appearance of a man who found life pretty good. He was wearing immaculate grey flannels and a loosely fitting but elegantly tailored sports jacket, and he meant to enjoy himself, though not quite in the way his fellow passengers might have imagined. Less than six hours sleep had sufficed to impart a springiness to his step and a renewed spur to his intention. The slight contretemps with Merson and the mystery of the cabin-trunk had given a flavour to this trip, which, he had feared, might be chiefly notable for many exasperating games of hide-and-seek with a maddening flirtatious blonde. But now there were distinct possibilities, and as he felt this mood should be encouraged, he made his way down to C deck, and to that part of the ship with which he was now very familiar.

It was an hour when stewards were much in evidence, but though he passed several of them, he had to hang about for a time before he saw the one for whom he was looking. The man was carrying a breakfast tray and disappeared into one of the cabins as Peter caught sight of him. He waited until his quarry emerged into the alley-way again, then accosted him brightly.

" Good morning, steward."

" Good morning, sir."

It was the conventional reply, and the man would have walked past him if Peter hadn't barred the way.

" You look very tired this morning," he observed, scrutinising the weak face. " I take a great interest in my fellow men. What time did you get to bed?"

The steward looked at him shiftily. He didn't quite know how to take this remark.

" Rather late I'm afraid, sir. But that ain't unusual."

Peter flicked ash negligently from his cigarette, the gesture thwarting the other's attempt to edge past him.

" It must have been after two a.m." he said reflectively. " And after quite a strenuous spot of work on your part. I— er—hope Mr. Merson paid you the fifty dollars?"

The steward swallowed heavily. All thoughts of eccentric humanitarians suggested by Gayleigh's opening remarks, were rudely dispelled.

" I—I don't understand, sir."

" Come, come!" chided Peter. " I saw you lug the trunk to the promenade deck. I was padding along behind, observing the good work. I also saw you heave it over the side."

There was a pause, the weak face presenting a picture of dismay. He cast a furtive glance over his shoulder, then lowered his voice.

" Are you a friend of Mr. Merson's, sir?"

" Hardly! I just happened to be around." Then in the same casual tone : " Do you know what was inside that trunk?"

The steward's mouth twitched. He stared into those lazy but very cold blue eyes and sensed that evasion would be futile.

" No, sir, I don't," he blurted out suddenly. " And that's the truth. Mr. Merson told me he wanted to get rid of some old junk, and asked me to help him——"

" In the early hours of the morning!"

" Yes, sir." He glanced over his shoulder again. " Course I knew there must be something fishy about it. But—well I didn't see no real harm in it, so I took a chance. I hope you ain't going to report it, sir?"

Peter merely looked at him.

" It's as much as my job's worth, sir," he whined desperately.

" H'm. You should have thought of that before. It's a bit late now, with Merson's bribe in your pocket."

" Strike me pink, I wish I'd never touched it! Straight I do. I've been wondering all night what was in that trunk. D'you know anything about Mr. Merson, sir?"

" Nothing more than you're thinking," said Peter. " And

if you're right you're an accessory after the fact, my friend. Don't forget that."

Judging from his expression there was not much likelihood that he would.

"If I were you I wouldn't repeat this conversation to Mr. Merson."

"No, sir."

"Otherwise I might say a few words myself."

"I understand, sir. And thank you, sir."

His cringing relief brought a disparaging twist to Peter's lips. There was nothing to be gained by prolonging the conversation, and stepping aside he dismissed the man with a curt nod. Very obviously this spiritless creature knew no more than himself. He watched him scurry away, mopping his brow with a handkerchief, then strolled back the way he had come. Breakfast, he felt, was indicated.

It was some distance to the saloon, and he was about to turn off one of the main alley-ways when he saw Merson appear at the other end. He began to approach slowly, deep in thought, his gaze on the floor. And he had not taken more than a few steps when the stocky American, Dave Lyman, turned the corner. He saw the other and hastened forward, greeting him with a hearty slap on the back which aroused him from his reverie with disconcerting suddenness. Anyone but Peter Gayleigh might have seen nothing unusual in this boisterous reunion. But recalling what he had noticed during the card game on the previous night he sensed that Lyman was acting a part.

As yet neither of them had seen him, and he suddenly decided that he would very much like to hear what they were saying. He looked quickly about him, but there was nowhere in that bare corridor where he could listen without being seen. Unless . . .

There was a door on his right. It was, he realised one of the doors to a suite. The apartment beyond might be empty : on the other hand it might not, and another man would have paused before taking the risk. But Gayleigh was not one to visualise difficulties before they arose. He tried the door, found it was unlocked, and pushing it open, peered quickly inside. A pair of dainty red sandals were lying on the carpet near a bed on which a white linen dress had been carelessly tossed. Elaborate toilet articles also indicated the sex of the occupant. But she was not there now.

Peter darted inside, and almost closing the door, stationed himself behind it.

The words he heard as the two men approached were not very promising.

" ——used to play most nights at Freddie's saloon on 52nd Street," Lyman was saying. "Bunch of right guys, too. I reckon we put down more liquor than a distillery. Now there's a game for you. Poker. Yeah, give me poker every time."

"Very interesting," muttered Merson in his precise, cultivated accent. "I prefer bridge myself."

"No, feller, you gotta hand it to poker. That's my game."

"I still prefer bridge."

"Aw shucks. Now listen . . . "

Peter was doing just that, but he felt he wasn't having much luck. By no stretch of the imagination could it be called intriguing dialogue. If it had been broadcast to the world not even a radio monitor could have found anything incriminating in it. He sighed as the two men passed out of earshot, Lyman still expatiating with boring insistence on this momentous topic.

And then:

"Well, make up your mind," said a girl's voice behind him. "Are you coming or going?"

Peter swung round in time to catch a glimpse of nicely filled cami-knickers and silk stockings fast disappearing beneath a silk robe. The rest of her he recognised as Marcia Gordon.

"Pardon my confusion," she went on coolly, doing some quick work with the girdle. "This is really so sudden."

"I suppose it had to be you," he said bleakly. "Lady I'm sorry. And that, I may say, comes from the bottom of my heart."

"You know, I felt you had plenty of initiative," she pursued chidingly. "But don't you think you're overdoing the Romeo business. Sneaking in on a girl at this time of the morning and in the hope of seeing a strip-tease act——" She shook her head in mock reproach.

"I've already said I'm sorry."

"All right. Don't stand at the door. Come right in. Don't

worry about me. I only dress here." Then, as she looked at him archly : " How did you know this was my cabin?"

" I didn't."

" Oh really, Mr. Munroe ! How can you say that. You just barged in hoping for the best. And if I hadn't seen you first you might have got quite an eyeful."

It was not often that Peter Gayleigh stared at anyone balefully, but he managed it very successfully now.

" Out of hundreds of cabins on this ship I had to choose yours !"

" Perhaps it's the magnetism in me," she suggested. " Sit down and make yourself at home. I don't think it's likely that father will come in. If he does I'll introduce you as my boy friend."

" That's fine ! If you don't mind I think I'll be going."

" If you do," said Marcia Gordon. " I shall take off my wrap and scream. And I don't mean maybe."

Peter eyed her askance. She didn't look that sort of girl. She had the appearance of a lady. But the firm set of her lips, and the disturbing light in those dark eyes made him pause uncertainly.

" You'd do that?"

" Huh-huh. Just try to go. You'll see."

" Very well." He was still looking at her as he opened the door another couple of inches. Her hands went to the girdle of her robe as she took a deep breath. He shut the door very quickly.

" All right. All right," he said, raising his hand placatingly. " So you weren't bluffing."

She released her breath slowly and triumphantly.

" I told you I wasn't."

" Okay. You've made your point. What happens now?"

" Suppose we have a cigarette," she suggested. And as he shrugged and came towards her : " Remember I can still scream if you don't behave yourself." She was eyeing him warily, and for the first time Peter smiled.

" Marcia, you astound me !"

" I'm not quite such a fool as I may seem."

" I'm glad to hear it !"

" But I'm determined that you and I are going to be very friendly during this trip." She dipped her cigarette into the flame of his lighter. "And now you know what you're up against. I've been very lonely, but I don't intend to stay that way."

"I've seen a lot of nice young fellows on this ship," said Peter helpfully, but she shook her head.

"No, they won't do. It's got to be you."

"I was afraid of that."

"All I'm asking is that you talk to me. After all it isn't much. I'm not so repulsive, am I?"

He took in the blonde cluster of curls, a little disarranged but nestling attractively against the finely shaped head; the delicately moulded and distinctive features. The fresh redness of her lips and the creaminess of her skin owed nothing to make-up, for she had not had time to put any on.

"No. I'd say you look pretty good—at a distance."

"I look pretty good in close up, too. Anyway you'd better get used to looking at me. Because before I let you leave this cabin you're going to promise that you'll stop treating me like a bad smell."

She held out her hand, the dark eyes half-veiled as she stared at him very intently, and with an expression that he couldn't quite fathom. She might be hiding something, but if so it wasn't girlish foolishness. He supposed she must be in her middle twenties, but that look alone told him she was far from being an adolescent. He wondered why she had behaved like one when he had first met her.

She said: "Come on, Peter. Let's make a deal."

She was still staring at him with that Mona Lisa smile when he took the cool slender fingers in his, grasping them firmly. Very slowly he nodded his head.

"Splendid! You can go now. Somehow I don't think you'll try any more disappearing tricks. But if you do—" She broke off meeting his gaze mockingly. "Get it—Peter?"

"I get it," he said grimly. "*Au revoir,* my sweet."

He stepped into the alley-way, and closing the door remained staring at it thoughtfully for a few seconds. He couldn't be absolutely certain, though he was certain enough . . . She had called him "Peter" a name he never used with Munroe. And she had done so very deliberately.

She seemed to be a very discerning girl.

II

There were four of them at the small breakfast-table—the broadcasting correspondent, Larry Becket, Dave Lyman, and last but not least the girl Sona.

Peter Gayleigh had discovered that Sona Boyd was on board shortly after the liner had left New York, and had asked to be placed at the same table. He hadn't seen Sona since she was a child. She was now almost nineteen, and but for her name he wouldn't have known who she was. He supposed he, too, must have changed a great deal during those intervening years, for when he introduced himself as Munroe she had not recognised him. But in response to a little discreet probing at dinner on the previous night he had learnt that her step-father, Jervis Grant, had returned to Europe on an earlier boat, answering the call of urgent business, and leaving Sona to follow later.

Peter hadn't known that Grant had been in New York, but meeting this girl provided a very pleasant link with the past. For he had met her step-father some twelve years before. He was a diamond-broker of international repute, and shortly before Peter had made his acquaintance had given the police information which had led to the arrest of a gang of jewel thieves. Some diamonds had come into his possession, and with his expert knowledge he had recognised them as part of the proceeds of a robbery carried out many months before. He had informed Scotland Yard at once, and as Detective Sergeant Herrington, as he then was, had been one of the police officers assigned to the case, Peter had followed it with considerable interest. He had been at Cambridge with Dick Herrington, and afterwards they had shared a flat together—until it had gradually dawned on the future Chief-Inspector that there was much more behind Peter Gayleigh than met the eye. He had been with Herrington when they met Grant, with whom he had become quite friendly.

But he had not seen Sona since she was six years old, a snub-nosed, vivacious but rather dumpy child, very different from the charming sprite she had become. Yet in a beauty contest he doubted whether she would have been noticed, for her nose was still a trifle retroussé, and her mouth was too large. Sona's beauty lay in her personality. Her charm was something inherent that could not be assessed. She was a gay, almost elfin little creature, brimming over with sheer *joie-de-vivre*. There was neither timidity nor boldness in the direct glance of those clear wide-spaced eyes as she listened to Larry Becket, nothing but healthy exuberance in the easy laughter coming so naturally from the generously modelled lips. She was wearing white shorts and a woolly jersey to match, the chic simplicity accentuating her daintiness, but one felt that her clothes didn't matter. She was a fairy, a sunbeam come to life. Sona, the Gaelic word for happy. How aptly she had been named, he thought. There was no room for guile or deceit in such a nature. Sincerity was printed on every feature of that joyous face.

Larry Becket, too, it would seem, had quickly fallen under her spell. They were discussing trivialities so intently that Peter found himself stifling a smile. Larry had knocked around the world quite a bit. He must have met many charming women, but judging from his expression none so wonderful as Sona Boyd.

" I met that guy Merson this morning," said Lyman suddenly, cramming buttered toast into his capacious mouth. " I bin telling him we ought to form a poker school."

" It's an idea," murmured Peter. He wondered if Lyman played poker better than he did bridge. He had partnered him on the previous night, and had struggled vainly to comprehend his maddeningly unorthodox play.

" I'll say it's an idea," said Lyman, chewing prodigiously. "But Merson don't see it that way. Poker is better'n bridge any day. I'm fond of poker," he added, making his point, and looking wistfully into space like a bloodhound deprived of its favourite bone.

He had a lot more to say on this subject, and a quarter of an hour later Peter felt he must have heard pretty well all there was to tell about Dave Lyman's poker-life. It was a very ordinary story of unbeatable hands which miraculously *were* beaten, and after a time he contrived to stimulate interest without listening very much. He noticed that Marcia Gordon was sitting at a nearby table, and catching her eye looked away quickly. Merson was breakfasting alone and

very glumly at the far end of the saloon. No doubt he had
plenty to brood over.

"Y'know," Lyman resumed after a short silence which Peter
had scarcely noticed, "I gotten a hunch I've seen your face
before, Munroe." He screwed up his heavy brows in a
tremendous effort of recollection. "Yeah it's kinda familiar.
Ever been in Texas?"

Peter shook his head.

"H'm, it's queer. Maybe I'll work it out later. Way back
I worked on a ranch in Texas. Used to play poker in my off
time with the cowhands . . ."

Peter sighed resignedly. Ten minutes later he was again
brought back to reality by another question.

"Doggone it I know your face! Ever been in Hollywood?"

"I have not. You flatter me, Lyman . . ."

"Aw call me Dave."

"You flatter me, Dave. I'm not a film star. I'm not even
related to one."

"You ain't?" He wrinkled his heavy forehead again,
baffled but by no means beaten. Evidently his appearance
was not his only likeness to a bloodhound. Fortunately Peter
caught a phrase of Becket's at that moment, and took the
opportunity to change the subject.

"So you've been investigating the ship's newspaper,
Larry," he put in promptingly.

"Yeah." His eyes twinkled. "Professional jealousy, I
reckon. Couldn't keep away."

"Always abreast of the news, eh!"

"That must be a change for you, son," Lyman interjected
good humouredly. "Kinda slow after being way ahead—I
mean being right there where the noos breaks."

"I've had luck," said Becket modestly, and, what was more,
looked as though he meant it. "I guess fellows like me have
gotten at least one thing in common with other successful
criminals," he added with a grin. "We gotta have luck."

"Oh sure." Lyman chuckled, but a moment later became
serious. "That reminds me of sump'n I wanted to ask you,
Larry. D'you happen to know whether they've gotten any
further with the Van de Kramer robbery?"

Mrs. Lesley Van de Kramer was worth several million
dollars, and the theft of her diamonds from the New York

residence in Riverside Drive was one of the most discussed topics in the news. The Van de Kramers entertained lavishly, and, it would seem latterly, rather unwisely. For there was every indication that one of their guests at a recent party had sadly encroached upon this hospitality. But if so, the thief had apparently been an uninvited guest, since every person who was known to have attended had been thoroughly investigated. The diamonds had vanished from the Van de Kramer's safe, and the District Attorney who was a friend of the family, and who had been at the party himself, had not enjoyed much conviviality since.

" No, I've heard nothing fresh," said Larry.

" I met Mrs. Van de Kramer once," Sona put in reflectively. " I feel very sorry for her. She's so generous and such a delightful person."

Peter nodded. " One of the few people in this world who really enjoy spending a fortune on others."

" Oh? Do you know her, Mr. Munroe?"

" Er—no," Peter lied quickly. " Only by repute."

" Queer about that robbery," mused Larry, fingering his chin. " Maybe it wasn't an inside job. Oh yes I know the police think it was, but that hasn't gotten them very far. There'd be plenty of ways of getting into that house while the party was going on, and I don't mean by a window or anything like that. After all, there were quite a few waiters hired for the occasion, all fresh faces. A burglar in waiter's kit could easily have slipped in and amongst without being noticed."

" Yes I suppose so." Sona inclined her head reflectively. " Was the safe forced? The papers didn't say?"

He looked at her with his slow and very attractive smile.

" 'Fraid I haven't an exclusive on that, Miss Boyd."

" I'd say it couldn't have been forced," put in Lyman. " It takes time to blow a safe, and there's a whale of a racket even if it's wrapped round with carpets. Best thing 'ud be an electric drill, but even then . . ."

" So we have a criminologist amongst us!" exclaimed Larry.

Lyman hung his head sheepishly.

" Nope. I jest read detective stories."

"Another of your varied interests, I take it," Peter observed dryly.

"Aw shucks. I should have kept my big mouth shut. Specially as I bet Larry here knows a lot more'n he's told us."

Peter thought this to be the most intelligent remark the other had made so far. He nodded slowly, helping himself to some more coffee.

"I got that impression, too. How about it, Larry?"

"No, you're quite wrong. I'm not in the know. Not this time. I'm just putting two and two together, that's all."

"And making what?" asked Peter.

"Well, maybe they add up to Louie Palmer."

He looked at each of them in turn, and saw their faces register different degrees of puzzlement. Peter Gayleigh raised his eyebrows in mild interrogation ; Dave Lyman frowned heavily, as though striving to grasp the point in one of the Funnies ; Sona Boyd merely looked at him blankly.

"If this is where we're all supposed to purse our lips and give a long whistle of astonishment," she said, "I'm afraid it's a washout. I'm sorry, but Louie Palmer doesn't mean a thing to me."

It meant quite a lot to Peter, but he didn't think it advisable to say so.

"Louie Palmer, or to give him his full title ' Louie-two-decks-Palmer ', is an international jewel thief," Larry explained. "He's also very handy with cards. He was sent down to Dartmoor, in England, twelve years ago for a five-year stretch. After his release he returned to America—he's an American citizen—and though it was known that he intended to get even with some guy who'd jugged him, he didn't get around to that before he was arrested again in New York for another jewel robbery. He was sentenced to ten years in Sing Sing, though, of course, he got remission of his sentences both in England and America for good conduct. To cut a long story short he was released only a month ago. And the Van de Kramer robbery was just the sort of thing he might have planned." He shook his head, pursing his lips. "Pity I never saw Louie Palmer. I often wish I had. He was making headlines before my time of course."

All of them considered this for a few moments. Then Lyman said : " I don't see it that way. If Palmer's just quit Sing Sing he's out on parole. The cops must be watching him."

" You bet they are. But I'm not saying he actually did the job. I've just gotten a hunch he might have planned it, nothing more."

" Maybe you're right at that," ruminated Lyman, sucking up a mouthful of coffee which had gone cold. " Maybe he gave the cops the slip."

" If he did he wouldn't get far before he was picked up again. He's known to every sleuth in the States."

" Including private detectives, I suppose," said Sona, as though enjoying some hidden thought.

He nodded, looking at her wonderingly.

" Yes, of course."

" Then perhaps the Van de Kramer diamonds are on this ship," she suggested surprisingly. " How frightfully thrilling if they were ! "

" On this ship?" Larry frowned. " I must be a bit dense this morning. How do you work that out?"

" Yes," said Peter, his face quite expressionless. " We'd like to know."

The girl opened her handbag, very conscious of the suspense, her cheeks slightly flushed. " I found something on the floor near Mr. Lyman's chair after we finished dinner last night. This." She held up a slip of paper. " I suppose you must have dropped it Mr. Lyman?" she asked mischievously.

Her words had a surprising effect on him. He frowned, then stretching out his hand, almost snatched the paper from her.

" I bin wondering where I dropped this," he growled uncomfortably, and his very evident concern wiped the smile from her face.

" I meant to return it last night, but couldn't find you."

He was still glowering at her when she placed her hand on his hairy paw. " Don't worry, Mr. Lyman, we won't let it go any farther."

Lyman pushed his chair back and got to his feet, his resentful scowl merging into a baleful look.

"I reckon if you hadn't found it somebody else would," he said gruffly. "You folk'll excuse me, I know."

He walked away very self-consciously, and after gazing after him both men turned questioningly to the girl.

"That slip of paper," frowned Larry. "What was it?"

"Well I don't quite know what you'd call it," she said. "But it has Dave Lyman's name on it, and gives him authority to act as a representative of Lishman's Incorporated."

"Lishman's!" He stared at her with quick comprehension. She nodded slowly.

"Yes. It's one of the biggest private detective agencies in New York, isn't it?"

CHAPTER THREE

IN WHICH HE ACQUIRES AN APPRENTICE, AND
ENTERTAINS A LESS ATTRACTIVE ALLY

I

THE games deck was ablaze with sunshine, the pure blue of the sky adding to the sparkling brilliance of the bathing-pool. Brightly coloured caps and swim-suits bobbed about in the water, overlooked by a few tables with red and green umbrellas. There was much laughter and good natured protest as white and tanned bodies splashed one another, dived, submerged and agitated the water in joyous abandon. To starboard some men in white shorts were playing deck-hockey, beads of sweat lining their foreheads, their tense exertions conrasting with a score of less energetically inclined onlookers. In the pool, Peter saw Sona, clad in a white swim-suit, doing a more frantic than elegant breast-stroke and swiftly pursued by Larry Becket, rolling through the water with an effortless crawl. Her shriek of apprehension was stifled as he reached her, pushing her under the water. Sona surfaced again spluttering and coughing. Larry brought her to the side, his arm about her shoulder, suddenly solicitous.

" You beast! " she gasped, almost as though she meant it and as soon as she had recovered her breath.

Larry looked tragically glum. " Sorry, Sona."

Peter smiled. The " Miss Boyd " already belonged to the past, he noticed. He did some brisk work with a towel, flung it over his muscular brown shoulders, and lighting a cigarette inhaled deeply. He had settled himself comfortably at the table where he had left his bathing-robe when a vision in an emerald green swim-suit appeared from somewhere behind him.

" Hullo! " said Marcia Gordon. " Have you been in?"

" No," said Peter darkly. " My hair often gets wet and mussed up like this. Water trickles off my legs, too. It must be something wrong with the metabolism."

She sat down beside him, as he was afraid she would, the dark blue eyes regarding him steadily.

"You don't associate me with very happy thoughts, do you?"

He shrugged. Nothing would have induced him to admit that she looked very lovely. Her dazzlingly white skin and blonde curls chimed pleasantly with the green swim-suit. She had a lithe supple body, and she carried herself well.

"I hope you're satisfied," she said coolly, noting his silent appraisal.

Peter grunted.

"Queer when you come to think of it," she said.

"Think of what?"

"Well, I've got much less on than when you saw me this morning, yet in the eyes of the world I am now decently clad."

"Have you no shame," growled Peter. "Such reflections might be misunderstood. If you won't go away, for heaven's sake lower your voice."

The red lips parted in a smile.

"Perhaps I'd better. You see I want to talk to you about the Van de Kramer diamonds."

Gayleigh drew deeply at his cigarette. A shadow seemed to obtrude itself, blotting out the colourful scene. Suddenly he felt quite alone with this girl, conscious of the intense stillness inside him, the mockery in that accusing gaze.

"So that's what you've been working up to. All right, let's have it."

"Here? Among all these people? You're not scared?"

"Why should I be?"

"I beg your pardon. How foolish of me. I forgot that you're Peter Gayleigh."

"You must be slipping," said Peter languidly. "I fancy that's the first time you've forgotten it since you recognised me. Should I know you? Have we met before?"

"Not before last night. I don't move in your rarefied atmosphere."

"You seem to gate-crash it pretty well."

She studied him in silence for a moment.

"You're just like I thought you'd be," she said presently. "You've got nerve. Aren't you afraid I might tell?"

"That bothers the hell out of me. Tell the whole ship if you want to."

"If I did it would make things very awkward for you."

Peter brightened his cigarette, eyeing her resignedly.

"Not awkward, just annoying. I'm not hankering after publicity. But if you want to see a man hounded for his autograph, spoken to by all and sundry, just so they can say they *have* spoken to him, ogled by females, and treated to unwanted drinks by pimply youths and middle-aged extroverts who get their thrills by proxy and have a line in small talk that would embarrass a moron—if you want to impose all this on a man simply because he's called Peter Gayleigh, go ahead, do your stuff. I've been through it before. I can take it again."

"I'm afraid you haven't quite grasped my point," she said. "What about the Kramer diamonds?"

"That seems to be your worry. It isn't mine."

"Are you sure? Mrs. Lesley Van de Kramer loses her diamonds and a few days later we find Peter Gayleigh making an ocean trip under an assumed name. Am I getting warm, or am I close to the ' ice '?"

It was then Gayleigh decided that this unwarranted suggestion had gone far enough.

"You've got a pretty line in criminal slang," he replied unconcernedly, "a pretty enough face and a fairly decent figure—"

"Thanks."

"——but it's quite obvious to anyone who rates an intelligent quotient that you're very, very dumb."

"Really!" She was more than a little peeved. Peter's mouth curled itself into that twisted cynical smile.

"If I'd stolen the diamonds do you think I'd have left New York so quickly, and taken the risk of being recognised by anyone who'd seen my photograph? That isn't the way things are done, my sweet."

"Isn't it? I think it's just what Peter Gayleigh might do. And right now I bet you're getting a great thrill out of it."

She was partly right, of course, and because he realised it, he threw back his head and laughed softly. Such an audacious get-away might have appealed to him in his more reckless moods, since its unoriginality would have loaded the dice heavily against him. It was certain that he would have come under suspicion, and that he would have been obliged to discard the evidence. Yes, it might have been fun —if he *had* stolen the diamonds. But, as it happened, he hadn't.

"You're almost too ingenious to be real," he chuckled. "If it will ease your mind, I've never seen or met Mrs. Lesley Van de Kramer."

"Even if you had you wouldn't admit it."

"Shrewd, very shrewd," he conceded. "But since you've got this queer idea why don't you go to one of the ship's officers and whisper knowingly into his ear. The last person you should tell is me. Aren't you afraid I might strangle you in the dead of night, and chuck you overboard?"

He found it impossible to treat her accusation seriously, equally impossible to believe she was thinking of blackmailing him. She was too transparently honest. Even her attempts at guile marked her out as the veriest amateur. She hadn't gone the right way about it. She was just a nice girl with a silly obsession.

"Do you really mean it?" she said. "You didn't do it?"

He shrugged "Sorry I can't oblige you. Some other time perhaps."

She was silent for a few seconds, nibbling at her lips. He thought she looked quite intelligent when she frowned.

"Anyway," she said at last, "as you're Peter Gayleigh you're sure to get into a spot of bother very soon. Then I'll be here to get you out."

"That will be a great help!"

For the first time she returned his smile naturally.

"You must think I'm an awful little fool," she said frankly. "But, you see, I've never met anyone who works outside the law. I've often wanted to—so I put on what must have seemed to you a rather ridiculous act. I've a confession to make Mr.—er—Munroe."

"Indeed?"

"Yes. My name isn't Gordon. I have to use that because it would seem odd if father and I had different names. My father's on this boat, too. But you'll never see him. He spends all his time working. That's why he booked a suite. His name, in case it means anything to you, is Miles Lawson."

" The mystery story writer?"

" That's right. I suppose, in his own way, he's about as famous as you are, and that, of course, is why he's travelling incog. He's hoping to do a lot of writing during this trip. He's crossed the Atlantic so often that it's lost all interest for him, and he's dictating and revising most of the time. He's a dear, really, but at times like this he forgets I exist. Which leaves me at a very loose end."

" I see. So that accounts for your frantic efforts to get a playmate."

" In a way—yes. But it doesn't explain why I've been throwing myself at you." She raised candid eyes to his. "You see, although father writes the most bloodthirsty stuff he's just a mild little man who wouldn't harm a fly. I'm tired of getting my thrills at second hand—by reading his books I mean. Just for once I'd like to experience the real thing. That's why I'm fastening myself on to you like a leech." She wrinkled her nose deliciously. " Honestly, Peter, do you really mind? I promise I won't get in the way too much. You can regard me—well as a sort of apprentice."

To one of Peter Gayleigh's calibre this suggestion was ludicrous. It was extraordinary, so utterly unexpected that he could do nothing but stare at her.

" Well, well," he said, recovering himself. " There are more things in heaven and earth, Horatio—— All right, stick around, if you want to. But for your private information I'm on vacation. I don't expect to commit more than a couple of murders on this trip."

Her eyes flashed her appreciation, and as she stood up, pulling him playfully to his feet, he somehow forgot all the more sophisticated women he had known. But only when they had scrambled, dripping, out of the pool ten minutes later did he pause to think how his feelings had changed towards this emerald nymph. He found it rather disconcerting.

II

It was not difficult to pick out Dave Lyman's chunky figure as he stood on the fringe of the little crowd watching the hockey-players. He remained there, rather self-consciously, speaking to no one. A cigar jutted from the corner of his mouth, and whenever Gayleigh looked in his direction he appeared to be completely absorbed in the game.

But there was no sign of Trevor Merson.

The Indian, in fact, was still in his cabin where he had returned immediately after breakfast. The chatter and idle frivolities of the upper decks held no interest for him. There was something to be done before he could relax. He, too, wanted a place in the sun. But because he thought of this in a totally different way from those lounging about on deck he had locked his cabin door. There must be no interference. It would be disastrous if he was disturbed.

For some time he stared, deep in thought, at the sword on the wall. Perhaps it was fortunate that Gayleigh had seen it, that he had noted the white sapphires in the handle. Had he touched the blade he would not have been alive : he would not have interfered again in matters that did not concern him. On the other hand, his death would have meant unwelcome inquiries. For Peter Gayleigh was not like that other man who had paid the full price for his curiosity. Gayleigh had been seen aboard. He would have been missed, even if it had been possible to dispose of the body. But this was merely a backwater in the swirl of Merson's thoughts. It had not happened. More, it could not happen—after his immediate work was done.

He continued to stare at the sword.

It had required courage to display it openly, but now everyone who was likely to enter the cabin had seen it. The steward, who had been of great assistance in the early hours of that morning, had seen it several times. In short it had lost its novelty. If necessary the man could testify that no attempt had been made to conceal it. Merson had hung it there shortly after he occupied the cabin, and to create this very impression.

He lit an Egyptian cigarette, and wondered if the police had traced the Van de Kramer diamonds to *S.S. Cornelius*. Every precaution had been taken, but it was just possible that he had been followed.   There might be a detective aboard. Or perhaps jewel thieves. There was Peter Gayleigh, for instance. He was worried about Gayleigh, but since he had seen the sword he would attach little importance to it if he ventured into the cabin again. Yes, all things considered the rearrangement he had in mind should be adequate, at least until the danger became more pressing.

There was a worn leather suit-case at the foot of the bed. Merson unlocked the suit-case, and removed the neatly folded clothes it contained, placing them carefully on a couple of chairs. Then dropping to his knees beside the empty suit-case he inserted dusky fingernails tentatively into each corner, releasing the tiny springs that he knew to be there. Finally he raised the false bottom revealing another sword.

It seemed to be the twin of that now hanging on the wall of the cabin. The two-edged blade was about two feet long, and the same Eastern characters were inscribed on the dull steel; the hilt presented the same vivid colours, and the same pattern had been scrupulously observed in the setting of the jewels, which, like those in its counterpart had not the brilliancy of diamonds. In every respect it appeared to be a replica of the other, yet there were essential differences. The blade had not been wrought in Brunei, it had never been in the possession of a witch-doctor, and it was not impregnated with poison. It had been fashioned in America only a few months before.

And it was infinitely more valuable than its twin.

Merson lifted it by the blade, eyeing the jewels in the hilt with the discernment of an expert. He had inserted each of those stones separately, and with the patience worthy of their value. And assessing the work critically he was convinced afresh that not even a connoisseur would have recognised those stones as the Van de Kramer diamonds. Only detailed scrutiny would have revealed them to be diamonds at all. They had the appearance of white sapphires, for Trevor Merson had not wasted the years he had spent in the East Indies.   Immediately after the robbery the diamonds had been recut to fit the settings already prepared for them. But before inserting them in the hilt he had covered them with an extremely fine coating of transparent lacquer. It was a trick he had learned from natives in Borneo, and it proved very effective. The brilliancy of the diamonds had been reduced by just that amount necessary to give them the sheen of white sapphires.

He had done this work with the aid of the magnifying glass which he now took from his pocket. He screwed the glass into his eye, satisfying himself once again that the lacquer had left no minute irregularities on the facets of the diamonds. Then thrusting the glass away he got to his feet, and went towards the less valuable but more deadly weapon on the wall. As Gayleigh had noticed, it was suspended by a strip of green leather tied about the hilt and the blade. Merson removed it, and carried it to the suitcase, depositing it inside as though he had been dealing with a deadly reptile. The strip of leather went with it, for he was afraid the end attached to the blade might have absorbed some of the poison, and that its virulence was not a myth he had very recent cause to remember. He went to a drawer, and taking out another length of green leather, prepared in readiness, tied the ends to the more valuable sword. It only remained to hang it on the wall, press down the false bottom of the suit-case, and pack it again with clothes. Then contemplating the sword once again he nodded his head.

Trevor Merson was a great admirer of Trevor Merson's audacity.

He had a great fondness for these particular diamonds. They constituted the first big coup he had achieved. But, he told himself, he must not forget that they were merely a nucleus, nothing compared with that which would accrue from the Greater Plan. It was interesting to reflect that Jervis Grant's step-daughter was travelling on the same boat. She seemed a nice kid. Too bad he was going to put pressure on her step-father. That worried him quite a lot! He felt almost as sorry for him as he did for Mrs. Lesley Van de Kramer, or that fool who had finished up so ignominiously in the cabin-trunk.

Suddenly he felt it would be amusing to mix with those unsuspecting idiots on deck. And it was a beautiful day for a swim. He undressed, donned swimming-shorts and a brightly coloured bathing robe, and very well pleased with the morning's work, left the cabin.

III

After the conversation at breakfast Peter Gayleigh thought he knew why Dave Lyman was so interested in Trevor Merson, and his own interest in the half-caste had increased accordingly. He saw Merson as soon as he stepped on to the sports deck, and decided the time was now ripe for a little research.

" Excuse me," he said, interrupting Marcia in the middle of a sentence. " I'll be back."

He snatched up his bathing robe, slipping it on as he went, heard the girl say sarcastically, " Well it's been nice knowing you " and was out of earshot. He stepped behind the broad funnel of a ventilator as Merson approached the pool, and a few moments later disappeared down the nearest companionway. He was certain that Merson had not seen this swift departure, equally certain that the door of the other's cabin would not present an impassable obstacle. He approached it in leisurely fashion, bided his time until there was no one in sight, then took some odd-looking pieces of metal from his bathing-robe. They were not ordinary keys, though in Peter Gayleigh's practised fingers they served the same purpose. Trial . . . Rejection . . . Trial. A few abortive attempts, and the lock snapped back. He darted inside and closed the door.

If his hunch was correct the Van de Kramer diamonds were in that cabin.

His gaze travelled round it slowly. It presented much the same appearance as before. A metal trunk, and a worn leather suit-case had not been moved, and the wardrobe door was slightly ajar. The drawers and the bed itself might also call for attention. And that was all. The cabin fittings on *Cornelius* shone with polished rectitude. They did not lend lend themselves to the concealment of gems. His survey took in the sword, and the jewelled hilt. He had never had much time for white sapphires. And these were not even the best sapphires, as he had seen earlier that morning. He stepped towards the metal trunk. It was not locked, in contra-distinction to the worn leather case. He was examining the lock of the suit-case when there was a sharp tap on the door.

Peter's head jerked round, his pulse racing. After a few seconds the tapping was repeated. Then in a tense whisper :

" Peter ! Why don't you answer ? I know you're there."

It was Marcia Lawson.

This realisation played havoc with Gayleigh's set expression, which now suggested that he was struggling to find an expletive strong enough to express his feelings. He opened the door cautiously, glanced up and down the alley-way, and pulled the girl into the cabin.

" So you followed me."

" Of course. I told you I wasn't going to be left out. And as I saw you slip into this cabin, and it wasn't yours, I came to help."

" Oh, you did !" He took a deep breath. " A little more of this, a very little more, and I shall wring your confounded neck. Now scram. Can't you see I'm busy ?"

" Very busy ! If someone else came to that door you'd be in quite a spot—unless you had me outside to warn you. Like this." She whistled a few notes very softly. " How will that do ?"

" Fine," he snapped, sourly. " I suppose you got that from your father's books. Its originality leaves me speechless."

He opened the door again, saw there was no one about, and began to push her outside. And since it seemed impossible to get rid of her :

" Okay you've got your first assignment."

He saw her eyes light up, edged her completely outside and shut the door again. It was quite probable, he thought, that she would walk about near the cabin, and as though butter wouldn't melt in her mouth. Everyone would know there was something phoney going on. He felt much less happy than he had done before. But he was not going to miss this opportunity, and there was no time to be lost. He went quickly through the contents of the metal trunk and the wardrobe, made a swift search of the drawers and the bed. Nothing. Nothing at all. He had left the suit-case until the last, since the locks would take some time to force. But he had overlooked the clothes Merson had worn that morning, and which he had tossed carelessly on to a chair. There was a wallet in the breast-pocket, but not the wallet he had examined earlier. It contained a few letters and papers of little interest. Or so he thought until he unfolded a sheet of notepaper on which a few lines of verse were typed. Coupled with the Eastern characters written underneath, and which reminded him of those he had seen on the blade of the sword the verse was very significant. He crossed to the sword and compared the two inscriptions. They were identical.

Puzzled, he read the verse again:

> " To him who would its weight assess,
>   Pause thou, consider and caress
>   This magic blade.
>   For it hath wondrous power and charm
>   If lightly poised upon the palm
>   Of those who scorn all earthly balm,
>   And palisades."

This was, presumably, an elaborate translation of the inscription on the blade. Evidently the weapon was credited with mystical properties. A native superstition no doubt. Interesting, but of little consequence.

It was not surprising that he failed to grasp the deadly implication behind these words. But despite his urgency they intrigued him. He wondered what was supposed to happen when the blade was " poised upon the palm." Possibly a half-naked savage might get a thrill out of it. Though he was cynical enough to believe that any transcendental feeling would be self-induced. The weapon had probably been used in some barbaric ritual. Among savages under the spell of a witch-doctor's personality it had perhaps been a very potent force. But now it was nothing more than a curio. And a legend like this would, of course, increase its value. No doubt its present very enterprising owner had thought of that, too.

He put the sheet of paper back in the wallet, and returned it to Merson's jacket, his brow still corrugated in thought.

Mumbo jumbo, of course. And yet . . .

On an impulse he went back to the sword, grasped the blade in both hands, and raised it slightly as though assessing its weight. He held it for a few moments, then lowered it again, turning away and flapping his hand at it disgustedly.

"Aw fooey!"

Now that he had satisfied his curiosity he felt annoyed that he had yielded to it, little realising that if he had amused himself in this way a little earlier he would have flirted with death for the last time.

He was approaching the locked suit-case again when he caught the sound of a faint but familiar whistle.

IV

Peter froze. He heard a man's voice in the alley-way. The words, muffled but distinguishable, were superimposed on the girl's valiant little tune.

"Good morning, lady."

It was Dave Lyman, and from what followed it seemed that he hadn't spoken to her before. She stopped whistling, returning his greeting rather curtly.

"You gotten yourself a good tune," he pursued with an elephantine attempt at friendliness.

"Indeed." Her tone was icy. "I'm glad you like it."

"Been here long?"

"Long enough," snapped Marcia. "D'you mind letting me pass?"

"No need to get all het up, lady. I was jest askin' a civil question."

"I've been asked questions like that before."

"Aw now, don't get me wrong." Gayleigh could picture his discomfort. "Maybe I spoke out of turn, but I'm lookin' for someone, see. The guy you was with at the bathing-pool fifteen minutes ago. Mr. Munroe. You wouldn't know where he is?"

"I'm sorry, Mr.—er—"

"Call me Dave. Er—Dave Lyman, miss," he amended rather hurriedly.

"I'm sorry Mr. Lyman, I don't know. Mr. Munroe was going to his cabin when I last saw him."

"He ain't there now."

"Then I'm afraid I can't help you."

Peter heard the distinctive sound of the girl's sandals, followed by the man's heavier tread as he continued in the opposite direction. The footsteps of both became inaudible, but Peter waited a full minute before he opened the door softly and peered outside. There was no one in sight. He closed the door, striding quickly after the girl. As he had guessed she was waiting in the adjoining alley-way.

"Thanks for the warning," he said tersely.

"Did you get what you were looking for?"

He shook his head.

"Then why didn't you stay? It was only a man called Lyman. He's gone."

"So it would seem," said Peter grimly. "And I mean just that. Lyman isn't a fool. He'll be back. I'll join you on deck presently."

"Why not now?"

"Because, my sweet, two can play at hide and seek," he rejoined enigmatically." And as he saw her frown. "No questions, I'll explain later."

"Everything?"

"Perhaps."

She glanced at him doubtfully, but grasping her arm he hurried her along. He had got rid of her before he reached his cabin, and one swift glance inside told him that his fears were justified. Someone had been there. The bedclothes were disarranged; his cabin-trunk, which had been closed, was now standing ajar; the drawer of the wardrobe was only partly shut, revealing a turmoil of underwear. Which meant that his cabin had been very hurriedly searched.

It didn't take him long to discover that none of his valuables were missing. He hadn't thought they would be. And he didn't think he would have to wait much longer before Dave Lyman paid him a call. In actual fact he had inhaled the value out of less than an inch of his cigarette when someone knocked at the door.

Peter opened it with a sardonic smile. "Come in, Dave," he said dryly. "I guess you know your way around."

"Yeah, I reckon we both been busy," said Lyman, eyeing him severely through the drift of cigar smoke. "Kinda catching, ain't it."

He edged himself into the cabin, pausing to squirt nicotined saliva over his shoulder into the alley-way. This was a representative of Lishman's Incorporated bent on serious business.

" Maybe I'd better shut the door," said Peter.

" Maybe you had." He waited until this was done, then eyeing Gayleigh with a fixed stare, shifted the cigar from a yellowish clamp on the right of his mouth to one on the left. The cigar might have been a miniature cannon through which he fired his next shot.

" How come you was in Merson's cabin just now?"

So there was to be no finesse at all.

" Was I?"

" You sure were, Munroe. Or maybe I should say Peter Gayleigh."

Peter simulated an expression of elaborate surprise.

" Some day you must tell me how you do it," he said. " Could it be from my photographs?"

" It could. I never forget a face. Recognised you jest as soon as I came on board. That's why I'm sitting at your table. That's why I wanna know if you found anything in Merson's cabin."

" The Van de Kramer diamonds perhaps?"

The other looked at him in exactly the same way that many harassed detectives in two hemispheres had looked at him before. There was doubt, suspicion, nicely blended with wariness in that fixed regard.

" Suppose we stop circling round each other and straighten things out, Dave," Peter suggested, helpfully. " I haven't got the Van de Kramer diamonds. I hadn't even an inkling that they might be on this ship until Miss Boyd pulled that trick out of the hat at breakfast. You ought to have told me you were a private sleuth," he added reproachfully.

" Yeah, I know. But that don't explain why——"

" Oh yes it does." He was smiling very sweetly. " You've had your eye on Merson ever since the ship sailed. I notice these things."

" I might have had my eye on you, too."

" That's just it. You might, but you hadn't, although you knew who I was. Which means you didn't suspect me. But you thought you had something on Merson." A smoke ring eddied leisurely past Lyman's left ear. "And with that flair for deduction that characterises my more lucid moments I wondered if your assignment concerned the Van de Kramer diamonds. It wasn't such a clever deduction, really, because I seem to remember that before Lesley Van de Kramer married his present wife he got all the evidence he needed to divorce his last one from a muck-rake employed by Lishman's." He shrugged and spread his hands. "So what was more natural than that Van de Kramer should give your agency the opportunity to win another medal. See what I mean?"

The stocky man continued to look at him steadily.

Peter asked : "You're working quite independently of the police, I suppose?"

"You tell me," growled Lyman, and as Gayleigh's lips twisted into that wicked smile. "Okay, bud, I've heard you're smart."

"Better. Much better." Peter smoothed his hand over his chin glancing askance at the other. "You followed me from A deck, and when you saw me go into Merson's cabin you thought you'd be smart, too. Who knows you might have found something interesting in here. Perhaps something connecting me with Merson. And why trouble to tidy up before you left. You didn't mind if I did know you'd been ferreting around. Since I was enjoying myself in the same way, there was no danger that I'd report your bit of fun."

"Maybe you're right at that," Lyman admitted weightily.

"I've got to hand another bouquet to you, too. The questions you put to Miss Gordon were masterly. You knew I was in Merson's cabin and that I should overhear, and because I'm not quite a fool, that I should leave it pretty quickly. You didn't want to waste time. You wanted to talk to me."

"You ain't bad at that yourself," Lyman muttered sourly. "With any luck I might get in more'n a couple of words sometime."

"I *beg* your pardon." Peter's voice was sweetness itself. "You were about to say . . . ?"

But now that he had the opportunity he wasn't overwhelmingly articulate. Actually he seemed to be struggling for words to express some finer feeling. He put the cigar back in his mouth, thrust his hands into his trousers pockets, and rocked gently for a few moments on his surprisingly dapper feet. His wrinkled brows suggested that he was slowly coming to a momentous decision.

"Listen," he said suddenly. "I bin checking up on you. I ain't denying that. But now I'm satisfied and—well, how about you and me teaming up?" He looked for somewhere to spit, found there was nothing handy, and stared very directly at Gayleigh. "That's a fair enough offer, ain't it?"

It was also a very good pointer to Lyman's thoughts. He didn't know whether Gayleigh was after the diamonds with the intention of returning them to their owner, or whether he hoped to keep there himself. But he knew that nothing he could do would prevent this notorious adventurer from carrying out his own investigations. It was better to have Peter Gayleigh as an ally, even one who wouldn't tell him very much, than as an adversary who wouldn't tell him anything at all.

"It's a fair offer, ain't it?" he repeated rather aggressively, for Peter's eyebrows had lifted in genuine admiration.

"It certainly is. It will be a pleasure to work with you, Dave."

The other rubbed his thick palms together, and Peter stifled a smile. Mr. Lyman evidently thought he was making excellent progress.

"We'll deal with this on our own, bud. Jest you and me. It ain't as if I was a cop, bound by rules and red tape. If Merson has those diamonds, and I'm darned sure he has, I reckon we'll get 'em, eh?"

And because Peter Gayleigh also liked to know what others were doing, including Dave Lyman, he said with the utmost enthusiasm : "I reckon we will, bud."

v

Such a partnership as this, Lyman evidently felt, should be cemented with something more than words. He fixed a hopeful gaze on Gayleigh's cabin-trunk, and said : "That looks like good Scotch you gotten in there."

"Very suitable to the occasion," Peter concurred. And as he produced the bottle and a couple of glasses : "The fact that this liquor is still here proves that you're an honest man, Dave."

"I'll say." His eyes were on the whisky as the other poured it out. "I always take mine straight."

Coming from Dave Lyman it was, thought Peter, quite an apt riposte. Lyman realised it, too, after a few seconds. His big mouth split into a belated grin.

"Gee, that's right," he said, wagging his head appreciatively. "I've come by this straight, and I like my liquor straight. What d'you know !"

Peter looked at him, then thrust one of the glasses hurriedly into his hand.

"Neat. Very neat, Dave," he applauded kindly.

"And folks tell me I ain't gotten a sense of humour."

"Do they?" He raised his glass. "A few of these and you'll be killing me with your cracks. Well, here's to success."

The stocky man nodded, and disposed of his drink at a gulp.

"I reckon it's no use going back to Merson's cabin now," he observed. "Maybe he missed both of us on deck. Anyway he's back. I passed him on the way here." He was looking speculatively at his empty glass. Peter took the hint and replenished it again. "We gotta wait our opportunity, bud."

"That's right."

"It's jest a matter of time."

"Have another," said Peter.

Lyman did. It was all very hearty and convivial. He didn't say how he had got on to Merson's trail, and neither mentioned the incident that had occurred earlier that morning. Peter told him that he had found nothing of interest in Merson's cabin, omitting all reference to the sword and its inscription. There was a great deal of talk that revealed nothing. The only thing they shared was the whisky. So it took Lyman a long time to realise that he was getting exactly nowhere.

"Well, I'll be on my way," he decided at last. "The idea is to search Merson's cabin. We'll fix that later."

As the door closed behind him Peter gazed ruefully at what had once been a full bottle of whisky. Entertaining

Dave Lyman was expensive, and, up to the present, scarcely worth the effort. But between them they ought to be more than a match for Merson. Altogether he was not displeased with the morning's work as he slipped off his bathing-robe and began to dress.

Marcia was sitting at a table near the swimming-pool when he returned to A deck and, as he had anticipated, her greeting lacked warmth.

"Oh, hullo!" she exclaimed tartly. "My name's Marcia. Remember? In the dim and distant past you said you'd join me here."

Peter offered an apology and a cigarette.

"Sorry I've been so long. I've been in conference with our Mr. Lyman. He waylaid me in my cabin."

"You mean he knew that you . . .?"

"Exactly. Suppose we take a stroll to a less frequented part of the deck."

A couple of minutes later they were leaning over the rail staring at the untroubled, sunlit water.

"Perhaps I'm taking a risk," he began doubtfully. "Ravishing blondes like you are just made for confidences, besides other things. But I've found they're not always on the level."

"There's nothing phoney about me." Her deep blue eyes rested on him anxiously. "I thought we'd settled that."

He wanted to believe her, and now that she was behaving naturally he felt inclined to take the risk. Those surprisingly dark eyes fascinated him. There was sincerity behind their loveliness, a promise to a man, though perhaps he didn't happen to be that man. She had been very quick to recognise him, but so had many virtuous and much less interesting women he had met. Of course there were several things he must check sooner or later. But perhaps they could wait. If she was really more subtle than he thought it would merely add to the fun. And so :

"It's settled now," he said decisively. "Forgive me, my sweet, I'm just naturally inclined to be cagey."

He didn't tell her about Merson's nocturnal exercise with the cabin-trunk, but with that sole exception he related all he knew, beginning with Dave Lyman and passing on to the Van de Kramer diamonds, and Merson's sword with its mystical inscription.

" So Merson has the diamonds," she commented as he finished.

" Perhaps. I've no proof that he has."

" H'm." She was silent for a moment. " It's jolly queer, isn't it? About that sword, I mean. I wish I'd been there when you handled it."

" If you had," he said sourly, " there would have been two of us looking foolish. I didn't feel anything unusual, and there haven't been any after effects."

" Then it must be a hoax."

" Yes, a profitable one, I fancy. Just another of Merson's sidelines."

Looking round he saw Larry and Sona, both fully dressed, coming towards them. As they drew level, Sona smiled roguishly.

" Didn't you hear the luncheon gong, Mr. Munroe?"

Peter introduced Marcia, and from the impish light in Sona's eyes realised she had spoken to him for that very reason. The two girls scrutinised each other critically, then after a few generalities Sona and her escort moved away.

" He's gotten himself a lovely, all right," commented Larry as soon as they were out of earshot.

The girl laughed, looking at him teasingly.

" Perhaps I ought to be jealous. But I'm not. And I agree with you. Did you notice the way she was looking at him before they saw us?"

He nodded. " Just in the way you look at me when you think I'm not watching."

Sona blushed, and as his eyes twinkled, reddened still more.

" Don't flatter yourself Larry Becket," she told him sharply, turning her head away. She felt very annoyed with herself —blushing like a schoolgirl. She didn't feel annoyed with Larry. But she wished he wasn't quite so observant.

CHAPTER FOUR

1

NONE of them saw Merson again during lunch, or throughout
the afternoon. He remained in his cabin, where he had
every intention of remaining until the boat docked. The
cabin had been searched, he had soon discovered that, and
though the intruder had taken nothing, and both swords had
apparently kept their respective secrets, he wasn't taking any
more chances.

After lunch Marcia settled herself on deck with a novel,
while Peter, to whom she had clung tenaciously, presently
found an opportunity to make some inquiries on the pretext
of regaling himself at the bar. He found the steward who
attended that very reticent fiction writer, Miles Lawson, and
as Peter Gayleigh had a way of acquiring information without
arousing suspicion, he soon learnt that Lawson's habits were
entirely in accordance with those of a busy author. So far
so good. Later he hoped to make his acquaintance.

In the cocktail bar he met Lyman, who was leaning glumly
against the wall, cherishing a double whisky.

"I bin hoping our friend 'ud show himself so's we could
get busy," he said guardedly. "Maybe he's wise to where
you were this morning."

"Does that surprise you?" Peter drew him to a spot where
they were not likely to be overheard. "It doesn't surprise
me. Merson's nobody's fool."

"If I hadn't interrupted you, you might have found
sump'n," growled Lyman. "Maybe I shouldn't have done
that. Now we gotta get him outta his cabin."

"True. Like easing a limpet off a rock. Of course you
could have a word with the captain, or better, advise the
Southampton police that . . ."

"Now wait a minute," Lyman interrupted hurriedly. "I'm

53

actin' unofficially on behalf of Mr. Van de Kramer. The cops don't know nuth'n about me. Besides, I'm not dead sure Merson has the diamonds. And if he hasn't—well I'm not askin' to join the bread line yet awhile."

Peter stared ruminatively at his drink.

"Much as I'm averse to behaving in an entirely praise-worthy and legal manner, I might do something myself," he suggested.

"And if sump'n went wrong, drag me into it. Yeah, that's a swell idea!"

"You underestimate me, Dave. I thrive on difficult situations. I could keep you out of it."

A retort which was met with a look of deep distrust.

"Keep me out is right. Out altogether. Maybe I'd be left to do the explainin' while you slicked after the diamonds. I wasn't born yesterday, bud."

Peter smoothed his hand over his mouth, hiding a smile.

"Hardly the team spirit, Dave. But if that's the way you feel we'll forget it. Got any other ideas?"

"No I ain't."

"Then we'll just go on hoping," said Peter philosophically.

"Yeah. And maybe sooner or later we'll get some place."

It was not an easy problem to resolve since Merson did not appear in the dining-saloon that evening, nor later at the dance in the centre lounge where Peter Gayleigh and Larry Becket, together with the two girls, formed a jolly little party. Lyman, whose passion for poker, or any other card game, seemed to have evaporated in Merson's absence, spent most of the night in the smoke-room. About eleven o'clock Peter saw him mouching about the deck, pausing occasionally to stare through the plate-glass windows into the brightly lit lounge. After a time Peter strolled towards him.

"If you must keep your eye on me, Dave," he drawled sardonically, "couldn't you manage to do it a little less obviously?"

The other merely grunted.

"Sea like a mill-pond," he growled laconically. "And Merson sea-sick."

"You don't say!"

"I bin talkin' to his steward. That's the excuse Merson's

putting out to avoid a personal appearance. I figure he'll be sick from now on."

"Never mind," Peter consoled him cheerfully, turning back into the lounge. "You can still watch me."

This impasse did not worry him unduly. Fate had pitch-forked him into this situation, and at the proper time he had no doubt that he would be given the opportunity to develop it. Until then he proposed to enjoy himself. Marcia Lawson had been thrust upon him, and he found her very adequate compensation for a stalemate in other matters. As the days passed he had no fault to find with this uneventful life.

It was on the last night before the liner reached Southampton that he received the invitation for which he had been angling.

"I've told father about you," said Marcia. "And he'd like you to dine with him tonight, in his state-room. He's taken his meals alone throughout the whole voyage. So you're greatly honoured."

"H'm. You haven't told him who I am?"

"Of course not. That's our secret. I've told him your name is Munroe."

Miles Lawson proved to be a man slightly below average height and inclined to corpulence. He was bald, except for a thin fringe of silvery hair that clung tenaciously to his ivory pate as though reluctant to relinquish possession. His eyebrows, too, were almost non-existent, curving like bleached commas over pale grey eyes. But the lower part of his face bore a marked resemblance to Marcia's, though the skin was dried and wrinkled like an old apple. He greeted Gayleigh rather abstractedly, and with a polite lack of interest which suggested he had been coerced into this meeting.

"Father has been working very hard today," Marcia thought it advisable to explain. "He gets frightfully absorbed in his writing. I'm afraid he's still in the clouds."

"Fortunately my daughter bears with me, Mr. Munroe." He smiled at her indulgently. "May I offer you an aperitif?"

Dinner was served, and as the meal progressed he became less preoccupied and talked, if not volubly, with the assurance of a man who was well informed. Despite his ineffectual appearance, his knowledge of crime and criminals was encyclopædic, and he had, it transpired, been present during police investigations in England and America.

"You must tell Mr. Munroe about the Van de Kramer case," Marcia reminded him presently, and with a conspiratorial wink at Peter. "Father got mixed up in that too, you know."

"But not from choice, my dear." He shook his head ruefully. "One might say that I was implicated."

"Oh don't be silly, father!"

Peter glanced at him, and saw that the pale eyes were twinkling as he went on.

"I know the Van de Kramers quite well, and it so happened that I was with the District Attorney at the party when the theft was committed. The D.A. is an old friend of mine. Very fortunately, perhaps, I was with him all the evening."

In reply to Gayleigh's question Lawson gave him a first-hand account of what had occurred that night, though he advanced no facts or theories that had not already appeared in the newspapers. In his opinion the diamonds had been stolen by an uninvited guest, and he seemed to think they were still in America.

From this the conversation veered to other topics of a more general nature. But not once did Lawson evince even a casual interest in his guest's personal affairs. He asked Peter nothing about himself. He seemed wholly incurious about his daughter's new friend. Unnatural in the circumstances, Peter thought—unless the other knew who he was. Perhaps Marcia had told him, though her manner suggested she hadn't. It was far more probable that this amateur criminologist had recognised him. If so, there was nothing remarkable in that, for a mere pseudonym was a thin disguise, and in his case not difficult to penetrate. He had been recognised many times before, and he knew he would be again. And so, when he left Miles Lawson's suite, he felt almost certain that neither the girl nor her father were anything more than they seemed to be.

11

Behind the locked door of his cabin Trevor Merson was a busy man that night. The sword, which had once held the Van de Kramer diamonds, lay discarded on the bed, the soft metal of the hilt mutilated and barren, only the tiny punctures, like blind eyes, giving any indication of former glories. Some of the diamonds were now in a tiny, glass ash-tray within easy reach of his hand, and he was sitting in a chair, a smart blue lounge suit across his knees. Years at sea had made him very proficient with a needle, and as he held the jacket up, gazing critically at the left shoulder he felt that his fingers had lost none of their dexterity. Lowering the garment again, he began to pick out the seams in the right sleeve, so that presently the padding in the shoulder was revealed. There was a considerable amount of padding, for Merson had the sloping shoulders of his Indian forebears, which the stylish artistry of the tailor had endeavoured to hide. His own conceit in such matters, he now hoped, would serve a very useful purpose.

Using a pair of fine tweezers he inserted the remaining diamonds, one by one, into the thick wad of material. Then, after passing his fingers tentatively over the cloth to ensure that no unevenness could be felt, he sewed the sleeve back into place with meticulous care. Finally he examined both shoulders very critically, and nodded his head. Even the most careful scrutiny would not reveal that the jacket had been subjected to this unusual treatment. But he had no illusions about the thoroughness of the search he would undergo if he were suspect. In that case the jacket would be examined by the Customs officers and the diamonds would, almost certainly, be found. That was a risk he had to take. But in the ordinary course of events he felt he had nothing to fear. The poison sword, too, should escape notice, though even if it were discovered in the false bottom of the suitcase, its malignant power would not be apparent.

It only remained to dispose of the worthless replica, and this he did quite simply by opening the port and flinging the sword into the moonlit sea.

At the same moment Larry Becket, who was leaning over the rail on the promenade deck, broke the silence, the very thoughtful silence that had enveloped Sona and himself. She was standing so close to him that he could feel the warmth of her vital young body. And he knew that her closeness was not accidental, that her thoughts matched his own. To-morrow the liner docked at Southampton. The tiny world contained in that floating hotel would be disrupted. Cosy intimacies would be shattered. Larry and Sona had a lot to think about.

" That's queer," he said suddenly.

The girl turned her head slowly towards him, her lips half parted, her eyes starry as they caressed his face.

" What did you say, Larry?"

" I thought I saw someone chuck something through one of the portholes. It looked—well rather like a sword."

Sona peered over, following the direction of his gaze with scant interest. There was nothing to be seen, and with a little smile she slipped her arm intimately through his.

" What does it matter anyway," she said.

Looking into that fresh young face Larry decided it didn't matter at all. Nothing mattered except . . . He turned towards her, and then she was pressing against him, urged by the pleasant compulsion of his arms about her, those inviting lips melting towards his. It was a lingering kiss, exquisite in its passionate sincerity, a mutual expression of feeling too deep for words. When the girl turned away gently, to peer silently over the water, his arm still rested about her. Presently :

" You will look me up, won't you, Larry?"

He looked at her in quizzical surprise.

" Need you ask, darling. This is only the beginning."

" I hope so. Oh I hope so," she said in a voice far beyond her years. " You know I've got a feeling it isn't going to be all—just like this."

" No," said Larry pensively. " Sometimes I shall have to leave you. That's the worst of my job. But," the pressure of his arm increased, " I guess I shall always take you with me in my thoughts."

" I hope so, darling."

He had misinterpreted her sense of vague uneasiness, of

impending disaster, but why worry him with fears that had their roots merely in a woman's intuition.

"You and I are just meant for each other, Larry. It seems strange when I think of it now—I used to wonder what being in love would feel like. And now that I know, it seems so natural. It's just a wonderful feeling of completeness."

"Yeah." He inclined his head slowly in agreement. "Though it's taken an angel to make me realise it. I used to think that love was just a physical and spiritual passion. But it's not. It's something much bigger than that."

The ship slid through gilded water, an unreal thing to the two who stood there, a chariot borne on the ethereal substance of an infinitely greater reality.

"I suppose you'll be very busy in London, Larry?"

He nodded. "Pretty busy I'm afraid. I'm broadcasting a kind of London News Letter, to keep the folk at home up-to-date with current thought over here. I reckon the broadcasts will be easy enough. It's collecting the dope that gives me a headache. Y'see I'm expected to put over something different."

"Something with the Larry Becket touch."

"Yeah. First thing I got to do is look up my old contacts."

"And your new ones, I hope," slyly.

There was no one about. She wouldn't have seen them if there had been, for her eyes closed happily as he bent towards her again . . .

III

Grey clouds hung over Southampton, bringing a persistent drizzle that partly shrouded the gush of passengers and baggage, the scurrying of porters and stewards, all the teeming activity inseparable from the docking of a big liner. *S.S. Cornelius,* tethered like some vast beast, seemed to be pouring out its life blood.

The great majority of the passengers had already disembarked when Peter Gayleigh strode towards the Customs' sheds, having bid farewell to Sona and Larry and to Marcia and her father. He hoped to see all of them again, and if Marcia's parting words were anything to go by, she would be renewing the acquaintance very shortly.

"I'll be seeing you," she had intimated very confidently. And with a smile that conveyed several possibilities: "As your apprentice I've still got a lot to learn."

She had gone ashore some time before with the others, for Peter had been in no hurry to leave the ship. A disinclination he shared with Dave Lyman. Both had sent their luggage ahead, yet neither moved from the deck until Trevor Merson made a belated appearance. He was now receiving the attention of a Customs' officer, while Lyman hovered in the background awaiting his turn. As Gayleigh approached, the American ignored him completely, keeping his eyes on his quarry.

Peter wondered where the trail would lead them. If he lost Merson after the train reached Waterloo it might be the end of this adventure, for if he was swallowed up in London's millions it would be extremely difficult, perhaps impossible, to locate him.

The Customs' officer was making a swift examination of Merson's luggage while he maintained an attitude of bored indifference which said much for his histrionic ability. The official chalked a hieroglyphic on the suit-case concealing the sword, and transferred his attention to the metal trunk. Merson lit an Egyptian cigarette, his dark eyes flashing towards Gayleigh, who seemed to be fully occupied in dealing with his own luggage.

"Have you anything to declare?"

"Nothing but cigarettes," said Peter, indicating an opened hundred packet lying on the top of his suitcase. He had less luggage than Merson, and with any luck should be free to pass on to the train in time to note where the other was sitting—if Merson was not detained for further investigation. But it seemed that he was not suspect, for as Gayleigh's luggage was being examined very thoroughly he saw Merson stride away. Lyman also was relocking the lid of his one capacious suit-case. And still the officer who, Peter felt, must have been wished upon him by a perverse fate, continued his laborious and maddeningly detailed inspection. He had removed several articles of clothing, a fact which brought a cryptic smile from Lyman as he gathered up his case.

"I guess I'll be seeing you on the train," he observed sardonically. "Better not let 'em keep you too long."

He moved away, his gaze fixed on Merson's receding figure, while Peter tried to control his mounting impatience. There had been something in the American's last remark that sounded suspiciously like a note of triumph.

It was ten minutes later before the Customs' officer completed his examination. He turned to another uniformed official standing nearby. After a brief colloquy the second man came towards Peter.

"I'm very sorry to detain you, sir, but I must ask you to come this way."

Peter frowned. "May I ask why?"

The other looked at him very straightly.

"You are Mr. Peter Gayleigh, aren't you?"

"I am."

"Will you please come this way."

From past experience Peter knew better than to argue with uncommunicative officials trained in the art of stolidly polite evasion. Inwardly fuming at this development, he accompanied the man to an office nearby where another uniformed official received them very solemnly. The braid on his cuff denoted that he was the Chief Preventive Officer. He looked at Gayleigh very searchingly for a moment. He was about to say something when Peter forestalled him.

"I know," he said bitterly. "I'm a notorious character. So what?"

"I'm afraid we shall have to search you, Mr. Gayleigh."

One might have supposed this was the last thing he wished to do. His tone implied that it was most regrettable, but that somewhere a hierarch at an infinitely higher level had forced this unpleasant task upon him.

"That, of course, is why I was brought here," said Peter. "This procedure is quite familiar. It has happened to me so many times before. But I really thought you'd outgrown this sort of foolishness."

"I'm very sorry, Mr. Gayleigh . . ."

"I suppose a man called Lyman tipped you off?"

It was galling to think that Lyman had got the better of him in this way. For the significance of that sardonic smile, and those parting words was now apparent. Lyman had got rid of him very neatly. He had eliminated competition and the possibility of further interference from an ally who was of no further use. There were hidden depths in Dave Lyman.

He didn't expect an answer to his question, and merely shrugged when the C.P.O. remained silent.

" All right. Let's get this over. I'm in a hurry."

Left in the very capable hands of a subordinate officer he submitted to being searched with what, he told himself, was exemplary fortitude. Every inch of his clothing was examined, from the neck-band of his shirt to the welts of his shoes. It took a considerable time. When at last he was released with apologies and much deferential politeness the train carrying Trevor Merson to London had gone. And, presumably, Lyman was now hunting his quarry alone with the blissful satisfaction of a job well done.

So that Peter Gayleigh was not in the best of moods when he arrived some hours later at his flat in Jermyn Street. His man, Carver, relieved him of his overcoat, and said : " I hope you had a pleasant voyage, sir?"

" Very," Peter told him shortly.

The other eyed him solicitously, misinterpreting this observation.

" I'll mix you a drink, sir. It will settle your stomach."

" I'm not suffering from *mal de mer,* Carver."

" No, sir, I understand—just sea-sickness. I know you're not partial to such fancy drinks, sir."

It was then Peter recalled what he had almost forgotten during his absence—that Carver's flair for intensely serious but quite illogical conversation was as natural as his look of hurt reproach when his weakness was pointed out to him. He eyed this faithful little man tolerantly, and was striding into the lounge when Carver informed him that there had been a telephone call.

" Less than an hour ago, sir. A person by the name of Lyman."

" Oh?" He halted rather abruptly, glancing over his shoulder. " What did he want?"

" He 'phoned to ask if you had arrived here. When I told him that you hadn't, he said he was very sorry to hear it. Rather peculiar I thought, sir. He didn't leave his address or his 'phone number, but rang off immediately."

" Sorry, eh!" Peter snorted his disgust. " If he said that

he was lying. In fact," he added as a bitter afterthought, "that man is very aptly named."

It took Carver some time to assimilate this, comprehension dawning slowly on his very earnest face.

"Oh no, sir," he protested, for he had a passion for exactness. "Mr. Lyman doesn't spell his name that way. I jotted it down so that there should be no mistake. If you'd care to see it . . ."

"Thank you—no."

There was a fierce light in his eye as he glared at Carver. This subject, he felt, had been pursued quite far enough.

CHAPTER FIVE

IN WHICH HE VISITS PINEWOOD, AND HIS DEPARTURE
IS ACCELERATED BY SPORTSMEN WITH UNKIND IDEAS

I

PETER GAYLEIGH had been accused of many things, but never of being a recluse. Indeed, it had been said by harassed police officials, and a veritable legion of undesirables whose endeavours had been thwarted by his impudent intrusions, that he was much too socially inclined. For when Peter Gayleigh enjoyed himself in ways that were no more reprehensible than those of any other man about town, he was apt to be credited with dark, ulterior motives which would later become painfully apparent. In point of fact this often was so, though many of his engagements were of a purely social nature, for Peter had many old and trusted friends. Most of these were in London, and during the diversions of the next few days he gave scant thought to the unsatisfactory ending of the affair aboard *S.S. Cornelius*. So far as he was concerned the Van de Kramer diamonds were of no further interest now that he had lost contact with Merson, who had probably disposed of them very quickly. Even if he had not, the matter could be left in the very capable hands of Dave Lyman. There had been no further word from Lyman. Hardly surprising since he had shown such a marked preference for working alone.

Peter was still under the impression that only the diamonds were at issue, so that his lack of interest was understandable. Actually, as he was to discover, they were of little consequence compared with the seething vortex of the Greater Plan.

It was on the third day after his return that a provocative fate lifted the veil a little more, revealing another facet of this gem of deception.

Marcia Lawson called unexpectedly.

Carver showed her into the lounge in the early afternoon, and with that speculative curiosity reserved for strange feminine visitors who possessed a liberal quota of physical charm. He cast a dubious glance at Gayleigh, and withdrew, shaking his head sadly.

" I'm so glad I found you in, Peter," she greeted him. " Gosh, it's good to see you again ! "

He took in the well-cut costume, the stylish little hat, and the elegant contours of expensive silk stockings, the attributes of a blonde perfection he had rarely seen equalled.

" It's good to see you, too," he said.

" This is not just a social call." Then, dryly, as she saw the admiration he was making no attempt to conceal : " So I hope you aren't feeling too uninhibited."

" I was thinking you might like a drink," said Peter.

" Were you? I don't think you were. But thanks for the hospitality."

He brought her a martini, and organised a whisky and soda for himself. He gave her a cigarette, lit it, and sat down facing her. Her eyes were clouded, and she was frowning slightly.

" I saw Sona today," she began reflectively. " That's really why I came. The poor kid's worried."

" All people in love are worried," he said cynically. " I suppose she hasn't seen Larry."

But she shook her head.

" Oh no, it isn't that. As a matter of fact she was with him today. I saw them having lunch together in Frascati's. I went across to say how d'you do, and they asked me to join them."

" You're not going to tell me you did ? "

" Huh-huh."

" Darling, have you no tact ! "

" I'll admit they weren't very pressing." A faint smile touched her lips. " But, you see, I'd noticed something strange about Sona. She'd lost that elfin gaiety. Larry looked very serious, too. So I sat down, made amiable conversation for a time, then brought the conversation round to you."

" I don't quite like the way you put that," he remarked dryly. " But let it pass. I hope my name wasn't taken in vain."

" On the contrary. It had a magical effect."

" What? Munroe? "

E

" No, I told them who you really were. And, of course, they were frightfully interested. I thought there was no harm in telling them now."

He shrugged, a twinkle in his blue eyes.

" I'm surprised you managed to choke it back so long. Tell me, my sweet, how did Sona react to this staggering revelation?"

" I wish you'd treat this matter seriously, Peter, and try to understand. I merely told them to pave the way, to create a more intimate atmosphere, because I hoped to find out what was worrying them. Don't you see?"

" No," said Peter flatly. " But the logic of the female mind often eludes me. How did Sona take it?"

" Well, you know her step-father, it seems. And after I told her who you were, she confided in me without any persuasion on my part. As an old friend of her step-father she felt you'd be willing to help. He's been acting strangely ever since she got back."

Peter pursed his lips, and got slowly to his feet. He returned his empty glass to the cocktail cabinet, paused before it a moment, then looked slowly over his shoulder at the girl.

" Of course I'll do anything I can. Suppose you give me some details."

" Wouldn't you like Sona to do that? I think you ought to hear her story at first hand."

" Quite. But as Sona isn't here . . ."

Marcia shot him a sidelong glance. She rose, crossed to the window and peered down into Jermyn Street, tapping on the glass and crooking a beckoning finger.

" Sona and Larry," she explained as she turned round. " I asked them to wait outside in my car. They're coming up."

II

Peter regarded her sombrely as she raised her chin slightly, displaying very even white teeth in a triumphant little smile.

" I see! You're rather good at paving the way, aren't you?"

" I like to think so," she said, and was still smiling as he went to admit the other two.

Both of them greeted him rather diffidently while eyeing him with considerable interest.

"We didn't mean to barge in like this," apologised Larry. "But Marcia said—well that you were Peter Gayleigh."

"Guilty I'm afraid," he admitted as they continued to stare at him very intently. "I hope I come up to expectations?"

"Oh gee, it isn't that," said Larry with an expression that was neither a frown nor a laugh, a crinkling of his eyes which suggested embarrassment. "It's simply that Sona and I haven't gotten over our surprise yet."

"My step-father often speaks of you," put in Sona. "And then to meet you on the boat like that!" She looked at him bewitchingly. "I do think you might have told us who you were."

"I'll admit the temptation was very strong." He included both of them in an easy smile. "Frankly I was quite jealous of Larry. I hated to see him getting so much attention."

He was leading the way into the lounge, and having proffered cigarettes and supplied Larry with a whisky, he lowered his lean, muscular frame into a chair and eyed them silently for a moment. Sona had lost that *élan* which was so typical of her. The generous lips that seemed made for laughter were drawn into a tight little bud of anxious preoccupation; her brows were wrinkled, and the fine eyes, through which sunbeams had peeped, held the wistfulness of a hurt child.

"Marcia tells me you're worried about your step-father," he prompted gently. "You can count on me to help you in any way I can."

"Thank you. I feel I need some help. You see, father has been acting very strangely ever since I got back."

Peter continued to look at her. Then: "Is it—that he seems afraid of someone?"

"Why, yes." Her eyes widened in surprise, before she shot a swift glance at the other girl. "But of course Marcia told you that."

"No." This was Marcia as she eyed Peter speculatively. "I must say that was a pretty good guess."

It was more than a guess. It was a hunch. For he was thinking of the international jewel thief, who, as Larry had told them a week ago, had been released from Sing-Sing—the man known as Louie Palmer. Peter had said nothing then, and now that the possibility he had envisaged was taking definite form he decided to wait before committing himself. But his wry smile gave no indication of this.

"Yes, just a guess. And I was trying to make an impression!" The transient smile faded as he turned to Sona again. "What is your step-father afraid of? Do you know?"

The girl shook her head unhappily.

"I only wish I did. But father—I've always called him that—hasn't said anything. You see, he thinks I'm still a child. Besides, he never has confided in me. I'm sure that if I asked him outright what was the matter he'd just smile indulgently and fob me off with some vague reference to business. He just doesn't realise I'm growing up. Though I think it must have dawned on him to some extent when Larry called."

"If it didn't," put in Larry, his heart in his eyes as they devoured her face, "he must be blind."

Peter's gaze flashed towards Marcia. Neither of them smiled.

"And when you called, did you notice anything unusual, Larry?"

"Why sure. The man's badly scared. There's no doubt about that."

"I realised it as soon as I got home," Sona continued, "although father did his best to hide his feelings. But I've never seen him so restless. He kept going to the windows and looking out as though he were afraid there was someone lurking in the grounds."

"You mean at Pinewood? I've never been there, but it's near the river at Hampton Court, isn't it?"

She nodded. "Yes, it's a rather gloomy old house, though I've got used to it."

"Far too many trees," put in Larry. "Apart from the trees around the house there's a small pinewood running along one side of the grounds. The house stands in about 15 acres. Sorry, Sona. Carry on."

"Even before dusk, on the day I returned, father had all the window-shutters closed. He went round every room examining the fastenings himself. And both the front and back doors were locked and bolted. When he went to bed he locked his bedroom door, too, a thing he's never done before. It was the same every night." She pressed her hands together on her lap. " Oh, in a dozen ways it's obvious—he's terribly afraid of something. Of course I asked him why he was taking all these precautions. He said there'd been several burglaries at Hampton Court recently. But even if it's true, I'm sure that isn't all that's worrying him. You see he used to go out for long walks. Now he never leaves the house."

" Tell them about the man who called a couple of days ago," urged Larry.

" Oh yes. You know, Larry, I'm certain I've seen that man before. I wish I could think where." She turned to Peter again. " He was rather handsome, and I remember he had long slender fingers. Perhaps that's why I noticed them. They were so delicate, and—well like a woman's. I'd been out shopping, and I passed him in the drive as he was leaving. Then, when I got back to the house, I saw the sword."

" The sword?" echoed Peter. His eyes narrowed, but there was nothing more than interested curiosity in his voice.

" Yes. It was about two feet long, with bits of glass in the hilt. Or they might have been semi-precious stones. And there was some writing on the blade. It was lying on the table when I came into the room. Father was examining it, with his back towards me. He was so absorbed he didn't realise I'd come in until I spoke. Then he jerked round as though I'd startled him."

" He was annoyed?"

The girl shook her head uncertainly.

" No, I don't think so. Just startled. Naturally I asked him about the sword, and he told me he'd bought it from a man who dealt in Eastern curios. He said it was a fine example of handwrought work from North Borneo. But until then I didn't know he was interested in such things. He took it to his study, and I haven't seen it since. Actually, I was much more interested in the man who brought it. It seemed strange that he should call and that father should see him, because he obviously didn't want any visitors. When I told him I'd invited Larry he asked me where I'd met him, and all about him. I really think he'd have refused to admit him if Larry's name hadn't been so well known. Even so, he made quite sure it was Larry before he let him come in."

" That's right," said Larry. " I felt he was scrutinising me all the time. I've seldom felt so darned uncomfortable."

Peter drummed his fingers on the arm of the chair. He could not account for Merson's visit, though he thought he knew what Jervis Grant feared. He must see him as soon as possible, he decided. He lit another cigarette, staring thoughtfully at Sona.

" Do you think the house is being watched?"

She did not reply at once, but he did not miss the uneasy glance she flashed towards Larry.

" I'm sure it is. I went to post a letter last night, and as I was coming back along the drive I thought I saw a shadow moving towards the pinewood. It looked like a man, though, of course, moonlight plays queer tricks sometimes, and I might have been mistaken. If anyone was there it couldn't have been one of the servants, because I found that none of them had been out. Then, only this morning, while I was cutting some roses in the garden, I had the unpleasant feeling that I was being watched." She smiled half apologetically. " Again, it might have been my imagination. I didn't see anyone when I looked round. But I don't mind admitting that I was scared. So I hurried back into the house and 'phoned Larry. I arranged to meet him at Frascati's."

" But that isn't all," frowned Larry, as she looked at him uneasily again. " Shortly after Sona met me in the grill room, this guy with the beautiful hands walked in. Maybe he'd followed Sona from Pinewood though she says she didn't see anyone on the way to Frascati's. This guy's face seemed familiar to me, too." He wagged his head with a puzzled frown. " I've been wondering if I saw him somewhere in New York. Anyway, we caught him looking in our direction. It might have been coincidence, or——" He spread his hands. " What do you make of it?"

" Just one more question," said Peter, turning towards Sona again. " When you left Pinewood this morning did you say where you were going?"

" Well—no." She looked rather sheepish. " I told father I'd promised to visit an old schoolfriend in Knightsbridge. You see, I often used to stay with Kathleen's people during the holidays when father was on business abroad."

" You did? Splendid!" He brought his palms down

decisively on the arms of the chair. " In that case I daresay you could arrange to stay with these people again?"

"Yes, I daresay I could, though Kathleen's got a job abroad—in Washington. But father . . . "

"Don't worry. I'll tell him where you've gone. I certainly feel you'd be better away from Pinewood for a while."

" I'll say !" emphasised Larry. " That's exactly what I said. How about it, Sona?"

"Well, I hate to leave father." She looked at them irresolutely. " But since you both think . . ."

"Then it's settled," Larry sprang to his feet decisively. " I'll see you get fixed up all right, darling."

"And I'll take you along to Knightsbridge in the car," Marcia volunteered. She glanced suspiciously at Peter who was eyeing her serenely. " But I'll be back. Incidentally, you haven't told us what you propose to do."

" I shall call on my old friend Grant. Just leave this to me."

He saw them to the car, and returning upstairs again picked up an envelope which had evidently been slipped under the door. It was unstamped, and it was addressed to himself in bold sprawling capitals. It had not been there when he admitted Sona and Larry. There was, he found, a sheet of paper inside. Written upon it in the same illiterate handwriting were the words :

" Grant has it coming to him. Keep out of this, or
        you'll get yours too."

Peter sighed. This was not the first time he had received such a warning, and there was a sameness about such crude discouragements which had begun to pall. He had hoped for something more original from Merson—or, as he now believed, his accomplice, Louie Palmer.

It was not until much later that he realised how very original Louie Palmer could be.

III

"Far too many trees," Larry Becket had said, and as Peter brought the Bentley to a standstill in the road running past Pinewood he found himself in complete agreement with this criticism. The house itself was not visible from the wrought-iron gates, sagging open, and so thickly coated with rust that it would probably have been disastrous to move them. The Ionic stone columns on either side presented a pock-marked decrepitude. The heraldic beasts surmounting them had also begun to decay, the English climate having put their noses and several other parts of their anatomy out of joint. Beyond the gates the drive curled round, losing itself almost at once in the dense foliage of the trees. Viewed from the road the whole of this small estate seemed to be woodland, contained within lichen-covered walls. But as he walked up the drive, peering with interest through the elms on either side, he saw comparatively few trees in the grassland immediately beyond, only a few sycamores and oaks. The pine wood Larry had mentioned extended from the wall on the right, continuing past the house and some distance from it, a thick, dark green mass raised on rusty-coloured trunks, impervious to sunlight.

Presently he saw the house, and found that it was smaller than he had expected—a squat, uninspiring building devoid of gables, towers, or any ornamental flourishes. Whoever had conceived it must, Peter thought, have been glad to get this load off his mind. He was nearing the steps leading to the equally solid front door when he saw the curtains at a lower window flutter significantly. His approach had been observed. But after what Sona had told him he had expected this precaution. He went up the steps to the front door, and pulled the very ancient bell.

The summons was answered almost immediately by an elderly manservant.

" Is Mr. Grant at home?" Peter asked.

" Yes, sir. What name shall I give?"

" All right Paynton," a voice interpolated behind him. " Come in, Gayleigh." And as Peter stepped into a rectangular hall, looking towards the man who had not ventured beyond the threshold of one of the rooms, " Shut that door, Paynton."

He waited until this was done, then came forward extending his hand. This was Jervis Grant, a man in the late fifties with strongly defined features and a chin—reminiscent of Punch—that seemed out of proportion to his tall, lean frame.

He was wearing a woollen dressing-gown, and, Peter noticed, a very careworn expression.

"Glad to see you, Gayleigh," he muttered gravely as they shook hands.

Peter had not seen him for almost a year, yet the impassive face registered neither surprise nor curiosity. He seemed too preoccupied, too absorbed in himself to ask why Gayleigh had called.

"This way," he said, indicating the room from which he had come. It was evidently a study, for it was equipped with a desk littered with papers. There were two leather chairs, and some good prints on the wall. There were no windows, and the electric light was switched on.

"Fate must have sent you here," he remarked in the same abstracted way in which he had greeted his visitor. "I'm more than glad to see you. My God, I need someone to talk to!"

He was very different from the smartly groomed man Gayleigh had known before. There were dark pouches under his eyes; he had not shaved; and his lank grey hair fell loosely over his forehead. And since this was obviously not the moment for polite generalities Peter came to the point at once.

"So I gathered. I've been talking to Sona."

"Sona!" His brows came together as he struggled to grasp this. "But you haven't seen Sona since she was a child."

"I met her on the boat coming over from New York."

"Oh I see." His frown deepened. "Strange, Sona didn't mention that."

"I travelled under an alias," Peter explained. "Fame has its disadvantages. Until today Sona didn't know who I was. She's very worried about you, Jervis."

The other turned away passing a hand through his hair. A black onyx ring on his little finger glinted under the light.

"So she's been talking to you, eh. Well I can't say I'm surprised. I wish she'd stayed in New York a little longer. Mind you," he added quickly, "I think she's quite safe here, otherwise I shouldn't have permitted her to remain."

Peter pursed his lips.

"She had lunch with Larry Becket today, and afterwards they came to see me. Becket called here recently, I believe."

"Yes. Seems a nice enough lad. So she confided in him. What did she say?"

"Simply that you were behaving strangely, not at all like your old self. She thinks this house is being watched. And she's scared, Jervis. I suggested she should stay with some friends in Knightsbridge. In the circumstances I felt that was advisable. Don't you agree?"

The other did not reply at once. He lowered himself into a chair, then getting up again restlessly, began to pace the room.

"You're right of course," he said presently. "This is no place for Sona. I ought to have realised that." He paused, turning to stare directly at Gayleigh. "I'm going all to pieces, and I think you know why."

"I can guess. Because of something that happened twelve years ago."

"Yes." He inclined his head slowly, his eyes half closed. "I wish now I'd never been mixed up in that business, but when the diamonds came into my possession what could I do?"

"You did what any other honest man would have done," said Peter, recalling how he had first met Jervis Grant.

"No doubt!" He spoke bitterly. "I went to the police. And now, twelve years after, I'm paying for it. It was my evidence that brought that gang to justice. The leader, you remember, was a man called Palmer. He got five years."

Peter nodded reflectively.

"Yes—Louie Palmer. I've never forgotten the look he gave you as they dragged him from the dock."

"I haven't forgotten it either! There was stark murder in that man's eyes." He resumed his restless pacing up and down the room. "That's why I left England when Palmer was released. After a time he followed me to America, but fortunately he didn't catch up with me. He was arrested for another jewel robbery over there, and was sent down for ten years. Recently I made inquiries about his remission of sentence. He was released on parole sooner than I'd expected. To be exact, just over a month ago."

"Which was why you took the first available boat back here."

"Yes."

" And you think he's followed you?"

The onyx ring flashed again as he spread his hands, shrugging wearily.

" I don't know. I just don't know. But I've had this thing hanging over me for years, and now I feel that it's drawing closer. Palmer is a man who never forgets. If he finds me he'll get me, even if he swings for it."

Recalling the livid hate he had seen on Palmer's face, Peter knew this to be no exaggeration. But he also knew that he would never see those twisted features again, that if he met Palmer the man would be unrecognisable. For after his release from Dartmoor he had changed his appearance. A facial operation. Plastic surgery. When arrested in New York he had not been recognised. His finger-prints had established his identity.

" As you know he's the worst type of criminal," Grant resumed after a pause. " And he's spent years in prison. He's had plenty of time to brood over his revenge. By now the canker must have eaten deep into his black soul. That man will show no mercy." His lips curled bitterly. " Ironic, when you think of it. I've done nothing illegal. Quite the reverse. Yet I feel like a man under sentence of death."

Gayleigh thought he looked like one too. The hunted light in those deep set eyes was as foreign to Jervis Grant as his careless appearance.

" I'm surprised you haven't got into touch with Herrington. He dealt with the case, and he knows all the facts. He could give you police protection."

" I've thought of that. But until I'm sure—". His teeth came together with an audible click, moving his very determined chin into even greater prominence. " I'm not easily intimidated. I'm merely taking precautions. It's possible this house is being watched; that Louie Palmer is here. But I've seen nothing conclusive. I've got a ghastly presentiment, that's all. I'll go to the police when I'm positive. Not before."

Obviously he had made up his mind, though the change in him was so marked, his nervous manner so much at variance with this stubborn resolve that Peter wondered if it had become an obsession. Or perhaps pride was forcing him to fight this battle alone.

" Sona must have found it very unnerving here," he went

on, changing the subject abruptly. " I'm glad that young
fellow Becket called."

" You've had no other visitors, I suppose?"

" No—oh yes, just one." He waved his hand negligently.
" But that's of no consequence."

" Someone you know, of course," Peter persisted casually,
flicking a speck of dust from his jacket with elaborate care.

" Actually, it was a man I met in New York. Fellow called
Merson. The sort of man one can't quite reckon up." He
wagged his head reflectively. " Y'know I think you'd have
enjoyed meeting him."

Not a muscle of Peter's face betrayed his reaction to this
opinion.

" Possibly I should."

" He's a dealer in Eastern curios. I can't say I've got much
use for such things myself, but Merson wanted me to accept
something in return for some business I put in his way. I
introduced him to several wealthy collectors in New York.
He gave me a sword which he said, once belonged to a witch-
doctor in North Borneo. Not a very attractive weapon to
look at, but "—for the first time his face relaxed into the
semblance of a smile—" it's supposed to possess magical properties. A lot of rot, of course."

" But interesting," mused Peter. " A magic sword, eh.
How does the charm, or whatever it is, work?"

Grant shrugged. He thrust his hand into the pocket of his
dressing-gown, and produced the slip of paper Peter had seen
in Merson's wallet.

" This bit of verse explains the procedure," he explained
dryly. " I understand it's a translation of an inscription on
the blade." He gave it to Peter. " Perhaps you'd care to read
it."

Once again Gayleigh scanned the familiar words :

" To him who would its weight assess,
　Pause thou, consider and caress
　This magic blade.
For it hath wondrous power and charm
If lightly poised upon the palm
Of those who scorn all earthly balm,
　And palisades."

" H'm." He cocked a disbelieving eyebrow, recalling how he had reacted to this injunction when he had first seen it. He handed the paper back. " Have you tried it out?"

The diamond-broker shook his head.

" I've got far too much to think about without indulging in such childish nonsense."

" Quite." Peter made a grimace. " Besides one couldn't exactly say that you ' scorn all earthly balm and palisades.' !" After his experience aboard *Cornelius* he was not interested in the sword. But he was very interested in Trevor Merson. And so : " Did this chap say where he was staying?"

" Why yes." Grant looked at him in surprise. " At a restaurant called the Four Hundred in Soho. Apparently the proprietor is a friend of his. But don't get any foolish ideas about Merson. I told you how I met him. He's got nothing to do with Palmer."

" Perhaps not. But we can't be too careful."

" We !" With belated hospitality he offered his visitor a cigarette from a box on the desk. " No, Peter, I'll fight this alone. If I want any assistance I'll let you know. Until then I'm not dragging either you or Herrington into it."

It would have been impossible at this stage to keep Peter Gayleigh out of it, for the scent of danger was strong in his nostrils. But as Grant evidently credited him with much less pertinacity than he possessed he did not disillusion him. Instead :

" I think you're being much too noble. Very foolish, if you don't mind my saying so. But, of course, if that's the way you feel—"

" I do. Most definitely." He struck a match, lighting Gayleigh's cigarette and his own. " And now, tell me what you've been doing, Peter." It was an attempt at heartiness that failed dismally. " It must be nearly a year since I last saw you."

His determination to change the subject was very apparent, and for a time they talked about personal matters of mutual interest.

" You'll stay to dinner, of course," he said presently.

" No, but thanks all the same. I've an engagement in town." He looked at his watch, for now that he had Merson's address he was anxious to do something about it as soon as possible. As it was he had prolonged his visit merely out of politeness, and because a hurried departure might have indicated his intention. "I merely dropped in to tell you about Sona."

"At least you'll have a drink before you go?"

He mixed whisky and soda from a decanter and syphon on an occasional table, and Peter had barely emptied his glass before a telephone shrilled in the hall.

"That's probably my office in Hatton Garden," said Grant as he opened the door. "For the past few days I've been attending to all urgent business from this house."

"In that case I'll be getting along." He gripped the other's hand. "And don't forget, I'm always available if you want me."

"Thanks, Peter. And thanks for coming. Don't think I don't appreciate it."

He moved towards the phone. Peter let himself out, and retraced his steps along the drive. After the artificial light in the study, and the air of fearful expectancy that impregnated the house, the trees, even the leaden clouds overhead, for it was a dull day, were a refreshing contrast. Sona had been quite right when she said that Jervis Grant was worried. He was so badly scared that Peter wondered if he knew more about Palmer's movements than he had disclosed. Probably he did, for surely the mere presentiment that danger was drawing closer, and, moreover, danger which had threatened him for years, could not have effected such a change in a man like Grant. No, he must have good reason to believe that Palmer had located him and was biding his time. And yet, very stupidly, Peter thought, he refused to inform the police.

He had almost reached the end of the drive before it occurred to him that in Grant's position he would have done exactly the same, and the reflection brought a wry smile to his lips. Had he been the central figure in this situation he would have revelled in it. But he would not have immured himself in the house as Grant had done. Peter Gayleigh believed in the maxim that attack is the secret of defence. The battle would have been carried into the open, and it would not have been without its colourful moments.

He had reached the gates when he saw the flat tyre on the

Bentley. A jagged piece of glass protruded from the rear wheel, so that it was not difficult to decide what had caused the damage. He might have collected that piece of glass from among the broken bits, seemingly those of a milk bottle, farther along the road. But he knew that he hadn't. That glass had not been there when he arrived. Which meant that someone had punctured the tyre deliberately. Perhaps someone who hoped he would change it for the spare. And while he was doing so with his back to the grounds. . . .

In that instant of realisation his spine seemed to contract under the touch of icy fingers. The ghostly tattoo extended to the nape of his neck, but he resisted the urge to look round. With scarcely a pause he continued towards the car.

IV

It must have seemed to anyone who was watching him that he had seen the flat tyre and was going to examine it. He did, in fact, bend over it for a moment, before moving with unhurried smoothness round the back of the car. The action suggested that he was going to inspect the spare wheel before dealing with the casualty. Again he stooped so that he was hidden from the drive and the more thickly wooded part of the estate. Then shielded by the Bentley, he darted to the far side, still crouching as he moved swiftly towards the bonnet, peering round it cautiously. But although he sensed that, somewhere among the trees, a pair of eyes were focused upon the car, he saw no one.

The chill feeling along his spine had now given place to a tense exhilaration, a tingling in his veins. A few minutes before it had seemed that the discussion with Grant, the realisation that his friend was asking for trouble, could not give birth to immediate action. Peter's sole hope in that direction had centred round his prospective visit to the restaurant in Soho. Yet danger had hatched out with glorious suddenness. He had been warned to keep out of this, and now he was in the thick of it. Nothing could have been more conducive to the joy of living. This, he decided, was where the flatulence of discussion ended and the real effervescent fun began.

He poised himself on his toes, and ran swiftly in front of the car to the shelter of the wall on the right of the drive. Whether this movement had been observed or not would depend largely on the view obtainable from the Unknown's position. Peter had to take that risk, but as nothing happened he decided he hadn't been seen. Perhaps there was no danger. Perhaps all this was unnecessary, and he was behaving like a fool. But faced with that flat tyre he didn't think so. And he knew that he wasn't going to adopt Grant's attitude and wait for developments. He was going to make a flank attack, and do some scouting which might shed some much needed light on this ambush.

That part of the wall against which he had flattened himself continued for more than a hundred yards. It took him half that number of seconds to glide, almost silently, to the end of it. Overhead the pine trees marked the beginning of the thickly wooded area extending right across this side of the grounds.

Peter waited a moment, glancing back again towards the Bentley. No one had approached it to find out what had become of him. The deceptively peaceful scene remained exactly the same. This lack of response was rather disconcerting, for he had hoped to arouse curiosity. Had he been seen? or could it be that the punctured tyre had been meant to convey nothing more dangerous than a second warning? That seemed unlikely, yet, if an attack had been planned, why hadn't it come while he was returning along the drive?

The wall was not very high. A lithe spring and he gripped the top of the brickwork. He raised his head, and peered into the wood, then hoisting both legs over the wall, dropped lightly down on the other side. He took his automatic from his pocket, and eased back the safety-catch.

The straight trunks of the pine trees reared up before him, the lower branches bare and sepulchral-looking in the half light beneath the thick green canopy overhead. And there was an awesome silence. It was as though he had descended into a dead and petrified world where no movement had ever taken place. He decided to cross the wood diagonally,

and then work along the inner fringe back to the Bentley.
In that way he might come upon the Unknown from
behind.

He began to weave his way between the trees, his gun
poised in readiness, the thick carpet of pine needles contribut-
ing to the silence of his movements. No birds sang in those
uninviting surroundings, and he knew that if he made the
slightest sound it would be heard by anyone lurking in the
vicinity. It was, therefore, the height of misfortune when a
dry twig, almost hidden by the pine needles, snapped under
his feet before he had gone fifty yards.

Peter stifled a curse. The rusty-coloured trunks crowded
closely together : his range of vision was limited, and though
he saw no one he thought he heard the sound of furtive
movement away to his left.

He waited, his gun at his hip.

A minute passed, during which the eeriness of the wood did
nothing to restore his confidence. But the sound was not
repeated, and picking his way with extreme caution he went
on again.

He was circling a slight rise in the ground when the shot
came.

The bullet smashed into a tree-trunk not six inches in front
of him, and as he flung himself down on his face he heard
the report, like the sound of a cork being withdrawn from a
bottle. Whoever had fired the shot was some distance away,
and the gun was equipped with a silencer.

The shot must have come from a rifle. Peter raised himself slightly on one elbow, glancing dubiously at his automatic. It was useless against a rifle—unless he could get
much closer to this sportsman. And he thought he knew now
why he had not been picked off while he was returning to the
car. The elm trees fringing the drive had partly shielded him
from view, and he had been walking fairly quickly. But if
he had presented his back to this sniper, while changing the
wheel of the car, he would have offered a perfect target to
anyone who had studied angles and chosen a position accordingly. This very methodical gunman had waited to make
certain he would get him with the first shot.

Well, it hadn't quite worked out that way. But his movements had obviously been noted. And the other had done

F

some stalking on his own account. Judging from the direction from which the bullet had come he must be concealed
somewhere near the drive.   Peter wondered if he could
shorten the distance between them sufficiently to use his automatic before the other scored a bullseye.   It was not a very
joyous prospect, and he could think of far better ways to
spend his time.   But because he was Peter Gayleigh he
decided to go on.

He remained motionless for a couple of minutes, then
began to edge forward very cautiously on his elbows and
knees.   Before he had gone twenty yards his immaculate
grey suit had suffered considerably, though, much more
important, his health remained unimpaired.   It was possible
that he was now out of view, so, seeking as much cover as a
clump of nearby trees afforded, he rose to a crouching
posture.   Nothing happened.   He set off again with rising
hopes stimulated by the thought of what he would do to this
sniper when they came to close quarters.

And then a second bullet removed a piece of cloth from his
sleeve.

Peter flattened himself again, waited, and as a third bullet
chuffed into the pine needles less than a foot away from him,
dragged himself on his stomach to the shelter of a shallow
depression.   Presently he resumed his former stalking tactics,
but he hadn't moved more than a couple of yards before
another bullet streaked past.

And it came from an entirely different direction.

Which could only mean one thing.   There were at least two
of these sportsmen, and he had got himself very nicely into a
position where he would be the target for continuous cross-
fire.   Not for the first time in his life he realised that he was
quite a spot.

To continue now would be sheer madness, since if he
located one of these gunmen, and attempted to come to grips
with him, he would probably be shot down by the other.   And
if there were more than two. . . .   He had been called fool-
hardy, but there were limits to the risk he was prepared to
take when there was no immediate chance of retaliation.   No,
there were times when a strategical withdrawal was justified,
and he had no doubt at all that this was one of them.   It was
a pity that he hadn't caught even a glimpse of his attackers,

but for the time being his curiosity would have to remain unsatisfied.

The beginning of the return journey was enlivened by several more shots, some of which went so wide of their mark that he knew he must be invisible so long as he kept close to the ground. He retreated on his stomach. It was not a performance that would rank as one of his most dashing achievements, but it enabled him to regain the wall over which he had climbed with such optimistic expectations. He covered the last few yards on his feet, and having made certain that none of the gunmen were waiting in the country road, climbed over the wall without further hindrance and walked rapidly away in the opposite direction to the Bentley. The scene at which he glanced back very frequently still looked very peaceful, but its deceptive serenity precluded all thought of returning to the car.

He was heading in the direction of Hampton, and it was quarter of an hour before he reached the village itself. He found a garage and arranged for the Bentley to be made roadworthy and brought in, since he felt there would be no danger in this, providing he didn't try to collect the car himself. While he was waiting he asked if he might use the telephone.

He rang up Jervis Grant.

Nothing, he was glad to learn, had happened to Grant. He had neither heard nor seen anything unusual since Gayleigh left.

"But why these cryptic questions?" he asked rather irritably.

Peter told him.

"Proof enough, I think that the house is being watched," he concluded, after several increasingly nervous interpolations from the diamond-broker. "Take my advice, Jervis, and phone Herrington."

This time he raised no objection.

"I'll do that," he said very promptly. "And by God I'll barricade the windows! Thanks for the warning, Peter."

Peter didn't offer to stay around, since he felt there was nothing useful he could do before the police arrived, and after that he didn't want to be subjected to the time-wasting business of an official interrogation. The divisional police should be at Pinewood in half an hour, perhaps sooner if a squad car was cruising in the vicinity. The matter could now be left to them.

The man who had gone to fetch the Bentley returned very shortly, having fitted the spare wheel. Peter did not wait for the punctured tyre to be repaired. He got into the car, and headed for the Four Hundred.

CHAPTER SIX

IN WHICH HE INVITES HIMSELF TO A PARTY, AND
TREVOR MERSON ISSUES ANOTHER INVITATION

I

OUTWARDLY the Four Hundred was just another restaurant in Soho, that Mecca of less exalted restaurateurs who, with limited capital but unlimited energy, cater for the culinary idiosyncrasies of a dozen nationalities. It presented nothing more than a large plate-glass window and a narrow entrance to passers-by in Dean Street, so that the name placarded above in red letters on a bilious yellow background and retraced in Neon tubing was somewhat pretentious. The dining-room immediately beyond the entrance was small but well appointed; the napery was spotless; the chairs were tastefully upholstered in green leather; and coloured plaques, the work of Soho artists, graced the walls. A casual visitor might have left with the impression that there was nothing unusual about the restaurant, that, compared with other more colourful resorts in the neighbourhood, it was not worth a second visit.

Yet it was this seeming lack of enterprise that had largely contributed to the success of its proprietor, one Mike Winniger, who had rented the vacant and larger premises adjoining with the intention, it was understood, of enlarging the Four Hundred as soon as labour for the purpose was available. It could not be denied that the restaurant was ordinary. It was, therefore, inconspicuous. Yet there were nights when it was well patronised, others when it was almost empty, and only some of the clientéle and the entirely male staff could have accounted for this strange fluctuation.

Mike Winniger knew they would be busy again that night, although the dish that had this magnetic effect was not on the menu. It was being prepared in a room at the back of the vacant premises, to which those who were privileged would find their way. There were shutters over the windows

of this room, so that no light escaped into the cul-de-sac outside.   The curtains and thick carpet—which deadened any
sound, besides imparting a more habitable appearance to the
apartment—had not been there half an hour before.   The
furniture consisted of a billiard-table and a number of
straight-backed chairs piled against one of the walls.

If Winniger had been questioned about this furniture he
would have said that it was stored there in preparation for
the new restaurant and club he had in mind.   Actually, he
had no intention of adding to his less profitable activities in
this way.   But as no one could be sure that he hadn't, this
explanation could not be disputed.

He had been a bootlegger in Chicago in less difficult times,
and most of his staff were recruited from racketeers who had
assisted him in these operations.   One of them, now acting as
a waiter, was busily rearranging the chairs.   Another was
setting out the equipment of a small, improvised bar.
Winniger, himself, attended to the billiard-table.   It looked
like any other full-sized billiard-table, but, as he proceeded to
demonstrate, the slate bed was reversible, the join being
hidden under detachable cushions.   On the underside, now
uppermost, was a roulette-wheel.   Winniger examined this,
then producing a small ivory ball, tossed it on to the wheel,
and set it in motion.   He watched it for a few moments, satisfied himself that the mechanism was in perfect order, and
turned to the waiter who was attending to the chairs.

" Okay, Tony, let's have the trimmings."

The man brought several boxes of different coloured
counters, and a roulette-cloth bearing the customary squares
and numbers.   He placed the boxes of counters near the
wheel, while Winniger took the cloth, unfolded it, and spread
it on the table.

" Anything else, boss?"

" Yeah.   The croupier's rake.   Fetch it, then give Joe a
hand with the liquor."

" An excellent idea," said a strange voice behind him.
" Between them they might fix me a drink."

The reaction to this remark came quite up to Peter
Gayleigh's expectations.   Three heads jerked round simultaneously; three pairs of narrowed eyes bored into him like
gimlets.   He was standing at the door, a cigarette protruding

at a jaunty angle from his lips. The grey suit looked even more woebegone than it had done when he left Hampton, but there was a joyous light in those mocking blue eyes.

He said: "We all seem to be enjoying ourselves. That's fine."

Very palpably Mike Winniger didn't agree with him. That basilisk stare could not possibly have been generated by good fellowship. Peter took in the wrinkled forehead, above slit-like eyes; the puckered flesh below both ears, scars which might have been left by knife slashes, or perhaps a facial operation; the blue chin, and hairy, very muscular hands. He was stockily built, and he wore pointed shoes. He looked what he had been. Any casting director would have typed him as a racketeer.

"Who let you in here?" he asked, in a way which boded ill for someone.

"No one let me in," Peter told him blandly. "I effected illegal entry by the window in the passage. As you may recall, it looks on to a cul-de-sac. You see I'm looking for someone—someone who doesn't like me very much—and I should have hated him to sneak out the back way while I was kept waiting at the front. See what I mean?"

"So you're jest looking for someone."

"Huh-huh." He removed the cigarette from his mouth, flicking ash with delicate precision on to the carpet. "I'm told he's staying here."

"Who?"

"A friend of yours. A bloke called Merson."

The lines in the wrinkled forehead deepened. Winniger thought all around this remark before he said tersely: "He ain't here."

"Of course you may be right," said Peter. "I didn't see him on my way in. But he may be lurking behind closed doors. He's good at that sort of thing."

"I've jest told you—he's out."

"Where has he gone?"

"I wouldn't know."

His eyes darted from Gayleigh towards the other two men and back again. Tony and Joe stepped forward very purposefully—until Peter did things with his right hand. Bluish steel leapt between his supple fingers.

" I wouldn't if I were you," he said gently, as he levelled the barrel.

Both men halted, looking at Winniger for further instructions which were not forthcoming. His eyes had narrowed, but he said nothing. Evidently he didn't underrate the man behind that gun. And though the mockery in Gayleigh's eyes had extended to his lips he was wondering why this gorilla hadn't asked him who he was. Perhaps he knew. Perhaps Merson had told him. And perhaps not.

He said : " This little hold-up is illegal, of course. But so are your party arrangements. So that makes us quits. Has Merson told you about me?"

There was no response, merely a pregnant silence.

" No one could say you guys talk too much," remarked Peter. " But if Merson is out he'll be back." He moved the gun to include the roulette-wheel. " And I'm pretty certain he'll be back tonight. Our Trevor loves taking other folk's money. He'd make a good croupier."

" You're wasting your time, feller." Winniger had found his voice. " Merson ain't here. I'd advise you to beat it."

" That's very kind of you, Mr.—er—? "

" The name is Mike Winniger."

"—Mr. Winniger. I barged in here quite accidentally and maybe I'll take your advice. But, of course, I shall be back."

" I wouldn't come back if I were you," said Winniger darkly.

" Quite. But, you see, you don't happen to be me. I repeat, I shall be back. And you'll welcome me as though you liked it. Because I'm fond of a flutter myself, and I intend to be included in the invitations. If I don't receive one I shall go to the police. I shall tell them that Mike Winniger's parties should be broken up, now and for evermore." He displayed his teeth in an angelic smile. " Mind you I should hate to do that. I'm all for free enterprise. It would hurt me like hell to put you out of business. But you see the way it is."

" If I raise my voice," snarled Winniger, " I can bring half-a-dozen of my boys in here."

Peter cocked his head on one side provocatively.

" Really? I didn't know you were a family man."

Winniger glared at him. He said : " Don't be a sap. Clowning won't get you outta here."

" No," said Peter, " always supposing your overgrown progeny manage to get in. If there's too much shooting the police might interfere. We don't want that, do we?"

The other said nothing, though his expression suggested a string of words which, Peter felt, would all have been quite unprintable.

" So I shall be seeing you later," he continued serenely. " When does the party begin?"

" Find out."

" That's what I'm trying to do," he said patiently. " And you're going to tell me. Unless you play ball with me "—his gaze darted towards the roulette-table—" you won't play ball at all. I think you know me. If you're sociable I shall keep my mouth shut. Otherwise——" He shrugged. " Well, the cops have their uses."

" We planned to begin at ten o'clock," growled Winniger.

Peter said : " I hope you will. I wouldn't put the party off. If you do a lot of men in blue uniforms and others in plain clothes will begin to take a great interest in the Four Hundred. And it won't make the slightest difference to me. I shall be back in any case."

A second later he had darted into the passage, and he was closing the door smartly behind him when he saw another waiter who seemed to have materialised out of the solid brick. He was standing against the wall which evidently divided the restaurant from the untenanted premises.

" Good evening," said Peter pleasantly. " I've just seen Mike. I'm the new chum."

The man stared at him blankly. Peter gave him a friendly nod, and turned in the opposite direction, striding to the window by which he had entered.

" Hi, you !"

The other had suddenly realised that all was not as it should be. He had thrown off his stupor and found his voice. But he lost it very promptly again as Peter levelled his automatic.

" Take it easy, pal," he said, halting him as he rushed forward. " We're not as friendly as all that."

He opened the window, and swung one leg over the sill and then the other, dropping lightly into the deserted cul-de-sac. The man was at the window glowering at him as he looked up. Peter raised a jaunty hand before striding away. No one had talked very much except himself. But they would be talking now. He wondered why his ears weren't tingling.

II

Since it was not yet eight o'clock he collected the Bentley from the car park in Soho Square, and returned to his flat.

And there he found Marcia Lawson.

She was sitting at a trolley-table, which Carver had evidently brought in, and she was rapidly disposing of some salmon mayonnaise. He had not expected, or indeed wanted to find her there. But she had obviously made herself at home.

"At last!" she exclaimed as he appeared. "I've been waiting for ages. I thought you'd be back long before this."

She had changed from the costume in which he had last seen her, and was now wearing a deceptively simple dress, a model of expensive elegance. The high neckline was relieved by a rope of pearls, but she wore no other jewellery, though the last rays of the sun slanting through the window seemed to create strands of pure gold in her hair. She looked regal, but not at all unapproachable. She looked much too desirable for a man's peace of mind.

She said : "Well, aren't you going to say how d'you do? And you needn't frown like that. I told you I'd be back."

Peter shrugged resignedly. This girl, he felt, might have been attached to his earthly sphere of operations by a piece of astral elastic which brought her bouncing back at the most inopportune moments.

"You should have brought your slippers," he said dryly. "You'd have been more comfortable. I suppose Sona is fixed up all right?"

"Yes, they received her with open arms. Larry made quite an impression too. I think she'll be very comfortable there—and so will Larry when he calls."

"So that settles that."

"And much more satisfactorily than the chauffeur act you knew I couldn't avoid," she pointed out shrewdly. "Oh yes, I could see what you were thinking. You hoped you'd get rid of me." She made a little pout. "And after I hadn't seen you for three whole days."

"Almost a lifetime!" He indicated the food on the trolley-table. "However it seems I failed, so carry on with the good work. At least no one can say I'm not hospitable. There must be some good in you, otherwise you wouldn't have got round Carver."

She laughed softly, applying herself again to the salmon mayonnaise.

"I told him you'd invited me to dinner, though I don't think he believed me. And he seemed very loth to provide food for a famished female with such adhesive qualities. I suppose it must have been my personal charm that eventually did the trick." She tilted her head provocatively. "Don't *you* think I'm rather attractive, Peter?"

"Absolutely marvellous," he told her, but with as little conviction as he could put into it. Which still sounded far too much.

"Thank you. A little tepid perhaps, but encouraging. Now tell me why your suit looks as though you'd been wiping it on the ground."

He regarded himself ruefully.

"Because I've been doing just that. There have been complications, Marcia my sweet."

"So that's why you've been so long. Tell me about it," she urged, leaning forward eagerly. "How did you find your friend Grant?"

He provided himself with a cigarette, lit it, and sank into an easy chair.

"Grant has got the jitters. And after what happened I can't say I'm surprised."

"Oh? Well—go on."

"He's afraid of a man called Louie Palmer."

She stared at him uncomprehendingly, a tiny frown ruffling her forehead.

"And who is Louie Palmer?"

Peter hesitated. It was just possible that Marcia Lawson had been foisted upon him by someone who was playing a very subtle game. He hadn't overlooked that, though he didn't want to believe it. But since every move he had made was known to the Others, nothing could be lost by telling her what had occurred.

"He's a very nasty bit of work. Twelve years ago he was the leader of a gang of jewel thieves operating over here." He outlined the circumstances culminating in Grant's evidence at the trial and Palmer's imprisonment. "It was quite obvious that he was out after Grant's blood. No one who saw the look he gave Grant from the dock could doubt that. Palmer meant to get even with the man who had testified against him."

"But surely your friend couldn't have done anything else when the diamonds came into his possession?"

"No," said Peter, "that's one of the drawbacks of being an honest man! But Palmer wasn't very fair-minded. He didn't see it that way. Though, fortunately, he didn't get the opportunity to settle the account when he was released from Dartmoor. He followed Grant to America. But Palmer hadn't been over there very long before he was arrested for another jewel robbery. He was sentenced to ten years. He was released on parole only a month ago."

"I see." She nodded slowly. "And now Grant thinks this man has found him."

"Exactly. If Palmer is in London he must have given the American police the slip. Sona may have seen him in the grounds at Pinewood. I don't know. But I do know those grounds are damned unhealthy. After I left the house a couple of sportsmen tried to put me out of the running. It's possible one of them may have been our old friend Merson."

"Merson. The man on the boat? But how does he come into it?"

Peter wished he could answer that question. For he felt that Merson was implicated in some way, yet to what extent, or how, he could not fathom. He thought there was much more behind Merson's visit to Pinewood than appeared on the surface. The fact that he had called on Grant at such a time might be sheer coincidence, but it was far more probable that he had an ulterior motive. Was he in league with Palmer? If so, what did Merson hope to get out of it? Where was the percentage? On the face of it, this was a simple case of revenge with no apparent complications. Surely a man like Palmer could have attended to this personal matter on his own. He might, of course, have enlisted the services of unimportant underlings. But it was difficult to visualise Merson in that role.

He got to his feet, and mixed himself a whisky and soda, deep in thought. Were the missing links to be found in Merson's association with Winniger. Who was Mike Winniger, and where had he come from? Later, he decided, he must delve a little into Winniger's past history. The man was obviously an American. Among other things it would be interesting to know how long he had been in London.

"Well?" prompted Marcia, and as he looked at her vaguely: "I asked you how Merson came into it."

"Merson comes into it as a dealer in Eastern curios. He feels under a deep obligation to Grant for putting some business in his way in New York. So he calls to see him, and presents him with the sword I told you about on the boat. Can it be that Merson does this out of the kindness of his heart? The answer is very definitely—nuts."

Marcia was frowning at him in perplexity. She said dryly: "That's beautifully clear! It might help if you told me what happened to you today. Or would that be asking too much?"

He chuckled. "All right," he said lightly as he took his drink to an easy chair, and sat down again. "The story begins with Uncle Peter stepping from his car before the outer portals of Pinewood. He observes the decrepit gates, wondering if they will fall on him as he passes through and flatten him on his pan. But no, our hero goes safely through, and being very observant, sees a pine wood. Immediately, and with that rare brilliance that characterises all his deductions, he realises that he has found a clue. He has done it again—he has discovered how the house got its name!"

"What a man, children! What a man!" put in Marcia with a sickly smile. "Uncle Peter will now tell you about the buttercups and daisies, and his girl friend who made a noise like a raspberry."

"To continue," he resumed, undeterred. "Your Uncle Peter . . ."

" Please !" She protested wearily. " Must you tell it this way? Or are you just stalling?"

His eyes were twinkling as he muttered a hurried disclaimer.

" Not at all. But I have my lighter moments. You must bear with me—as the fat old dame said to the gigolo when she sat on his knee."

" Do be serious, Peter. I want to know what happened."

" Very well. You shall have a straight, unvarnished narrative."

It was not entirely that, for Peter Gayleigh had yet to tell a story of his own exploits which was not sprinkled with absurdities. Long ago he had learned to laugh at himself, and when asked about his adventures he always passed the joke on. His flippancy served to disguise the understatements when the story he had to tell was rather grim. And more than once a smile flickered on the girl's lips as he passed on from his conversation with Grant to a detailed and largely apocryphal description of his intimate contact with the pine needles in the wood, and sundry stinging insects which had, apparently chosen the most inconvenient spots on his anatomy to get rid of years of accumulated inhibition. The men with the rifles had been very poor shots it seemed, and the only reason why he had grovelled his way back was because he thought they might improve, and because unwanted friends imposing on his hospitality were eating steadily through him.

" There is a further instalment," he went on, after a pause. " As Grant had given me Merson's address, I thought I'd go along to the Four Hundred. I didn't see Merson there, although I saw a lot of other interesting people—and things."

He gave her an account of his visit, omitting his own very pertinent remarks, and the byplay with the gun. But he described Mike Winniger, and the preparations he had been making for the roulette party.

" I bet they looked pretty sick when you interrupted them like that. And they might have tried to prevent you from leaving," she said innocently. " Weren't you taking an awful risk?"

" A terrible risk. It appals me to think of it. Winniger is a man of few words, but strange as it may seem, he invited me along to the party. It begins at ten o'clock, and whether he abandons the idea or not—and somehow I don't think he will—I shall be there." He looked at his watch. "As I may not have time to grab some food outside I'll get Carver to bring in some more of that appetising salmon mayonnaise."

"And then both of us will be fit for the fray," said Marcia smugly. "If we eat anything at the Four Hundred they might put poison in it."

Peter looked at her.

"Perhaps I haven't made my meaning clear. I'm going alone."

"Oh, no, you're not!"

"But, my dear girl, this is no job for you. It's apt to be dangerous."

"That's why I'm going with you," she said emphatically. "If I don't, there ain't going to be no gambling party."

"What do you mean?" There was dark suspicion in his gaze.

"After what you've told me I could tip off the police. I could spoil everything." She looked at him very sweetly. "So from now on I join in the fun—or else! Short of stopping me by sheer force—and only a brute would do that—there's really nothing you can do about it, is there?"

Peter looked at her admiringly. If there had been a female Peter Gayleigh he felt she would have talked like this.

"I mean it," she went on firmly. "It's up to you, Peter darling. You've got your choice. What are you going to do?"

Ruefully he shrugged his capitulation.

"All right, honey, it's a date. But don't blame me if things get a bit hot."

"Do I look as though I should?"

"No. You look too good to be true."

The *double entendre* was not entirely unintentional, but he felt glad when, without hesitation, she took it as a compliment.

"Perhaps some day you'll forget yourself, Peter, and say something nice you really mean."

"Perhaps." His shrug conveyed all the indifference he could muster. "Just keep on hoping. Now, how about a drink . . .?"

III

Peter Gayleigh dismissed the taxi before the Four Hundred, and together with the girl, walked into the restaurant. Beneath his tuxedo his automatic rested in a spring shoulder-holster. He was prepared for anything in the way of surprises, for he was not expecting a cordial reception from Mike Winniger. It was also extremely unlikely that Merson, if he happened to be around, would display any noticeable bonhomie. Nevertheless Peter hoped to see both of them, and possibly other folk he knew whose fondness for gambling might have drawn them to this deliciously illegal party. He had thought of several amongst his multifarious acquaintances who might be there. But by a curious oversight he had not thought to meet the most likely person of all.

So he was mildly surprised to see Dave Lyman.

He was sitting at an inconspicuously-placed table, and he appeared to be absorbed in a newspaper. But as Peter and the girl glanced towards him he looked over the top, stared at them very intently for a moment, then lowered his eyes again significantly.

Marcia tugged at Peter's arm.

"Look! Over there," she whispered. "It's——"

He nudged her hurriedly, and catching the look in his eye she broke off quickly. A waiter, whom he had not seen before shepherded them to a vacant table, hovering over them in the way of his kind.

"Two sherries," said Peter. "We'll order later."

The man moved away, and Peter gazed casually round the half empty restaurant, taking in the slight movement of Lyman's thick forefinger as he turned over a page of the newspaper. He had pointed directly towards a door on which the one illuminating word *Gentlemen* was inscribed. A few moments later he rose, strolled casually towards it, and disappeared inside. Peter looked quizzically at Marcia.

"Excuse me," he said, pushing his chair back and getting to his feet."

She had followed the American's movements and was frowning slightly.

" You're going to talk to him?"

He nodded.

" But you'll come back?" she added quickly.

" Just as soon as I've powdered my nose."

He found Lyman alone in his retirement. He was standing before a mirror picking his teeth with a match.

" Well, how've you been, Dave?" he greeted him dryly. " It's always good to meet an old pal."

" Yeah." He flicked the match on to the floor with his thumb-nail, and turned to eye Gayleigh sombrely. " I've kinda missed you. You ain't bin around lately."

" After you brushed me off at Southampton I lost interest," said Peter sourly. " I felt hurt, Dave. It almost broke my heart."

" Brushed you off?" His surprise had all the appearance of being genuine. " I figured sump'n had happened when I found you hadn't gotten on the train. Trouble with the Customs, I guess."

" Just a little. But, of course, you wouldn't know about that. It's taken me a few days to catch up on the general situation. And now that I have, I'm expecting real co-operation from you, Dave. If I don't get it, I shall spill the beans, so far as you're concerned. You see, they know who I am here. They take a great interest in my movements and intentions. But if you're as good a detective as I think you are they won't know about you. It would be a pity to spoil their peace of mind, wouldn't it?"

Lyman eased a cigar from his waistcoat-pocket, chewed off the end, and spat it out as though it had done him a personal injury. He looked at Gayleigh and shook his head. His faith in human nature, it seemed, had been shattered.

" You're mighty sore with me, ain't you, bud."

" What acumen!" said Peter. " What astonishing perception! I'm different from other people. I like being given the run around. But don't do it again."

He showed his teeth in a pleasant smile that lacked nothing but good natured amusement. Lyman kindled his cigar, and shook his head sadly.

" This is a helluva business, Gayleigh. Fact is, I ain't making much progress, and everyone's lammin' into me. I got a cable from the boss at Lishman's today. He says Van

de Kramer is gettin' impatient. He says to shake the lead
outta my pants and get cracking. But it ain't easy. All I
can do is tail Merson, jest hoping he'll flash the jewels some
place. If I put the finger on him, and he hadn't got 'em,
I'd look sorta foolish. Besides, after that, I guess I couldn't
go chasing him around any more." He passed stubby fingers
over his chin. " Yeah, it's a helluva business."

Peter had never seen him so depressed. He looked as though
he thought a world that owed him a living was forgetting
to square its account.

" Why not try being straight with me, Dave. Then, maybe,
I can save your payroll. I take it you've been following
Merson ever since he left Southampton?"

" Yeah." He nodded lugubriously. " That's all I could
do. And I ain't doing that very well. I lost him this afternoon. That's why I came back to this joint. Merson's
rooming here with a guy called Winniger—the fella who
runs the place."

" So I gathered. Winniger is an American. Have you ever
run into him in the States?"

There was a perceptible pause while he considered this.

" No," he said carefully. " He's a new one on me. But
he's a tough guy. I reckon he's much tougher than
Merson."

" H'm." Peter didn't pursue the subject, though he felt
that Lyman hadn't told him all he knew about Mike
Winniger. Ideas about men like Winniger might be very
profitable to a private detective. If Lyman thought he had
something he would naturally keep it to himself. Peter, too,
had thought of vague possibilities concerning Winniger. But
as yet they lacked confirmation.

" Merson came back about an hour ago. Since you've
gotten here yourself, maybe you picked him up?"

" Not quite," said Peter. " Perhaps later we'll let down
our back hair and have a heart to heart talk. But not now.
I'm not aiming to spend any longer than is necessary in this
salubrious retreat, so I propose to skip a whole lot of detail.
A roulette-party is being held here tonight, Dave. At least
I hope so. It should have started already. The locale is a
heavily curtained room in what are supposed to be empty
premises next door."

The American inclined his head ponderously, sucking his teeth.

"So that's the set-up. I bin thinkin' sump'n must be going on. Couldn't figure why this joint was so popular tonight. Other nights it's bin almost empty. Yeah, that accounts for some of the swell dames and slickers I seen driftin' through a door out there. Doggone it, I'd like to get in meself."

"Sorry, Dave. That's impossible without an invitation from Winniger. Besides, they don't know about you yet. In the roulette-room you'd be too conspicuous."

The hopeful light faded from the other's eyes. He knew that Gayleigh was right.

"By staying in the restaurant you might help me, and incidentally yourself quite a lot. I can do with a second string. Because Miss Lawson and I are going to follow the example of those other people you saw. We've been invited to this party."

Lyman screwed up his forehead in disbelief.

"Sounds phoney to me. Maybe this is jest another smart idea to keep me in the dark."

"That doesn't need any bright ideas of mine, Dave."

"Aw shucks."

"Stick to me long enough and you'll see some light. I saw Winniger this afternoon. I'll tell you about that."

He did this as quickly as possible, while Lyman stared at him with owlish intensity, puffing cigar smoke out of the side of his mouth. It was impossible to tell what he was thinking, but Peter felt it didn't amount to very much. The more he saw of Dave Lyman's soggy face, the more he noticed the absence of any sparkling intelligence.

"We hope to leave in one piece," he concluded, "though Winniger and his boys may have other ideas. That's where you come in. If we're forcibly detained you might help a lot by advising the police. And after that you might join in the merriment yourself, if you can do that without spoiling your own plans."

"Yeah, I gotta think about myself. I'm jest a wage earner." He massaged his chin again, glancing sideways at Peter. "Okay, I'll stick around. But I guess you and me are goin' to have a real talk later."

"Sure," said Peter, and made a motion with his hands. "After you, Claude. We'd better not leave together."

Lyman returned to his table, and after a short interval Peter did likewise. Marcia, who was sipping her sherry, looked up at him inquiringly.

"Yes, I think it's about time we paid our respects to Mr. Winniger," he said, deliberately misinterpreting her unspoken question. "Wait here. I'll attend to the preliminaries."

On the opposite side of the dining-room, at the point farthest from the street entrance, there was a door which, he had noticed while returning to the table, bore the significant word *Private*. It was screened from the greater part of the room by mahogany panelling jutting from the wall, and since one of the waiters was sitting in this narrow space, ostensibly resting until his services were required, Gayleigh had no doubt that it led to the more exclusive part of the establishment. He sauntered across the restaurant, and moved behind the panelling. And as he had expected, the waiter rose immediately to confront him.

"Sorry, sir," he said very firmly. "You can't leave this way."

"I have no intention of leaving," said Peter. "Would you tell your boss that Peter Gayleigh and a lady friend are here."

"Mr. Winniger is expecting you?" His expression was politely deferential.

"Unless I miss my guess," said Peter. "You know perfectly well that he is. I saw you take a quick peek at me as I came in."

The man stared at him for a moment, then called to another waiter now hovering conveniently only a few yards away.

"This gentleman says Mr. Winniger is expecting him," he explained unnecessarily. "He has brought a lady with him. Would you let Mr. Winniger know."

"*Toujours la politesse*," smiled Peter. He found this suave reception rather amusing. "Do your stuff, my little man. I can wait. But you might tell Mike I shan't wait very long."

The man shot him a sidelong glance, and vanished through the door. Gayleigh lit a cigarette, inhaled deeply, eyed the other up and down and said : "You know where to find me." Then turning on his heel, he strolled back to Marcia and sat down. He looked thoughtfully at the glass of sherry, but did not touch it. Perhaps it was all right. It didn't seem to have affected the girl. But it would be a pity if the night's amusement was spoilt by a doped drink.

"Well?" asked Marcia.

"Everything is being made ready for our reception." His eyes took on that mocking light. "Would you believe it, Mike didn't know we were here." He blew a smoke ring, sent another chasing after it, then saw the excessively polite waiter emerge from his cubby-hole and nod towards him significantly.

"Now for it," he muttered. "Of course if you'd rather stay here——"

Disdaining to reply she stubbed out her cigarette and got to her feet. Gayleigh crossed the room again, and rounding the panelling found the second waiter had returned.

"Mike says okay."

He opened the door, stepped into what was evidently a small private office, and motioning them after him closed the door again. A second later a key clicked in the lock on the other side. Involuntarily Marcia gripped Peter's arm, her heart thumping. For the door by which they had entered was apparently the only exit. But a moment later their guide strode past them to a bookcase against the far wall. And as though accustomed to this procedure he thrust a hand under one of the shelves and pressed on the woodwork. The bookcase swung inward, disclosing the passage with the window at one end. It was here that Peter had seen the waiter who had seemingly materialised out of the solid brick.

"Thanks, pal," he said. He brushed past their escort, and with the girl at his heels strode swiftly towards the door of the roulette-room. He opened it smartly and saw at once that the game had not been abandoned. There were perhaps thirty well dressed men and women huddled round the roulette-table, some of them standing behind the chairs. But most of the view was blotted out by Mike Winniger, who confronted them as they entered.

"You don't scare easily, I see," said Peter, lifting his hand to include the room.

The other shook his head slowly, his narrowed eyes darting towards Marcia.

" I'm figuring to play it your way, Gayleigh. I don't like your methods. But I guess there's no reason why you and me should fall out."

" Meaning you're expecting to make quite a packet tonight."

Winniger shrugged. " This game's straight. So don't get any queer ideas. But at roulette the odds favour the bank. I don't take this risk for nuth'n."

Peter looked over the man's broad shoulder, glancing searchingly about the room.

" He ain't here, feller. Merson didn't seem pleased when I told him you'd be back. He left right away."

" That's too bad," deplored Peter. " You know, I was rather afraid he wouldn't be here."

" I've heard tell you're a gambler yourself, Gayleigh. From now on you're jest another guest. Join in the game if you want to. Only don't cause any trouble. Get it?"

" I think so." He smiled thinly. " I gather there's liable to be some unpleasantness if we attempt to leave before the party breaks up—say in time to tip off the cops."

" I'll say." His thick lips tugged down sardonically. Then as he turned away : " Okay, make yourself at home."

Peter took out his cigarette-case and proffered it to Marcia, his clean cut features quite inscrutable. And he was not staring at Winniger as he moved away but at one of the roulette players, sitting with his back towards the door. The man was partly hidden by one of the other players standing behind him, but the set of his shoulders and the back of his head was familiar. And then as Gayleigh lit his cigarette, the man looked round as though suddenly conscious that someone was staring at him.

At the same moment Peter's stomach seemed to execute a nose dive into sheer space before righting itself. For the pale eyes which met his were those of the crime novelist, Miles Lawson.

IV

Marcia was still eyeing Winniger dubiously as he went towards the tiny bar, so that she did not see Gayleigh's taut expression. Not immediately. Then glancing up at him she followed the direction of his gaze, and gave a little gasp of astonishment.

He eyed her sharply. But she was still staring, and with a puzzled frown, at the man who was now disengaging himself from the group about the roulette-table.

"Why, father!" she exclaimed, as he approached. "What are you doing here?"

"I might ask you the same question, my dear." He glanced at Peter. "Good evening, Gayleigh. Er—this is quite a surprise."

"In more ways than one," said Peter. "When we last met you called me Munroe."

"Munroe?" The bleached, almost non-existent eyebrows came together slightly. "Ah yes, so I did. I thought you'd prefer me to keep up your little deception on the boat. I recognised you when you came to dine with us."

"You did?" This was Marcia. "So you knew all the time. You didn't say anything to me."

"Why should I, my dear. It was so obvious that you knew all about Mr.—er—Munroe." He turned to Peter. "I must say I'm rather surprised that you brought my daughter here."

There was disapproval in his voice. His tone suggested that she would hear more about this later, and that he was not pleased to see her with a man like Gayleigh. But he did not put this into words, for he was obviously very conscious that his own presence in that room required some explanation.

"You needn't blame Peter. I made him bring me along," said Marcia. And then archly: "I didn't know you were a secret gambler, father."

"People in glass houses, eh?" He looked at her ruefully. "Yes, I admit I'm not in a position to throw stones. Actually, I went to a great deal of trouble to get myself on Mike's invitation list."

"Indeed." Peter was looking at him very straightly. "May I ask why?"

"Simply because I've never been to a gambling party like this before. The more select parties in the West End—yes. But not one at which one sees such a varied assortment of types, mostly drawn, I should say, from the lower middle

class. These people interest me, Gayleigh. Also our host
and his boys."

" Professionally, I suppose."

" Precisely. Though I won't deny I find all this very exciting, and pleasantly dangerous. Incidentally, I see Mike
is looking at us very keenly. H'm, I wonder why?"

Peter could have told him. For if his story was true, and
this was purely a fortuitous meeting, this would be the last
party he would attend. Mike Winniger would see to that,
working on the very sound assumption that any friend of
Peter Gayleigh was a potential menace. But if Lawson's
story was a smooth invention it would be interesting to know
just why he was there. Marcia's astonishment had seemed
genuine enough, and a less dangerous-looking man than
Miles Lawson it was hard to imagine. So Peter was prepared
to keep an open mind for the present.

" Perhaps Mike would look a little less like a thwarted
gorilla if we lost some money," he suggested, nodding towards
the roulette-table. " Shall we try our luck?"

Luck, he realised, as they obtained a closer view of the
play was very definitely the operative word. For on this
particular wheel there was not one zero, nor even two, but
three, in addition to the customary thirty-six numbers.
Which meant that the odds were heavily on the side
of the bank. The game might not be crooked, but Winniger
had not exaggerated when he had said that he was not taking
this risk for nothing.

" *Faites vos jeux,*" intoned the croupier, whom Peter had
no difficulty in recognising as the former waiter, Tony. His
French lacked the Parisian accent, but nobody cared. Hands
stretched out from the human caterpillar round the table,
some decisively, some uncertainly, depositing various coloured
counters on the numbers. None found their way into the
rectangles marked Pair, Impair, Passé and Manque. These
people were inveterate gamblers, scorning to waste time on
even chances.

" *Rien ne va ploo,*" Tony commanded in his execrable
but determined French. Then as the fateful little ball came
to rest : " Numero twenty-five—*vant sank.*"

A second croupier standing at his elbow wielded the rake
with a snake-like proficiency that suggested that if he was

another disguised waiter he had missed his vocation. In ten seconds the cloth was bare again except for the counters, flicked expertly in coloured spouts, to the few fortunate backers.

"*Faites vos jeux . . .*"

The wheel was spun again. The game went on, while Peter took stock of those about him. As Lawson had said they were not the kind of gamblers who frequented the more select parties in the West End. There was a man whom Peter recognised as a dance-band leader at one of the lesser known restaurants; another paunchy, podgy fingered male who looked like the cartoonist's conception of a bookmaker or prosperous publican, but for that very reason probably wasn't; and there was a man who looked like a solicitor's clerk. The rest of the men couldn't be classified very easily, though none of them looked as though they rated that very elastic term—gentleman. As for the women, most of them were of doubtful middle-age, some of them flashily beringed and with wrinkled faces excessively rouged and powdered. Marcia alone among the younger women looked as though she was not accustomed to this very intensive pastime.

The maximum stake, he learnt, was £10. But even with this comparatively low limit, Winniger should be able to pay his boys a very nice little bonus.

He bought some counters, and having given half of them to Marcia, lost all his own while showing her how the game was played.

"You're not very good at it, are you," she said rather unkindly. "Now watch me."

She put the equivalent of ten shillings on Number Eight, and it came up. And while Peter, who had been keeping a furtive eye on Winniger saw him stroll towards the door and leave the room, she was so busy checking her winnings that she forgot to remove her original stake. When Number Eight came up again her eyes sparkled with excitement.

"You see!" she exclaimed delightedly, and Peter nodded his congratulations.

"You'll be able to play quite a time before you lose all that," he said.

Lawson, who had lost consistently, smiled ruefully.

"Beginner's luck, my dear. You *will* lose it, you know. The odds are all against you."

Somewhat defiantly she put a neat pile of counters on Number Eighteen, and Peter smoothed a hand over his mouth to hide a smile as, flaunting the infinite permutations of chance, the ivory ball came to rest in Number Eighteen, utterly confounding Miles Lawson, who stared at his daughter with something akin to awe.

" You see !" said Marcia again on a rising note of triumph. " It's not a difficult game, really."

Lawson looked at Peter, who pursed his lips. He waited until the wheel was slowing down again, and, while both of them were watching it intently, strolled towards the tiny bar where the waiter named Joe was presiding.

" Drinks are on the house I suppose," said Peter. " I'll take a double whisky."

Joe poured out the spirit with frowning reluctance, placing it on the miniature bar counter without a word. Peter picked up the glass, and as the man turned away to attend to other thirsty patrons, strolled to a small collapsible table on which a variety of delectable snacks had been spread. At this juncture he caught Marcia's eye across the roulette-table, and indicating the food, raised his eyebrows interrogatively. Politeness, he felt, demanded this suggestion, but he was not sorry when she shook her head, and switched her gaze back to the table. For he had ideas, much more fascinating than roulette, that clamoured for expression.

There were a few others round the buffet, and as though inspecting the eatables farthest away from him, he manoeuvred nearer the door. The rest was simply a matter of timing. He disposed of his whisky, and waited until Joe was busily employed. The backs of the two croupiers were towards him. Marcia and her father were absorbed in the play. Very casually he edged to the door, opened it, and for the enlightenment of any of the guests who might be looking that way, nodded to an imaginary person in the passage.

Then with a final glance over his shoulder he stepped outside, and closed the door.

To his right he could make out the skilfully camouflaged outline of the entrance in the wall, but only because he knew it was there. At the end of the passage was the window by which he had arrived earlier, now hidden by a shutter, while at the other end there was a stout door, presumably leading into Dean Street. The door was festooned with cobwebs, and quite evidently had not been opened for years. There was also a flight of stairs in this direction, obliquely opposite and beyond the concealed entrance. It was these stairs which had suggested interesting possibilities to Peter Gayleigh.

He moved swiftly along the dimly lit passage, and began to ascend them, bringing out his torch and switching it on as he reached the dark landing above. The doors of two empty rooms were ajar, and having flashed the light inside and satisfied himself that they were in fact empty, he glided over creaking floorboards to another passage directly above that on the ground floor. Like its counterpart below, it ran from the front to the back of the building, and although the beam of his torch did not extend that far he knew there should be a grimy, but unshuttered window at the far end. He had seen that window when he had used the one immediately beneath—also the jutting stonework, forming a ledge which might prove very convenient. By working his way a few feet along the ledge he could reach a window giving access to one of the rooms above the restaurant itself. Once inside, the way would be open for further exploration. Sooner or later he might come across Trevor Merson.

Before proceeding along the landing he slipped his hand-kerchief over the bulb of his torch, directing the attenuated beam towards the floor. If there should be anyone in the cul-de-sac a light seen shining through the window of an empty building might create unwelcome complications. He passed several doors on his left, all of them opening into dust-laden rooms or shelved closets, which must once have served as store rooms or cupboards. Only one of the doors was locked. He stooped and peered through the keyhole, but could see nothing. The room was obviously in darkness, since no light showed beneath the door. There might be something interesting in there, but in all probability there was not. Possibly an accumulation of junk, or decorators' materials, on which it would be foolish to waste his time. The roundabout route he had been obliged to take was simply a means to an end. He hadn't expected to find anything on this floor, and he continued past another empty room to the window. It was secured with an old-fashioned catch which, he realised, would not delay him very long. He had thumbed it back when he heard a sound that seemed to pluck at every nerve in his body. A loud click, as startling as a pistol shot, had come from the brooding blackness behind him.

He switched off his torch, and leaping back, flattened himself against the wall. For it had not been difficult to account for that sound.

Someone had turned a key in the door of the locked room.

There was no one on the landing, but a thin sliver of light now showed beneath the door. If someone came out of that room he would be seen. But the door remained closed, and after waiting a couple of minutes he edged cautiously towards it. Quite distinctly he could hear someone walking about in the room. And there was nothing furtive about the sound. Whoever was in there, evidently thought he was alone. In the circumstances this illusion was understandable, but Peter felt that it should be dispelled at once.

He stretched out his hand, gripped the handle of the door, and flung it open—to find himself staring into the barrel of an automatic.

" Come in, Gayleigh," said Trevor Merson encouragingly. " I've been expecting you."

CHAPTER SEVEN

IN WHICH MARCIA LAWSON SEEKS EXCITEMENT,
AND GETS MORE THAN SHE ANTICIPATED

I

HE was standing at the far end of the room, near an oil-lamp on the floor, his macabre shadow on the wall writhing as though with fiendish glee. And he was not alone. Two other men, incongruously attired as waiters, stood on either side of the door. Their hands were in the pockets of their jackets, and their attitude suggested that very unpleasant things would happen to Gayleigh, if he attempted to shield himself by jerking the door shut.

"Come in," said Merson again. "Mike tells me you want to talk to me."

Peter did not move.

"Why is it, Merson," he observed sadly, "that I always find you skulking behind locked doors?"

The quip was ignored. Merson spoke sharply to the other two.

"Search him."

"Haven't you missed out a line?" Peter asked coolly. "There's a set routine about this sort of thing, you know. You haven't asked me to raise my hands."

"That won't be necessary."

Just why it wasn't necessary he learnt with stupefying suddenness. The man on his left prodded him with a gun, and as he looked quickly towards him, the other man brought the butt of his own weapon down with shattering force on to the back of Gayleigh's skull. He had a vague recollection of sinking to his knees as the room dissolved into a throbbing agony of blinding light, and a myriad dazzling stars, which grew fainter and fainter as he fell with nauseating speed into a bottomless void. . . .

The return to consciousness was equally unpleasant. He was swept with a momentum that jarred every bone in his head towards a tiny point of light that grew larger and larger, pervading everything, before presenting its nucleus as the flame of the oil-lamp. He had opened his eyes, and almost simultaneously came the realisation that he must have been out for some considerable time. For he was lying on the floor, his wrists and ankles bound tightly together with a very adequate length of window-cord. The man who had stunned him had his torch and gun, and he had no doubt that a telescopic set of jemmies he had brought with him, and his shoulder holster, had also changed hands. He wondered if they had found the safety-razor blade which he invariably carried in a tiny leather sheath in the lining of his hip-pocket. But even if they hadn't, it would be difficult, perhaps impossible, to reach it, for his hands were tied in front of him.

"I see you've helped yourselves," he said wryly. "Okay, where do we go from here?"

"We don't," snapped Merson. "At least, you don't. Not for the time being. Later on we hope to give you a change of scenery."

Gayleigh's lips twisted into that crooked smile which no misfortune could dispel. He was not feeling so good, for apart from his predicament, a pneumatic drill seemed to be disporting itself on the top of his head. But at least he was still alive. His recklessness had been rewarded in this way many times before, and he had faced more formidable adversaries than Trevor Merson. The man was a small-time crook, and always would be, however much he tried to raise his criminal status. For the moment he had the upper hand. That was all. And with that eternal optimism that made life such a great adventure for Peter Gayleigh, he wondered how long it would be before the tables were turned.

He said : "It's a pity you didn't wing me at Pinewood, Merson. Then you'd have saved yourself all this trouble."

The dark eyes contracted the merest trifle.

"You're pretty smart, aren't you."

"Sometimes," Peter admitted modestly. "Though I can't fathom why you called on Grant."

"Didn't he tell you?" The thin lips drooped cynically.

"He did. But his explanation wasn't very convincing, though I've no doubt he told me all he knew. Why did you give him that sword? Don't tell me it was for services rendered."

"You don't believe that?"

Peter shook his head very decisively. It made him feel a little dizzy, but it gave added emphasis to what he had to say. "Surely you don't think I'm such a dope. The sword, and the delightful sentiment which went with it, was merely an excuse for your visit. As for that mumbo-jumbo about its mystical power—well I'm not a great believer in magic, though I liked your poetic efforts. But even if the sword *is* dangerous in some way, I'd still say it doesn't matter two hoots. Because you and your pals have no intention of killing Grant. Not yet. I don't know what your game is, but I admire your build-up. There must be something pretty attractive behind it."

It was a telling little speech, and even after he finished, Merson continued to stare at him with hawk-like intensity.

"I didn't think you were quite so dangerous, Gayleigh."

"And yet you sent me a warning."

He didn't expect to learn anything from this quick riposte, but it had no sooner left his lips than he realised his assumption was incorrect. Merson hadn't sent that note. The flicker of puzzled incomprehension in the chocolate-coloured eyes told Gayleigh that. Who then was responsible? Had Winniger written it, or the man who was no more than a name—Louie Palmer. Even so, there was something wrong, something intangible which he felt was persistently eluding him. He had no doubt now that there were undercurrents in this conspiracy. It was by no means as simple as it seemed.

"All right, we'll skip that," he said as Merson frowned. "I'm not such a bright boy, really, otherwise I shouldn't be here. Were you waiting for me very long?"

"Not very long," said Merson. "We thought you'd leave the roulette-room pretty soon, and come this way. There's a window on the landing which might have been very useful."

"So we figured we'd better wait in here," put in the man who had taken Peter's gun.

"And you locked the door to arouse my curiosity, of course. When I didn't drop in you turned the key in the lock to give me a little encouragement. All right. We've all had fun. I'm to be taken for a ride, but not, I think, until the roulette-party breaks up."

"Maybe we should get back." This was the other man, and he spoke as though Gayleigh's remark had started a train of thought, as though further preparations must be made to put the finishing touch to this hospitality.

"I shall be seeing you again, I fear," said Peter, "and possibly your boss, Scarface. Maybe you boys can tell me when he had his face lifted?"

It was a shot in the dark, and the reaction was rather disappointing. Merson looked at him sourly, while one of the other men said:

"Another crack like that, and I'll lift yours. The boss got them scars in a rough house in Chicago. So what's funny about that?"

"Nothing. Nothing at all. I'm just naturally curious."

"All right, Ed, gag him," Merson instructed. "I'm getting tired of this small talk."

The man who looked as though he might have been with Winniger in Chicago produced a roll of adhesive tape, evidently brought for the purpose, and a pocket-knife. He cut off a suitable length, and stepping towards Gayleigh clamped it over his mouth, pressing the gag down with practised fingers.

"Okay, that should keep him quiet." Merson picked up the lamp and strode to the door, motioning the other two after him.

"Yeah," frowned Ed. "We gotta get the dame."

So they had not overlooked Marcia. Peter had clung to the faint hope that she would be told some plausible story to account for his disappearance, and that she would be allowed to leave. Now he knew that Winniger and his crowd were much too thorough to take a chance like that. Realisation brought a pang of self-reproach. For, of course, he needn't have brought Marcia. He had admired her nerve and had capitulated willingly, whereas he could have stressed the danger and indicated his intentions much more plainly. And if she had insisted, if it had been impossible to dissuade her, he needn't have come himself. But it was a bit late for such self-recrimination. He had got her into this, and now she was to pay for his crass stupidity. It was not an up-lifting thought.

Ed and the other man followed Merson on to the landing.
He was about to shut the door when he thrust his head back
into the room, eyeing Gayleigh sardonically.

"There's one thing I forgot to tell you. If you do
manage to reach your hip-pocket, it won't do you any
good."

And he held up a tiny, leather case, just large enough to
hold a safety-razor blade, dangling it provocatively. A
moment later the door closed behind him. Gayleigh heard
the grating of the key in the lock, followed by the sound of
their retreating footsteps.

The cord securing his wrists was bound tightly round his
body, so that he was unable to reach his ankles. In fact,
after some minutes of strenuous effort, he realised that if he
managed to free himself unaided it would be a miracle. And
the fruitless exertion had increased the throbbing in his head
to an agonising hammer-beat. He had never been trussed
up more efficiently. He flexed his powerful shoulder and
arm muscles with renewed determination, but the cord did
not give. In effect, he might have been encased in a straight-
jacket, and surrounded by Stygian darkness, a prey to uncomfortable introspection, the thought engendered another.
He wondered suddenly if the blow on his skull had made him
light-headed. For above his heavy breathing he thought he
heard a muffled whisper. He screwed up his eyes, blinked,
and listened intently.

"Peter, are you there?"

Unless he was suffering from hallucinations it was Marcia's
voice. And it came from beyond the door. How she had
got there he didn't trouble to think, for a wild surge of hope
obliterated such trivial considerations. He called out as
loudly as the gag would permit, achieving a sub-human sound
that might have come from a depressed puppy. But it was
the best he could do, and he hoped it would carry beyond the
door.

Evidently it did, and apparently the girl had realised his
predicament. She did not speak again for almost a minute,
though, in the intense silence, he could hear the rubbing of
her fingers as they explored beneath the door. Then :

"Can you hear me?" she whispered anxiously.

Again he produced the sub-human affirmation.

H

"All right. There's a space under the door. I'm going to push my nail-scissors through." He heard her suit the action to the words. "Hurry, I can hear someone coming."

He rolled towards the door, manoeuvring with difficulty, until at last he managed to grip the scissors. They were even smaller than he had expected, and he realised it would take him some time to free himself. Meanwhile, the girl had tiptoed away along the landing. The sound of heavier footsteps had become louder, but they did not approach much closer.

As he pressed the tough cord between the tiny blades again and again, fraying but not snapping it, he could guess what had happened. They had discovered that Marcia had slipped out of the roulette-room, and this floor was now being searched. It wouldn't be very long before they found her.

A section of the cord snapped under his fierce onslaught. He managed to free his wrists. By doubling up his legs he could reach the knots tied about his ankles, though his arms were still tightly bound to his body.

A couple of minutes passed. The heavy footsteps had become much louder. Then he heard one of the men on the landing outside the door. If he was interrupted now——But to his infinite relief the man passed on. Gayleigh wrenched the cord from his ankles, and could have groaned with frustration as the scissors bit with maddening slowness into the strands still pinioning his arms. He felt he had made very little impression when he heard the girl's voice raised in alarm, and the threatening tones of a man.

So they had found her! And he was still almost helpless.

He heard another man pass the door, hurrying to assist the other. At any moment now they might come into the room. If he was to take advantage of that moment he must get to his feet. He swung his legs round so that his back was against the wall, and began to force himself upright. From the sounds on the landing, it seemed that Marcia was being dragged towards the door. But he was on his feet, and waiting, poised for action when for the third time he heard a key turn in the lock.

II

The door opened slowly, spilling an increasing patch of light into the room. But as he was pressed against the wall, he saw nothing more than a man's hand, quickly withdrawn to deal more effectively with the struggling girl on the landing. He heard a vicious curse, and a stifled cry from Marcia. Then she was pushed very forcibly through the doorway. The man whom Merson had called Ed was striding after her when Gayleigh's shoulder crashed against him. Caught off his balance, he staggered against the door, clutched at it wildly, and as it swung further open, fell to one knee on the floor. The taller man behind him, who was holding the oil-lamp, deposited it quickly on the landing. But before he got rid of it, Peter grabbed him by the lapels of his jacket; jerking him violently into the room. He stumbled over Ed, as Gayleigh darted nimbly aside, and went careering past Marcia towards the far wall.

The element of surprise had served Peter well. Moreover there was no sign of Merson. Evidently these two constituted the whole of the opposition, but in the circumstances it was quite formidable enough. Unless he could free his arms, life might quickly assume a less roseate hue. His only hope lay in swift, elusive movement, using his knees and feet whenever possible. The doorway was still blocked. But he was ready for Ed as he came lunging at him. He moved very slightly to one side, and, as a ham-like fist went over his shoulder, sank his knee into the man's stomach. As Ed doubled up Peter's knee flashed up again, smashing under a bony jaw. Then swinging round, he saw that the tall man was dragging a gun from his pocket, while Marcia was clinging frantically to his arm. Peter dropped his head, and leaping forward, drove it like a battering-ram into the twisted features. The impact sent a wave of throbbing agony coursing through his tender skull and down his spine, but the man staggered backward followed by Marcia, who flung her arms in anything but a loving embrace about his neck, and assisted by his momentum dragged him to the floor.

Just in time, Peter saw that Ed was also fumbling in his

pocket as he crouched, gasping, one hand pressed to his
stomach. Peter's foot shot out, and the man withdrew his
tingling fingers from his pocket very suddenly, only to find
his wrist seized in a vice-like grip. Gayleigh tried to wrench
the man's hand behind his back, but before he could do so,
a muscular arm clamped about his neck. He jerked his knee
up again, but although the pressure on his neck relaxed
instantly the effort threw him off his balance, and realising
that if he once lost his feet it would be the end, he had to
release the other's wrist in order to right himself. But he was
free, while the bulky Ed was clutching his diaphragm even
more concernedly than before, gulping in air like a winded
bullock.

Peter's gaze swept towards Marcia. She was writhing on
top of the tall man, clawing at the automatic which he had
now managed to drag into view. Her skirt had worked up
to a most indelicate height, and there was a lavish display
of silk stockings and other things. But as she was kneeling
on the tall man's face this lack of modesty seemed to be justified. Peter decided that his immediate assistance might
change the whole aspect of the contest, and covering the few
yards separating him from the tall man, he took a running
kick at the hand holding the gun. Again he lashed out with
his foot. The gun slid from the numbed fingers on to the floor.

It hadn't taken long, but long enough for the panting Ed
to resume the attack. Peter hadn't time to evade the next
wild rush as the man came at him, his fists flailing. One of
the blows thudded against Peter's chest, and he stumbled over
the legs of the man on the floor. Then he was down with
the bulky Ed on top of him, unable to defend himself against
the blows that crashed into his face and ribs. The man made
the most of his opportunity. He had taken a lot of punish-
ment, and now he had a chance to even the score. His teeth
were bared in savage pleasure as his fists crashed home again
and again. Gayleigh was wondering how long he could
endure this onslaught when he saw that Marcia had gripped
the barrel of the gun. Evading the tall man's efforts to stop
her, she raised it above her head and brought it down
squarely between his eyes. The man fell back like a log.
She thrust a strand of hair from her eyes to stare at him
with fierce satisfaction.

" That'll teach *you* !" she panted triumphantly.

The vehemence and the implication in these words penetrated into the bloodthirsty mind of the man who was battering Gayleigh. Ed jerked round, knocking the girl back with a powerful sweep of his arm as she scrambled towards him. And in that instant Peter got one of his knees up, then before Ed could begin pulverising him again, squirmed from beneath him. He had both feet free now, and planting them against the man's shoulders sent him reeling backward towards the door.

" Put up your hands," panted Marcia.

She was on her knees, fumbling with the gun as she transferred her grip to the butt. But though she hadn't quite accomplished this, her tight lipped expression indicated that Ed might expect a bullet just as soon as she got the gun straight. He didn't wait for this fateful moment. He was near the door, and he darted through it, slamming it quickly behind him. Darkness claimed the room again. Peter heard the much too familiar sound of the key grating in the lock, followed by an exclamation of frustration from Marcia.

" Damn, he got away !"

It was Gayleigh's heavy breathing which brought her thoughts back to more pressing matters.

" Peter, are you all right?"

She waited for him to reply, forgetful of the gag that still sealed his lips, then frowning at herself crawled towards him, and eased the adhesive tape slowly away from his mouth.

" Thanks," he said tersely. " The scissors. Quickly. Near the door."

" Okay. I've got a lighter in my handbag."

She groped about in the darkness, and eventually retrieved the bag from the floor. Her lighter spurted into flame. The bright steel of the scissors winked in the light, and she picked them up. Peter's gaze shot towards their silent companion. The man was still lying with his eyes closed, his peaceful heavy breathing and flaccid limbs indicating his total lack of interest in this dénouement.

" That was quite a useful tap you gave him," he observed as she set to work on the cord. " I don't think he'll need another just yet."

" If he does I shall enjoy giving it to him. The beast!
I've never been so mad."

Peter smiled thinly.

" Atta girl. I liked the way you put your knee in his eye.
All-in wrestlers have nothing on you."

He felt the cord snap, and helped her to remove it by
raising his forearms and hunching his shoulders. They had
heard the discreet Ed hurrying away along the landing. By
now he must have imparted his sad tidings to the others. It
wouldn't take them very long to get organised, and although
Gayleigh's lean fingers closed in anticipation about the gun
he took from Marcia, he felt that no insurance company
would have considered either of them a good risk if they
had to leave that room with a gang of very determined hoodlums waiting on the landing.

He dragged himself to his feet, massaging his bruised ribs.

" I don't hear anyone yet, do you?"

" No—not yet."

But a moment later they heard someone padding stealthily
outside the door.

Neither of them moved. The unexpected sound, like the
tread of a ghost, had an eerie quality that somehow seemed
in keeping with their macabre surroundings. Peter was
staring fixedly at the door, his eyes half-closed. Even the
grotesque shadows cast by the tiny flame seemed to hover
expectantly on the wall. Then this tableau suddenly came
to life as the girl clutched his arm.

" They can't have come back," she whispered, as though
trying to convince herself. " We should have heard
them."

Peter said nothing. Could it be Merson? Had he
remained somewhere in the background when Marcia had
been thrust into the room? It was possible, for he looked the
type of man who would quickly efface himself when things
went wrong. But whoever it was, she was right. This prowler
could not have returned by way of the stairs. The creaking
floorboards would have advertised his approach.

Very deliberately Peter levelled the automatic.

" What are you going to do?"

" Shoot away the lock. That sentry has it coming to him.
We've got to get out of here before his pals arrive."

He took careful aim, and was about to squeeze the trigger when a nasal voice suddenly called to them urgently.

"Take it easy in there. Go easy with that rod. I gotten some keys here."

Peter lowered his arm, his tenseness dissipated by a surge of relief that smoothed out every ripple of apprehension. He glanced quickly at Marcia, and saw that she was staring vacantly at the door, her mouth open in incredulous astonishment.

"Okay, bud," he called out. "Go right ahead."

"Why—why it's Dave Lyman!" she managed feebly.

"True." He was eyeing her quizzically now. "But I'm afraid we can't afford to be too exclusive, darling. After all, Dave has his likeable moments. It seems that for once he hasn't been wasting his time."

III

There was no denying that when it came to opening locked doors Dave Lyman had a way with him. One moment he was probing tentatively through the keyhole, the next he had snapped back the lock with a celerity that brought a little gasp of relief from Marcia. The door opened abruptly, and the thin beam from a pencil torch stabbed into Peter's eyes, darted to Marcia, and finally swept round the room to settle on the man on the floor.

"Gee, who's the guy?"

"That," Peter explained, "is just another Beautiful Dreamer. Or at least he was. But as he seems to be awaking unto me, and as none of us want him very much, we'll change the theme song. Another little tap won't do him any harm."

While he was speaking he pocketed the gun, bent down, seized the man by the shoulders, and raised them from the floor. The last word was punctuated by a thud as he brought the other's head down violently. A bemused murmuring in the man's throat died at birth. Peter studied the fixed, inane, expression judicially for a moment, then straightened himself, rubbing his hands together as he turned to the door. There was no need to ask how Lyman had arrived so silently, for the landing window, which Peter had unfastened, was now wide open.

"We're expecting visitors, Dave. Some more of Winniger's mob. So, if you don't mind, we'll save all the floral tributes we owe you until later. Maybe you'd go first and give Miss Lawson a hand."

"Sure." He went to the windows and peeped out. "There's no one around." Then glancing back over his shoulder. "They're comin' back you say. I don't hear 'em yet."

"You will," said Peter decisively, "unless you put a jerk into it. Get going, man."

The distance from the window to the shadowy pavement of the cul-de-sac was not more than twelve feet. Moreover, the ledge formed by the brickwork ran three feet below the window. Lyman stepped on to the ledge, lowered himself to one knee, gripped the jutting brick with his fingers, and swung himself towards the pavement. A short drop, and he stood waiting for Marcia. He grasped her firmly as she hung from the ledge, and lowered her almost silently to the ground. Half a minute later Peter swung himself lithely to the pavement beside them. He had heard no one on the landing and he was frowning slightly.

"Not a peep out of them yet," he said. "They ought to be back by now."

Marcia looked at him with a queer little smile.

"You sound almost disappointed."

"No, just puzzled."

"Anyway, I'm more than grateful to you, Mr. Lyman," she said, turning towards him. "We thought you'd still be in the restaurant."

They were moving rapidly away from the window, along the short Z shaped length of the gloomy cul-de-sac.

"I jest thought I'd come round the back for a look-see, miss," he explained. "I figured I might get into the rooms above the restaurant somehow. Then I saw a light in that window. Seemed it might be an oil-lamp."

"It was," said Peter. "A thug called Ed dropped it on the landing."

"Yeah? I reckoned there didn't ought to be a light in an empty building. So I waited until it went out, then shinned up to the window. It was unfastened so I hopped inside. And then I heard you two talkin'. Sump'n about shootin' the lock off the door. As I was jest outside, it didn't sound so good." He halted before the dark mouth of a passage leading into Dean Street. "I gotta get back. Merson's my meat, and I'm sticking right on his tail."

He was staring at a cut on Gayleigh's cheek, a memento left by the stone in a cheap ring worn by the hopeful Ed. Until that moment Peter hadn't realised that blood had trickled down his face, and that he presented a very misused appearance.

"Yep, I reckon you two'll want to tidy up a bit. If I was you I'd get a cab in Hollen Street. That's maybe thirty yards further on. 'Taint so light as in Dean Street, an' you don't want a cop eyeing that cut and them dusty clothes and thinkin' you've been in a street fight. So long, I'll be seein' you."

He disappeared into the black maw of the passage, where Peter would have followed him, for he was not fond of even well meant advice, if Marcia hadn't restrained him.

"He's right, Peter. I don't know what I look like, but you look like a hospital case."

"H'm." He glanced back towards the window they had left. It was still in darkness. "All right, we'll make for Hollen Street."

They had reached the first bend in the cul-de-sac. To their left the sky above the roofs of the houses was brightened by the lights of Oxford Street. The sound of traffic, even the raucous cry of a newsvendor, came to them clearly. Yet, like many tiny off-shoots from London's thoroughfares, the cul-de-sac seemed to brood in forgotten solitude. Ahead of them, just before the second bend, a street lamp cast a broad fan of light on to the pavement, and directly in front of one of several narrow passages leading to the backs of the houses. Across the street the buildings were steeped in shadow, the openings to the passages resembling tiny caves in the sullen light.

They were almost level with the lamp-post, caught in the patch of light, when the attack came.

IV

A bullet smashed into the grimy brick not an inch behind
Peter Gayleigh's shoulders. It came from the other side of
the road, and was followed by two more shots, both fired from
silenced pistols. The second bullet streaked past the spot
where his head would have been if he hadn't ducked
instinctively, dragging Marcia down with him. It came
from the same direction.

The third bullet whistled over their heads from behind
them.

On their right was the entrance to the passage facing the
street-lamp. The passage was the only available refuge, and
Gayleigh sprang towards it, dragging the girl after him. He
had his gun in his hand as he swung round just inside the
narrow opening. With his other arm he swept Marcia behind
him.

" So this is why they didn't come back!" he said through
his teeth.

" You mean—they let us escape?"

" Just that."

" But—but why?"

" Because they didn't want any shooting in the house.
There isn't a silencer on this gun. It makes a lot of noise."

He peered cautiously into the street, but saw no one.

" They're pretty smart. Smarter than I thought. In the
house it would have meant shooting it out. This way they
might have got us before I could fire a shot."

One of the men who had attacked them must be lurking
in a passage farther back along the cul-de-sac; the other
man, on the other side of the road where it curved round
into Hollen Street. The ambush had been very cleverly
arranged. If Peter and Marcia took a chance and darted
round the corner, they might be able to evade the man who
had fired from behind them, but the other man would have
plenty of time to drop them in their tracks, since he would
have an uninterrupted view. On the other hand, if they
remained where they were, both gunmen would have to shift
their positions before they could fire into the passage. If

they did, Gayleigh thought, he would see them while they were moving to fresh vantage points. He could use his gun. For the moment they were safe.

But a split second later he realised this assumption was premature. He caught the sound of stealthy movement behind him in the passage.

" Peter ! "

The warning cry was wrung from the girl's lips as she clutched his arm frantically to attract his attention. But already he was swinging round on his heel. He saw the man who had opened the door at the end of the passage, the levelled automatic, and the grim expression behind it. And in that instant Gayleigh's reaction was purely instinctive. There was no time for thought. No time for anything save a lightning response. The man's finger was tightening on the trigger.

Without compunction Gayleigh shot him through the head.

The report shuddered about them, and through the wisp of smoke he saw the man crumple at the knees. Then, as he pitched forward on his face into the passage, the door closed smartly behind him.

Marcia's face was deathly white as she flashed a significant glance at Peter.

" The door. Someone shut it."

" Yes, there's another of 'em in there." His eyes were like cold steel as he nodded towards the dead man. " Get his gun. Quickly !"

She was trembling, and she felt that her legs might give way at any moment, but she forced herself to obey. Gayleigh shot another swift glance into the street, then switched his gaze back to the closed door. He saw her bend down shakily, and ease the gun from the limp fingers.

" Now watch the door like a cat. If it begins to open, shoot first and think afterwards."

She nodded dumbly. Her brain seemed frozen, but with an effort she managed to level the gun. It was Peter Gayleigh's thin smile that steadied her nerve. For incredible though it seemed, she saw that he was smiling. More, a fierce enjoyment blazed in those cold blue eyes.

" As an apprentice you're not doing so bad," he observed

encouragingly. "Remind me to buy you a new dress when we get out of this."

The glint in his eyes was like a tonic. Tightening her lips she held the gun firmly.

"Good enough. Just hold that position and you can't miss."

He might have been instructing her in a harmless game of target practice, and overriding the horror of this situation she experienced another feeling. Momentarily she forgot the dead man, the sickening danger that still threatened. Gayleigh's strong personality had enveloped her, transmitting some of his own calm assurance. She had merely heard of Peter Gayleigh's exploits, the amazing things that happened to him, but, until that night she had not shared any of the danger. And now she knew that his brand of courage, his infinite faith in himself, was something quite remarkable. He had gone to the Four Hundred, knowing about Winniger and his gang, deliberately inviting trouble, and simply because he wanted to talk to Merson. He had paid heavily for his insatiable curiosity. And he was still paying, though it didn't seem to worry him very much. His eyes were alive with eagerness, and a devilish smile lurked at the corners of his lips. If he had said "We're having a great time, aren't we?" she might have wondered if he was being ironical or not.

A couple of minutes passed. The cul-de-sac was still seemingly deserted. The sound of the shot had not attracted attention. No doubt it had been put down to the back-firing of a car—except by the man behind the door, and his accomplices in the street. Peter saw no sign of them, though he sensed they were still there. They had realised he would dive into the passage, of course, if the first shots failed to find their mark, for the entrance was facing the street-lamp. And they had even prepared for that eventuality. Another man had been waiting behind the door of the house, to which they obviously had access if they did not use it habitually. He had intended to shoot them in the back. It had all been planned to the last detail, but fortunately it hadn't quite come off.

Nevertheless, the dead man presented an additional complication. Before this incident Gayleigh had decided that, as a last resource he might fire his gun several times. The gesture could not have failed to attract attention. But if he did so now, and the much needed assistance came, he would be obliged, sooner or later, to give a very detailed explanation to the police. He had killed a man and, very naturally, they would want to know why. The very fact that he was Peter Gayleigh would go against him, and, of course Winniger and his hoodlums would deny all knowledge of the affair. With no one but Marcia to support his statement he would find himself in a very difficult position.

And so the last person he wanted to see was a policeman.

V

Winniger's men must have realised this. Evidently they had guessed what had occurred, for they made no attempt to force the issue. Perhaps they hoped that he would be discovered with his victim. In that event he would not trouble them again for some considerable time.

Several more minutes past, and he grew increasingly uneasy. Short of venturing into the street, or trying to force the door at the end of the passage, there was nothing he could do. And neither of these alternatives would be conducive to a peaceful old age. If he had been on his own, he might have made a dash for it along the street. He might have escaped with a flesh wound, for he knew that was the best he could hope for, since the man obliquely opposite would have time to fire half a dozen shots. But with the girl to think of, such recklessness was out of the question.

Suddenly he thought he saw something move in the shadow on the other side of the road. His grip tightened on the automatic, but he was not anxious to use it unless he could be sure of his mark. He found himself wishing that he had taken the dead man's gun, fitted with a silencer, giving Marcia the other one. But as he stared, tense and expectant, towards that moving object, it emerged from the shadow and padded unconcernedly across the road.

Peter released his breath audibly through his nostrils. He had been staring at nothing more dangerous than a stray cat.

In Hollen Street, so near and yet so far, he could hear a car starting up. It must be very close to them, he decided,

probably just at the end of the cul-de-sac. Not that it
mattered very much, unless——. The purring note of the
engine grew louder, and presently he saw the reflection of
the rear light in a window across the street.

The car was backing into the cul-de-sac.

The pounding of his heart against his ribs was like a
triumphal tattoo heralding the birth of new hope. The idea
came to him with all the startling clarity of a bugle call. For
he knew now what he had to do, just as he knew that his
guardian angel had not failed him.

" Manna from heaven !" he breathed to the girl at his
elbow. " That car. D'you hear it ?"

There was a light in his eyes which caused her to frown
slightly as she nodded.

" It sounds fairly close."

" Close enough. This is where we make a dive for it. Give
me your gun." He took it quickly from her. " Ready ?"

Her lips tightened as she inclined her head almost imper-
ceptibly. She had gone even paler, and swallowed heavily.

" Okay. Keep behind me—near the wall. Come on !"

He seized her arm, and swept her after him out of the
passage, and on towards the corner only a few feet away,
and round it as a bullet fanned his cheek. Another pierced
his sleeve as they covered the remaining few yards separating
them from the car. Then the chassis was between them and
the gunman. If their arrival had been timed to a second it
could not have been more opportune, for the car was beginning to move slowly forward. And they moved forward with
it, using it as a shield, until they reached Hollen Street.
Only then—when it was apparent that the driver intended to
turn to the left, still providing a very adequate screen—did
Gayleigh spring on to the running board, hauling the girl
up after him.

" Hey, what's the idea ?" the driver demanded.

" You'd be surprised," said Peter. " We need your help,
brother. You look like a married man. Are you ?"

The other screwed up his forehead. His expression was
a mixture of puzzlement, irritation, and alarm.

" Well, are you ?" persisted Peter.

" Now look here . . ."

" I thought so. And your wife probably thinks that out

of umpteen available men she had to pick you. If so, she does you an injustice. Brother, you look like an angel to me!"

Meanwhile, as he had intended, the car was carrying them quickly away from less delightful realities. They had almost reached Wardour Street when the driver stopped listening to this foolishness, and put his foot down hard on the brake.

"Well, thanks for the buggy ride," said Peter. "Sorry you've been troubled."

He dropped lightly to the road, pulling Marcia after him. Out of the corner of his eye he saw the man leaning out of the car, to stare after them as if trying to decide whether they were escaped lunatics, or just drunk.

"Thank heavens we made it!" gasped Marcia. "Look, there's a taxi!"

It was approaching along Wardour Street, and if there was any element of fairness in the occult forces that shaped his fate, such luck, he felt, was his due.

"Of course, my sweet. It's all part of the Peter Gayleigh service. You'd better hail it," he added advisedly. "Ed's artistic efforts haven't improved my appearance. We don't want the driver to swoon, or turn awkward."

"All right. And you'd better slip inside quickly. You look really awful."

She stepped forward and raised her hand. Peter was inside the taxi almost as soon as it stopped.

"Where to, miss?" And as she hesitated:

"Jermyn Street," instructed Peter.

She sank down thankfully beside him, and the taxi moved off.

"Life with you is rather hectic, isn't it," she remarked dryly.

"Sometimes."

"And moderately exciting."

"It can be. But I thought you wanted excitement."

"Yes, in small doses. Not in bucketfuls. If my legs don't carry me out of this taxi, you'll know I'm not the girl I thought I was." She shook her head doubtfully. "I'm afraid I've been very much of an also ran."

"Of course. My impression is that we both ran like hell." She gave him a fleeting smile.

"We certainly did! But you know what I mean."

"If," he reminded her, "you hadn't nosed your way out

of the roulette-room we should never have got past the post
at all. I should still be trussed up in the dark. Lyman
wouldn't have seen the light in the window, and he wouldn't
have troubled to investigate. No, my sweet, as the backer
said to the bookie : ' I owe it all to you.' "

"Of course you did a little, too," she conceded dryly. " I
wonder how many other girls you've worn out in this way?"

It was not a question he cared to answer. It opened the
gates to a long vista of memories, some of them gay, all of
them exciting. For there had been others, many others,
whose lives had been vitalised for a brief space by Peter
Gayleigh; who had shared the thrills and dangers of an
episode before his restless energy swept him away to fresh
paths of adventure.

"The first dose is always the worst," he said, as the taxi
turned into Coventry Street. "You'll get used to it in time."

"Shall I?" She shivered slightly. " I can't forget that man
—the one you shot."

"It's not a thing one does forget. But it was either him
or us."

"Yes." She was silent for a few moments. " Of course
there'll be an inquiry when the police find the body."

"*If* they find it," he said grimly. " Somehow I don't think
they will. Winniger and Co. will take care of that. Right
now I could use a drink."

"So could I. And when we get to your place I'd like to
tidy myself up a little."

"Then I'm going to pack you off home," he said firmly.
" I prescribe bed as a sedative for the nerves."

The taxi deposited them in Jermyn Street, and having
asked the driver to wait they went up to Peter's flat. Marcia
sank down thankfully into a chair. He eyed her without
comment, then crossed to the cocktail-cabinet, and poured
out two stiff whiskies.

"Drink this," he said, handing her one of the glasses.
" Cigarette?"

"Thanks."

He gave her one, and helped himself. Presently :

"Roulette is quite exciting, isn't it?"

"There *are* more exciting games," she replied dryly.

"It's the first time you've played, of course?"

"Huh-huh. And I was winning a lot."

"Y—es," he said in the same casual tone. "It's a pity you had to break off."

"Perhaps. Though I should probably have lost it all."

He took a deep drag at his cigarette. His eyes did not leave her face.

"When I nipped out of the room you seemed to be completely absorbed in the game."

"I was—so much so I didn't see you leave."

"Yet you must have followed me almost at once."

She smiled reminiscently.

"I'm afraid I'm not so sharp as you seem to think. It was father who saw you slip out. But, of course, I realised you were up to something, so, as soon as I could, I slipped out, too. You'd disappeared when I looked along the passage. Then I saw the stairs, and guessed you must have gone that way."

"I see." He eyed the spiral of smoke from his cigarette, his lips tilting into that crooked smile as he went on disarmingly: "You know, if I were you I wouldn't tell your father too much when you get home. Even parents who enjoy a spot of gambling are apt to take a poor view of fellows like me."

"Oh don't worry about father. I can handle him. He may have seemed a bit standoffish, but he's rather a dear, really."

He did not pursue the topic. He finished his drink and looked at her inquiringly.

"Just one more for the road?" And as she hesitated: "Nothing like it for steadying the nerves."

"Very well. Then I really must make myself presentable. I've a feeling I look like the morning after the night before."

Quarter of an hour later Peter, too, had improved his appearance. He went down with her to the taxi and saw her inside, gazing after it thoughtfully as it moved away. Then returning to the lounge he picked up the telephone. Two very determined attempts had been made to get rid of him since he had seen Grant, and though he had said nothing to the girl he had been wondering how Grant himself had fared. Presumably he had phoned Herrington, and since the Yard man had now been brought into this, perhaps a little more information might be gleaned from him. But it was most unlikely that he would be at Scotland Yard at that hour. Peter considered a moment, then dialled Herring-

ton's private number. Almost immediately a familiar voice
came over the wire.

" Herrington here."

" Splendid. This is your *bête noir,* Herrington."

" Who?" It was not a good line, and Peter could visualise
the other's puzzled frown.

" Peter Gayleigh. Tch! Tch! Have you forgotten me
so soon?"

The answering grunt carried a wealth of meaning. For,
as those who have followed Peter Gayleigh's career will know,
Chief Detective-Inspector Herrington's recollections of the
many occasions on which fate had thrown these two together,
were not of the happiest. It was true there had been times
when Gayleigh had been of great assistance to him. It was
equally true that each had a great admiration for the other.
But when Peter Gayleigh offered his assistance, he invariably
withheld essential information which, while it enabled him
to pursue his own lighthearted and frequently illegal investigations, made it impossible for Herrington to do anything
about it. He had no delusions about Gayleigh. He knew
exactly what he was. But Herrington had never been able
to prove what he knew. Some day he hoped that he would,
and in pursuance of this noble resolve he was prepared to
cultivate this unusual friendship. So that his interest on this
occasion sprang from both hope and misgiving.

" You've been a long time getting into touch with me,"
he said after an appreciable pause.

" Quite. Since I saw our friend I've been very busy."

Rather to his surprise Herrington did not pursue this
reference to Grant.

" Which means, I suppose, that I shall shortly be very
busy, too! You arrived in London three days ago . . ."

" So I did," interpolated Peter. " How nice to know that
you're always thinking about me. Who tipped you off?"

" The New York police. They informed us that you were
travelling under another name on *Cornelius.* They thought
you might be mixed up in the Van de Kramer diamond
robbery, and I can't say I blame 'em, though you had
an alibi, it seems. Anyway, we made very sure you hadn't
got the diamonds when you arrived at Southampton."

Peter blinked. There was a pause.

"You mean the Customs' people acted on your authority?"

"Don't tell me you didn't know!"

So he had misjudged Lyman. The American hadn't tried to put him out of the running, after all. The New York police and Scotland Yard were responsible for that set-back. And while he was being searched very thoroughly the man who probably had the diamonds had slipped through their fingers. His lips curled ironically.

"As a law-abiding British subject I deplore such base methods," he said. "They are so foreign to my nature they never occurred to me. Now about our friend Jervis."

"Jervis?"

"Jervis Grant."

"Well, what about him?"

Peter took a deep breath.

"I'm very tired, Herrington. I want to go to bed. Suppose you quit stalling. I'm in this business, and I mean to stay in. But perhaps Grant didn't tell you. I saw him today before he rang you up."

"Rang me up?"

"It might help," said Peter patiently, "if you stopped repeating everything I say. Try thinking out a sentence for yourself. I happen to know that Grant 'phoned you this evening to ask for . . ."

"Now look here, Gayleigh," Herrington broke in with exasperation. "What the devil are you talking about?"

"I'm talking about Jervis Grant."

"But in heaven's name, why?"

Peter frowned. "Do you mean to say he didn't 'phone you?"

"That's exactly what I do mean."

His tone left no room for further doubt. For some reason Grant had not asked for police protection, yet he had been on the point of doing so when Gayleigh had 'phoned him from Hampton. Had he changed his mind, or——. Very grim possibilities occurred to Peter, but there was no indication of this in his extremely casual reply.

"Maybe he'll 'phone you in the morning. Better late than never."

But as he pressed down the receiver-rest, stifling the Chief Inspector's justifiable protestations, he wondered if it was too late already.

CHAPTER EIGHT

IN WHICH JERVIS GRANT PRODUCES WHISKY, AND PETER GAYLEIGH SLEEPS IT OFF

I

THE number he had used that afternoon was fresh in his mind, and in less than a minute he was through to Pinewood. He could hear the ringing note. He waited anxiously, but there was no reply.

In his mind's eye he saw the telephone in the gloomy hall . . . Jervis Grant's windowless study. If he was in that room he should have answered the 'phone before this. If he was alive!

Brrr...Brrr...

The sound seemed to acquire an increasingly ominous note as he waited for what seemed an interminable time. His tense expression gave place to a heavy frown. Abruptly he glanced at his wristlet-watch. Half-past eleven. Perhaps Grant and the servants had gone to bed. If so, he might have to wait for some time. But even if his fears were justified, even if something had happened to Grant, surely one of the servants would answer in due course.

Brrr...Brrr...

Still no response. He decided to ring Herrington again. It would necessitate an explanation, of course, but that was inevitable if anything had happened to Grant. Herrington could get through to the divisional police who would investigate the matter at once. This was not the time to satisfy his own craving for excitement, for if he went himself, valuable time would be lost. Grant's life was at stake. Yes, Herrington must be informed.

Then suddenly the ringing note stopped. He had not been cut off. Someone had lifted the receiver at Pinewood.

"Hullo!" he breathed urgently.

"Hullo? Who's that?"

132

It was a querulous voice, the voice of a man who resented being disturbed. But, unmistakably, it was Jervis Grant.

"This is Gayleigh. My God, Jervis, you had me worried! Are you all right?"

"Quite all right. Sorry I couldn't get to the telephone sooner. I was in bed—and sound asleep, too. Sheer exhaustion, I suppose. First time I've slept for days."

"I'm not surprised. If you'd taken my advice you'd have had police protection by now. I thought you were going to 'phone Herrington."

He had to wait several seconds before the answer came.

"At the time I certainly meant to 'phone him," said Grant slowly. "But almost immediately after you rang, someone else called me up—er—one of Them."

"I see." Peter's eyes were stony. "Not your friend Merson by any chance?"

"No. This man spoke with a pronounced American accent. I'd never heard the voice before. You realise I can't discuss this over the 'phone, but, in short, I think I may be able to buy Palmer off."

"You don't say," grimly.

"Either I submit to his demands, or—well, you understand."

"And that's your reason for not calling in the police!" His tone was scathing. "You must be insane! If you pay now they'll go on bleeding you."

"Not necessarily. I hope to avoid that."

"By slipping away? And suppose you do elude them for a time, you'll have this hanging over your head for the rest of your life. No, Jervis, you've got to nip it in the bud now."

"I don't agree with you. I've quite made up my mind."

Still this stubborn determination to fight alone. Peter almost groaned with exasperation and dismay. How could Grant be such a fool? This was not the time for pride, or even more noble sentiments. How could he possibly hope to get the better of gunmen like Palmer and his accomplices who would stop at nothing? Peter himself might have done so, but his faith in his own capabilities did not extend to those of this law-abiding diamond-broker.

"All right," he said decisively. "I'm driving over to Pinewood right away."

" Now?" The querulous note was back again. " Really, Peter, that's quite unnecessary. I can take care of . . ."

" There's been some mild excitement since I saw you," he broke in quickly. " It may surprise you to hear that your friend Merson is one of the shining lights in this set-up."

" Trevor Merson!" He sounded incredulous.

" Yes. He's in cahoots with an American called Mike Winniger—possibly the man who rang you up. However that may be, they're a pretty unscrupulous couple. And I should know, because I've just returned from the Four Hundred restaurant. Perhaps I should say, *only* just. Merson and Winniger did their utmost to prevent me from leaving. So, you see, I've quite a lot to tell you."

There was a short pause while Grant digested this.

" Incidentally," he went on, " I'm almost certain that Merson was one of the sportsmen who tried to get me when I left your place this evening."

" You mean——? I find that very hard to believe, Gayleigh."

" No doubt. But now you realise why I must see you as soon as possible."

" H'm." There was another pause. " You'll have to come through the grounds, of course. After what happened before you'll be taking a big risk."

Peter's eyes gleamed.

" As you know, I hate taking risks," he said sardonically. " I suppose you've got the front door locked and bolted?"

" Yes."

" I'll give four distinct knocks when I arrive. That should be in less than an hour. G'bye, I'll be seeing you."

He put the 'phone down, and went into his bedroom where he had left the two automatics. He examined the one with the silencer, satisfied himself that it was fully loaded, then slipped it into his pocket. A small torch replaced the larger one that had been taken from him. Then pausing only to collect a dark overcoat in the hall he left the flat.

II

Quarter of an hour later he was sitting at the wheel of the Bentley, the cool rush of air fanning his cheeks and brightening the tip of his cigarette as he drove through the remnants of London's night traffic. He guided the big car with effortless ease, one hand resting lightly on the wheel, and, as always, he found the smooth movement, the humming of the engine, and the glare of the headlights as they devoured the road, conducive to clear thinking.

He knew very little about this conspiracy, he reflected. All the finer points—and he felt there were a great many— still eluded him. Why, for instance, had Merson called on Grant, presenting him with the sword? Merson must have been very sure of himself since he had given Grant his address, although in the circumstances, there was every likelihood that Grant would disclose it to the very man Merson was trying to avoid. He might have slipped up there, of course, but somehow that seemed incompatible with the very thorough way in which this scheme had been planned.

Peter shook his head in perplexity, switching his thoughts to broader issues. The only indisputable fact was that Merson was working with Winniger. As for Grant, he believed that he was being hounded down by Louie Palmer. Anyone in Grant's position would have thought the same. Yet, conceivably, this scheme was based on that very assumption. According to Grant, he had seen nothing which definitely proved that Louie Palmer was in London. He might still be in America. He might know nothing about Merson's subtle game. The idea provided food for thought, though he realised it was merely a possibility, nothing more. Nevertheless, it was a point that Herrington could clear up. Palmer had been released from Sing Sing on parole. The American police would be taking great interest in his whereabouts. Herrington could easily find out whether they had lost track of him or not. If they hadn't, then this conspiracy was a frame-up. He decided he would put this to Herrington. If Grant refused to help himself somebody must do it for him.

He had reached Wandsworth, and as the Bentley purred rhythmically along the Kingston Road he eased his foot forward on the accelerator. Across Putney Heath, then on towards Kingston Hill, and finally Kingston itself. Here he slowed down considerably, maintaining the same easy pace as he left the town behind and continued in the direction of Hampton Court. Pinewood was still more than half a mile away when he killed the engine and switched off the head-lights, coasting silently towards a country lane into which he negotiated the car. Quarter of a mile away he could see the trees, indicating Pinewood, appearing as a faint shadowy mass against the sky.

He approached the entrance to the drive as silently as possible, then buttoning up his overcoat to hide the white-ness of his dress shirt, glided into the blackness beyond the gates.

Nothing stirred. The silence was funereal. But while it induced a feeling of eerie suspense, it had its advantages. He would hear the faintest sound made by anyone in the vicinity. Moreover, he must be almost invisible himself. He moved forward a few yards, and paused to listen, repeating this pro-cedure as he flitted from tree to tree along the grass-fringed border of the drive. But when, presently, he reached the dark hulk of the house, he had neither heard nor seen any-thing suspicious. Quickly he mounted the steps to the front door, gave four very distinct taps upon it, and pressed him-self against the wall to one side. Perhaps these elaborate precautions were unnecessary. He hoped they were, but only after Grant had admitted him, closing the door sharply again, did he feel safe.

The diamond-broker was wearing the woollen dressing-gown, over his shirt and trousers, in which Gayleigh had seen him before. Evidently he had dressed himself again in preparation for his visitor. Or perhaps he hadn't undressed at all. He looked even more gaunt than before, but there was a decisiveness in the set of his features, a keenness in his eyes, which Peter noticed at once. He had the air of a highly strung man who was on the verge of accomplishing something.

"So you made it," he said. "Did you have any difficulty?" Peter shook his head.

"No. I fancy Merson and his crowd are much too busy disposing of the evidence."

Grant frowned. "What evidence?"

"There was a roulette-party," he explained quickly, for there were certain incidents he had decided to omit from his story. He had no intention of telling the overwrought diamond-broker, or anyone else, that one of Winniger's men had died very suddenly. "As I told you I've been to the Four Hundred. It's quite a go-ahead restaurant."

"That's where you got that cut on your cheek, I suppose?" He was eyeing Gayleigh wonderingly.

"Yes. From a hoodlum called Ed. One of Winniger's men."

"H'm." He led the way into the windowless study where he had evidently been waiting, for a half-smoked cigarette lay on an ash-tray. And as Gayleigh took off his overcoat, and tossed it over a chair : "Y'know, Peter, I can scarcely believe that Merson is mixed up in this. As for this man Winniger, I'd never heard of him before you phoned." He picked up the cigarette, and puffed at it jerkily, the onyx ring on his little finger sparkling as it caught the light from the glowing tip. "An American, you say?"

Peter nodded. "And the proprietor of the Four Hundred. But the restaurant is merely a cover for more profitable activities. He holds roulette parties in the empty premises next door. After I left here, I managed to get an invitation to the one he'd arranged for tonight."

"You mean you knew about this man Winniger and his parties?"

"Not until I went along to the Four Hundred for a look-see."

He made himself comfortable in an easy chair, then went on to relate how he had interfered with Mike Winniger's very private arrangements. Grant stared at him with increasing wonderment.

"I've known you a good many years, Peter," he remarked, shaking his head, "but you still continue to astound me. Personally the last thing I should have done would have been to return to the place later on."

"It was almost the last thing I did, too," Peter returned dryly. "I daresay I should have been all right if I'd stayed with the other guests in the roulette-room, but, you see, I wanted to talk to Merson. He wasn't around, and I'd a hunch he was keeping out of my way."

"But why should he?" frowned Grant. "I can't understand why, in the first instance, you didn't call quite openly. You'd never met Merson, and you'd no reason to believe that he was anything more than an acquaintance of mine."

Peter looked at him speculatively.

"I'm afraid that's not quite correct. As a matter of fact, I met Merson coming over on the boat. I didn't mention it before because he—er—doesn't like me very much. We had a slight difference of opinion about a card debt. Maybe I'll tell you about that sometime, but it's not important now. All that matters is that I happen to know, and from personal experience, that Merson is a crook."

"I see." The other's unhappy frown had deepened. "Well, go on."

"So I slipped out of the roulette-room to look for him. I couldn't get back into the restaurant, but I'd got other ideas which I needn't go into, because I wasn't given the chance to carry them out. I was on the floor above the roulette-room when things really began to happen. Merson and a couple of Winniger's not so tame thugs were waiting for me there."

He explained what had occurred, relating his brief conversation with Merson, but omitting all reference to the sword, and the part Marcia and Lyman had played in his escape. He made his story as short as possible, since the sole purpose of this recital was to convince Grant that he had been very much mistaken about Merson.

"They left me bound and gagged in the room. And I've no doubt that I should have been taken for a ride after the roulette party broke up. But to cut a long story short, I managed to get free. I hopped through the window overlooking a cul-de-sac at the back of the place, and escaped." He lit a cigarette eyeing the other thoughtfully as he sank down into a chair. "Mind you, Jervis, my own opinion is that Merson is just an underling. Which brings us back to Louie Palmer. You said you hadn't actually seen him."

"That's true."

"But you'd recognise him if you did?"

"Oh yes, undoubtedly. I saw him in Court when the case came up in New York—after the operation on his face. I made a point of going, so that I should recognise him again."

"Yes, I can understand that. Did you see him very closely?"

"Close enough! Though actually I was at the back of the Court. But why do you ask?"

"Because an operation like that might leave tiny scars under the ears."

"H'm, I didn't notice anything. Scars like those in an ordinary face-lifting operation, you mean?"

Peter nodded. "Winniger has scars like that, Jervis, and he's about the same build as Louie Palmer. But his chin and nose are not those of the man I remember, although his eyes are the same cold shade of blue."

"You think this man Winniger may be Palmer." Grant got restlessly to his feet again. "You may be right, of course, but as I've never seen Winniger I can't say. A mere description conveys very little. I wonder how long he's been over here?"

"I intend to check up on that." He drew deeply at his cigarette, keeping his eyes on Grant. "But if there's anything in this idea, Herrington could prove it much quicker than I could."

"I daresay he could." He turned away irritably. "But as I've told you I've decided to pay up. The sum demanded is £10,000. That's a lot of money, but it won't break me. And I'd rather lose it than get a bullet in my back. As you've good reason to know, this house is being watched, and I've been warned not to try any tricks. After I've paid the money I shall be safe—at least for a time."

"Perhaps."

"Almost certainly. And I want to go on living just as much as the next man, Gayleigh. After I've met this initial demand, and before they try to blackmail me again, I shall go to the police."

Peter fetched a deep sigh. It was hard to believe that such an astute business man could be so ingenuous, such an unwarrantable optimist. Moreover, even if he did manage to safeguard himself later on, it would be like bolting the door after the horse had gone.

"But good heavens, man," he protested. "All you need do is pick up the phone now! The police will be here in half an hour."

It was some time before Grant replied. Then:

"No," he said very slowly. "If you must know, I haven't told you everything. The situation is much more complicated than you imagine."

III

Gayleigh was to remember those words later, the amazing significance behind them. But now they merely excited his curiosity, which he realised, as the other went on, was not to be satisfied.

"I'm sorry, Peter. I appreciate all you're trying to do, and I'm grateful. But, believe me, there's a very good reason why I must keep certain things to myself for a few days."

He thrust a strand of limp grey hair from his forehead, paused thoughtfully for a moment, then went towards the desk. He opened one of the bottom drawers and took out the sword, holding it by the hilt.

"I can't understand Merson's game at all," he muttered, staring at the weapon with a baffled frown. "Why did he give me this? If he's as big a hypocrite as you say, it just doesn't make sense."

"It doesn't make sense to me either," said Peter, who wondered if Grant had told him all that had occurred during that meeting. "It might if I had the whole story."

The other looked at him in surprise.

"You don't seem to understand. The details I'm keeping to myself concern the arrangements for paying over the blackmail money. I'm as much in the dark about Merson's visit as you are. As you know, I had no reason to suspect him. But now—" he brought his gaze slowly back to the sword —"well, as I see it, he must have had some ulterior motive when he called."

"There's not much doubt about that."

"And as he said nothing of any consequence it's only

logical to assume that there's more behind this sword than we realise. Do you thing there *could* be anything peculiar about it?"

Peter smiled thinly.

"'To him who would its weight assess, pause thou, consider and caress this magic blade,'" he quoted ruminatively.

"Yes." Grant inclined his head slowly. "And how does it go on: 'For it hath wondrous power and charm, if lightly poised upon the palm.'" He bent his wrist so that the blade was across his body. "Well, maybe I'm a credulous fool, but I can do with a bit of magic right now."

He brought his other hand up, and was just about to grip the poisoned steel when the stub of his cigarette burnt down to his fingers. With a muttered imprecation he dropped it hastily into the ashtray.

"Here, you try, Peter," he frowned, handing the sword to him, and looking round for another cigarette.

There was an unopened packet on the desk, and while he was breaking the wrapping, Peter eyed the weapon critically. He had no reason to believe that it was not the one he had handled in Merson's cabin. It seemed pointless, therefore, to repeat his former experiment. On the other hand it could do no harm, he thought, and it would satisfy Grant, besides obviating the explanation that might be necessary if he refused. Already the other was frowning at him impatiently, fumbling in the pocket of his dressing-gown for his lighter.

"Heavens above, man!" he growled. "What are you waiting for? Frightened of the damned thing?"

It was a challenge that could not be ignored. He looked sardonically at the diamond-broker.

"Yes, I know," said Grant, as he thumbed his lighter into flame. "We're behaving like a couple of kids. And it's a fine time for that. But grip that blade, or give it back to me, and I'll try it."

"Okay," said Peter, humouring him, and was never nearer death than at that moment. As the other had done, he raised his hand to grip the steel. Grant sprayed out a fan of smoke towards the ceiling. Evidently his faith in the sword's power matched Gayleigh's, for he seemed to have forgotten it as he said :

"You understand that no one must know about my dealings with Palmer, or, if you like, Winniger and Merson. You haven't told anyone, of course."

Peter dropped his hand again.

"Only my girl friend," he said casually. "I forgot to mention it. She was with me tonight."

"There was a girl with you!" He suddenly snatched the sword from him, and flung it peevishly on to the desk, where it lay unheeded. "What the devil do you mean?"

"There's no need to work yourself up about it," said Peter calmly. "Marcia is very discreet. As a matter of fact, if it hadn't been for her I shouldn't be here now. She helped me to escape from the Four Hundred."

"You didn't say so."

"Simply because I didn't think you'd be interested. If I'd brought her into the story I knew you'd want to know how she knew so much. And that would have meant telling you some more about Merson."

"The more I know about that scoundrel the better," Grant snapped balefully. "So you've not told me everything! Incidentally a drink wouldn't do us any harm." He looked towards the whisky decanter, saw it was empty, and cursed roundly. "I'll get some more. I sent the servants away after you left this evening. Thought it best in the circumstances."

He spoke petulantly, and picking up the decanter left the room without another word."

Grant's nerves, Peter thought, were in a dreadful state. More than ever now he was determined to bring this stubborn wreck of a man to his own way of thinking.

It was several minutes before he returned with the replenished decanter, and muttering something about a defective electric-light bulb in the cellar. He poured out two drinks, squirted soda into them, and handed one to Gayleigh.

"All right," he said. "Let's have the whole story."

Peter told him how he had met Merson aboard the *Cornelius,* and went on to relate the incident of the cabin-trunk. He spoke of his alliance with Dave Lyman, and his more interesting association with Marcia Lawson. He did not say that he had searched Merson's cabin, or that he had, as he believed, seen the sword before. But he explained what had occurred when the liner had docked at Southampton, and that he had lost track of Merson until Sona's anxiety culminated in the visit to Pinewood that day.

Grant had finished his cigarette and lit another. Now, as Gayleigh finished, he thrust his hands despondently into the pockets of his dressing-gown.

"H'm, very interesting. Though it doesn't help much."

"I didn't say it would. It's just background material."

"Merson may have the Van de Kramer diamonds as you suggest, or he may not. Frankly I don't care a damn either way. I've more personal matters to think about." He thrust his hair from his forehead again, where it fell back almost immediately. "Perhaps some day we'll get to the bottom of his game."

Peter Gayleigh got slowly but purposefully to his feet.

"We're going to do that now," he said very decisively. "For the last time, Jervis, are you going to phone the police —or must I do it myself?"

He disliked issuing this ultimatum, but there was no alternative, since Grant refused to confide in him. It was the only way to save him from his own folly, and there was stern, unwavering resolution in Gayleigh's strong face as the other jerked his head up to stare at him in resentful astonishment.

"What? You can't mean that. I tell you——"

"Yes, I know. You've fixed everything. You want to handle this your own way. And a fine mess you're making of it. Well, all that's finished, Jervis. From now on I'll do the thinking. Are you going to put through that call?"

The other continued to stare at him resentfully, then suddenly dropped his eyes, like a thwarted child, before that dominant regard.

"No," he growled flatly. "I won't do it. This is my affair, and if you want my opinion——"

"I don't," snapped Peter. "Out of my way."

He thrust the frowning man aside, and striding past him into the hall picked up the telephone. He held it to his ear for a second, then pressed the receiver-rest slowly up and down, while a premonitory tingle between his shoulder blades telegraphed realisation to the sinking void of his stomach. After a few moments he examined the flex, pulling at it gently. There seemed nothing wrong with it.

Yet the line was dead.

" What's the matter?" This was Grant who had now appeared in the doorway.

" Nothing at all—except that we're too late ! Either this line has broken down, which I don't believe, or it has been tampered with since I phoned you."

" My God !"

" You've only one line, I suppose?"

" Why—yes." He passed his tongue over his lips, all his recent antagonism gone.

" Then we're cut off."

There was a pregnant silence, a stillness that had the potential of a lighted fuse burning steadily towards an explosive.

" Where's the nearest public phone?"

Grant blinked at him dumbly. Then as he raked his fingers through his lank hair again :

" About—about half a mile away. Near Hampton."

Peter's brows came together as he recalled the road along which he had hurried that evening.

" Yes. I remember it. All right, I'm going there now."

" But—but don't you realise ! They're probably waiting outside the house."

" That's why it appeals to me," he drawled, though his eyes were like chips of ice. " I'm one of those impulsive people who look for trouble. You needn't come with me if you don't want."

The diamond-broker turned back into the study, and as Gayleigh followed him, picked up his whisky and drained it at a gulp.

" Well?" prompted Peter.

He shrugged helplessly. " I'm sorry. I'd be no use to you. As you can see for yourself, I'm about all in—I didn't expect this."

Peter Gayleigh looked at him with all the tolerance of the strong for the weak.

" Well, perhaps you'll be safer here," he said. " Lock the front door after me, and keep your fingers crossed."

He picked up his overcoat and slipped it on, buttoning the collar round his neck. Grant stared at him doubtfully. Then as his unhappy gaze fell on Peter's half finished whisky :

"You'd better drink that. I fancy you're going to need it."

Peter lifted the glass and disposed of its contents, setting it down with a crooked smile.

"Well, anyway, thanks for the hospitality, Jervis. That's good whisky, but I shouldn't drink any more yourself. You've got a gun, I suppose?—just in case anything happens before I get back."

The other nodded, and Peter produced his own gun from the pocket of his jacket.

"Okay. Keep your chin up."

He went out of the room, and turned towards the front door. He withdrew the bolts as quietly as possible, and unlocked it.

"All right. Turn out the light."

He waited until the hall was in darkness, then opening the door slightly peered cautiously outside. He listened keenly for a few moments before he groped behind him for Grant's arm, and pressed it reassuringly. Then he was beyond the door, and the silence was broken by the faint sound of the bolts as Grant thrust them hastily back into place.

IV

Very possibly unseen eyes were staring at him through the blackness, though nothing happened as he descended the steps very softly, and glided to the shelter of the trees on the left of the drive. Here he waited for a time, his gun poised, the safety-catch pressed back. The silence remained unbroken.

So far so good. Perhaps he had managed to leave without being seen, though it was a little early for such optimistic reflections. This time he had no intention of returning along the drive or even of keeping to the grass-fringed edge. That was the obvious route, and it must be avoided. His best plan, he decided, was to cut straight across the tree-studded grass-land to the wall enclosing the grounds, keeping well away from the pine wood on his left, where the darkness was so intense that it seemed to be vibrating.

He moved lightly away from the drive towards a tree, peering keenly about him as he went, and screwing up his eyes. He felt he was not as alert as he should have been.

K

Evidently the whisky had affected him slightly, but, if so, the effects would soon wear off in the crisp night air. Pausing under the shelter of the thick branches he shook his head to clear his brain, and set off again. Not only the blackness of the pine wood but the darkness all about him was vibrating now, and to his intense annoyance, he realised that he was staggering slightly. Once he almost fell, and beads of perspiration stood out on his forehead as he recovered his balance and by a sheer effort of will reached the welcome support offered by the trunk of another tree. So far as he could tell, no one was following him : there didn't seem to be anyone lurking in the grounds, though, as yet, he had covered less than half the distance to the road. He wasn't clear of danger yet, not by a long way. Moreover, his unaccountable heaviness gave him grave cause for concern. He knew that three small whiskies, all he had had, could not have affected him in this way. His legs felt weak and unstable, and a heaviness that he could not shake off, seemed to be settling deeper and deeper in his brain. He felt as though he had been drugged. But surely that was impossible, since he had been with Grant. Though now he came to think of it, the whisky he had gulped down immediately before leaving had tasted rather bitter. But he was letting his imagination run away with him. Jervis Grant would never have drugged him. Grant was in a tight spot. He needed assistance.

Peter felt his chin drop to his chest, and jerked it up fiercely, fumbling in the pocket of his overcoat for a handkerchief. For this effort to think logically, his iron determination to overcome the lethargy that claimed him, had brought out fresh beads of perspiration on his forehead. His fingers touched the handkerchief—and something else. A folded sheet of paper which he knew had not been in his pocket before. Only one person could have put it there. Jervis Grant. Peter remembered that his overcoat had been lying in the study when he had gone to the telephone.

He braced himself, gritted his teeth, and withdrew the slip of paper, and still refusing to yield to the paralysis creeping along his arms he put his gun away, unbuttoned his overcoat, and produced the torch he had brought with him. He pressed it on, directing the light against the tree trunk as he leaned heavily against it. Then forcing his other arm

to obey his will he unfolded the sheet of paper, and brought
rt under the light.

He saw some words scrawled in pencil, and his lips curled
bitterly as he read :

"Sorry, Peter. The whisky was drugged. I did it to
gain time. At this point the police would ruin everything.
But if anything happens to me tonight, I'm relying on
you to tell them all you know."

Gayleigh crushed the paper angrily between his fingers. It
was true that Grant had not asked for his assistance, but he
had done his best to help him, little thinking that he would
go to such lengths to get his own way.

The wave of disgust that swept through him sent fresh
vitality into his veins. He crammed the note and the torch
into his pocket, and plodded forward again. But the effect
of the drug could no longer be denied. Before he had taken
half a dozen paces he staggered and fell, and though he
dragged himself to his feet and lurched on doggedly, the dull
weight on his brain seemed to be crushing it into oblivion.
He did not feel his legs give way beneath him, only the cool
dew of the grass as it brushed his cheeks. Then the ground
seemed to dissolve into infinity, and there was nothing but
absolute blackness.

v

When he opened his eyes again he found that he was still
lying where he had fallen, face downwards on the grass, and
under an oak tree that hid the drive from view. He blinked,
and raising himself on one elbow, shook his head. Then
staring vaguely at the hands of his wristlet-watch he saw that
it was nearly half-past six. The greyness of the dawn was
rapidly being dissipated by what seemed to be bright sunlight
coming from behind him. There was also the distant sound
of voices, and of general activity which seemed out of place
in those surroundings and at that hour in the morning. At
the same time he was conscious of drifting smoke, and the
very pronounced smell of burning. He screwed up his eyes
again, rubbed them with his hands, and peered round.

Then suddenly he was wide awake.

What he had imagined must be sunlight was a fierce glare in the sky above Pinewood. He couldn't see the house itself, only the dense clouds of smoke rising above the trees. But the voices and other sounds needed no further explanation.

How had the house caught fire? What had happened while he had been lying there? Had Grant escaped, or had he been trapped by the flames? Questions swept down upon him like an avalanche. Only one thing was clear. During the commotion caused by the fire no one had seen him lying there. For once in his life he had been completely ignored.

Scrambling to his feet, and heedless of his bedraggled appearance he ran back towards the house. The glare was becoming fainter and fainter, but clouds of acrid smoke enveloped him as the breeze swept them across the grass. His eyes were smarting and he found the heat almost overwhelming when he emerged from the singed trees at the top of the drive. Powerful jets of water from two fire-engines were playing on the crackling building, the snake-like hosepipes trailing along the gravel. Behind the helmeted figures the fireman who seemed to be in charge, and a police sergeant, were staring critically at the flames.

Peter dived back amongst the trees, and crossing the drive came up behind the two men.

"Tell me," he said, grimly, tapping the fireman on the shoulder. "How long has this been going on?"

Both men turned to stare at him in astonishment. His stiff shirt had become limp while he had been lying on the ground, and it was smeared with grass stains and earth. There was some more earth on his face, and his hair hung over his eyes. He looked like a man who had really been making a night of it.

"Who are you?" demanded the police sergeant. "How did you get in here?"

"Meaning, I suppose, that you've got some of your men stationed at the gates to keep sight-seers away."

"Never mind what I mean." He seized Gayleigh's arm. "Answer my questions."

"All in good time. Where is Mr. Grant?"

"The occupant of this house? That's no concern of yours. Now will you——"

"Listen," he interjected fiercely. "I've been in the grounds all night. Never mind why. But when I left this house some hours ago, my friend Grant was inside it. He had no intention of leaving. I want to know where he is. Have you got him out?"

The Sergeant and the fireman exchanged significant glances.

"Well? It's a perfectly simple question. Can't either of you answer it?"

It was then he saw the blanket covering something only a few feet from where he stood. And as the men's eyes darted towards it Gayleigh wrenched himself free from the policeman's grip. He reached the blanket, and before the other two could stop him, pulled it back.

He saw the charred, unrecognisable body of a man.

And as he stared, horrified, his eyes darted to the onyx ring on the little finger of one of the blackened hands.

Then the Sergeant seized him very firmly and dragged him back.

"I don't know who you are," he scowled, "but you're coming with me. So you've been in the grounds all night, eh! You've got a lot of explaining to do."

Peter scarcely heard him. He continued to stare, appalled, at the ghastly sight which the other man was now covering up again. So much for Jervis Grant's puny intentions. He had made his plans, adhered to them stubbornly, and a cruel fate had laughed at him, cancelling everything, giving him nothing but a wreath of flame.

"Poor devil," he muttered sadly. "They won't trouble you now, Jervis."

The Sergeant was eyeing him curiously.

"He was an intimate friend of yours?"

Peter inclined his head slowly.

"Yes. I never thought he'd come to this." He gave a deep sigh. "All right, Sergeant, get me to the police station as soon as you can. I've a statement to make."

"Oh you have!"

"But not to you," he went on grimly. "For your information my name is Peter Gayleigh, and I shall talk to no one but Chief Detective-Inspector Herrington of Central Office."

CHAPTER NINE

IN WHICH HE MAKES A STATEMENT, AND
HERRINGTON HAS THE LAST WORD

I

IT was some hours later, approaching eleven o'clock that morning, before Peter Gayleigh finally saw Herrington. In part, this delay was caused by his insistent refusal to make a statement to anyone but the Chief Inspector, and by the reluctance of the police to call a Central Office man into what seemed to be a purely divisional matter. But when, at last he left Kingston Police Station in a police car en route for Scotland Yard, he felt that he had spent his time very satisfactorily. For he had not only got his way, but had managed, when he was not shaking his head to progressively higher ranking police officials, to write out a very carefully worded statement of the facts leading up to the death of Jervis Grant.

It was a strictly relevant statement. That and nothing more. For while it contained everything that Grant had told him, and certain apposite comments on Merson's and Winniger's activities, it did not include very much about his own. There was no reference to Dave Lyman, Marcia Lawson, or her father, and no mention of a very dead hoodlum whose body, Peter hoped, had now been decently if secretly interred by those who had as much to lose as himself by its discovery.

In short, he was prepared to collaborate with Herrington —but, as usual, only up to a point.

And Herrington was fully aware of this intention. Not for a moment did he imagine that Gayleigh would tell him all he knew. That, he had learnt from past experience, was too much to expect. But as it seemed that he was to be told more than anyone else, he received Gayleigh with hopeful expectancy, tempered with distrust.

" Sit down, Peter," he said, as soon as they were alone in his room. " I understand you want to make a statement."

"Yes, about our old friend Jervis Grant."

"H'm." Herrington shook his head sadly. "He was almost unrecognisable when they got him out, I'm told. You suspect foul play, I suppose?"

Peter nodded, for he had thought this over very carefully and had revised his initial impression.

Herrington looked at him shrewdly.

"Anything to do with Louie Palmer?"

"You've got a good memory," said Peter. "The answer is yes, and no. Grant thought he was being hounded down by Palmer. But I'm not so sure about that."

"I see." He took out his tobacco pouch and began to fill his pipe. "You know Gayleigh, it's a pity you're so independent. If you hadn't cut me off on the 'phone last night, if you'd told me a few things then, Grant might be alive now. At least, that's how it looks to me."

Peter inclined his head gravely. The rebuke, he felt, was fully justified.

"I'm not denying it," he admitted quietly. "Though last night I was certain his life wasn't in danger. He was being blackmailed, and he decided to pay up. He was prepared to part with ten thousand pounds. So I can't understand why the blackmailer should want to kill him. But, somehow, I don't think it was an accident. And I don't think he committed suicide. But, of course, you're wondering how I came to be in the grounds this morning."

"That," Herrington returned heavily, "is just one of the things about your recent movements which is rather obscure. I can hardly wait for you to tell me why I shouldn't hold you, pending further inquiries."

He pressed tobacco into his pipe with his little finger, and looked very hard at Peter, who favoured him with that crooked and often infuriating smile.

"You wouldn't do that," he said blandly, "because you'd have to release me, and then you'd look very foolish. And when it comes to dealing with me, you never do anything foolish, Herrington. You use me, just as I use you. Our beautiful friendship is based on give and take. As I've said before, how well we understand each other."

The detective lit his pipe. He made quite a business of it. Gayleigh smiled at him wickedly.

"Never mind, Herrington. When you do think of a suitably cutting retort, send it to me on a postcard. Time marches on." He produced the statement he had prepared, and tossed it on to the desk. "Meanwhile you might find some inspiration in that. It gives you the whole story in chronological sequence, and in my own fair hand. You'll find quite a lot about a half-caste called Trevor Merson. You let him through the Customs at Southampton, and possibly with the Van de Kramer diamonds, while you had me prancing about in my birthday suit. But read it. Then, if you've got the face, tell me I'm not an asset to the community."

He crossed his legs, and leaned back comfortably, lighting a cigarette, while Herrington, after a swift glance at him, lowered his eyes to the closely written sheets.

After reading a couple of pages he looked up again very dubiously.

"If you were so sure this man Merson had the Van de Kramer diamonds I'm surprised you didn't search his cabin."

Peter lifted a reproachful eyebrow.

"Surely you're not serious? That would have been illegal!"

"Quite," was the sour response. "That's why it isn't in this statement. Very interesting about the sword, though. I'm glad you included that."

Peter said nothing, for he had never thought that Dick Herrington was a fool. He went on reading, and though the tiny groove between his eyebrows gradually deepened, he made no comment, even when he had finished the last page. Pushing the statement away he leaned back in his chair, deep in thought.

"Now you understand why I can't be sure that Louie Palmer comes into this," Peter observed presently. "Merson and Winniger may have planned everything themselves. Palmer may be entirely ignorant of the whole business. He may still be in America. Of course the police over there could probably settle that."

But Herrington shook his head.

"No," he said very slowly. "They've lost track of Palmer. He was last seen in New York a fortnight ago. The New York police cabled us to that effect, since, of course, he might have found a way to return to this country. That rather complicates matters, I'm afraid." He pointed to the statement with the stem of his pipe. "I notice you give a detailed description of Winniger. Why?"

"All right, you've guessed it. He's an American—an ex-racketeer. Or, if he isn't, he's just made for the part. He has scars under both ears, though his appearance doesn't suggest that he went to a beautician. And he's about Palmer's build. I'm wondering how long he's been in London."

"H'm, it's a long shot. But I'll check up on that."

"Splendid. Now I'm really getting some co-operation. He's in cahoots with Merson, at least some of his strong-arm men are, which amounts to the same thing. But I don't know how far he's implicated. Merson may have promised him a rake-off. Or they may be partners."

The detective sucked at his pipe, drumming his fingers on the desk.

"Anyway, according to your story, he organises roulette parties. We can't pull him in, of course, on a gambling charge unless we catch him in the act. But if you're prepared to make a charge of assault . . ."

"No," said Peter hastily. "I'm not anxious to thrash that out in public. Since I was caught napping, it would make me look rather foolish, if y'see what I mean."

"I see what you really mean," Herrington amended sapiently. "Someone probably got hurt pretty badly before you left those vacant premises. Or perhaps you helped your-self to a little financial compensation on the way out. Mind you, I'm not saying your statement isn't true—so far as it goes."

"For those kind words, many thanks," said Peter gravely. "But the villains in this piece are Merson and Winniger. Remember?"

"That's what you say. I've only your word for it. All right, Peter," he went on resignedly, and stifling further interruption. "I'll admit you've given me enough information to put both of 'em through the hoop. A hint that we know about his roulette parties may induce Winniger to talk. That should be a very useful lever. As for Merson he'll have to produce some very good alibis to get himself out of this." He puffed vigorously at his pipe. "I'd like to know a little more about that sword."

"A romantic weapon," murmured Peter. "But methinks its magic powers are vastly overrated. When I last saw it, it was lying on the desk in Grant's study."

"Then someone must have moved it. When the house was burning it was seen in the flower-bed in front, plunged to the hilt into the ground. Maybe it did that all by itself. Or perhaps someone wanted us to find it there."

Peter frowned. "Where is it now?"

"It's being examined by Dr. Winston, one of our pathologists. Winston is also conducting a post-mortem. You see, your suspicion was right. There are very obvious indications of foul play, or to put it more specifically, murder."

"H'm. You haven't been long getting off the mark." He flicked ash meditatively into an ashtray. "I think the statement I've given you entitles me to a *quid pro quo*. I'd welcome a little more information."

"So should I! Naturally we haven't got very far yet. But, I understand there are very clear indications that Grant was shot before the body was burned. He was shot twice. Once through the back of the head. The second bullet must have been fired from the front. It shattered his jaw. But the body was so badly charred, I daresay you didn't notice that."

Peter shook his head, and Herrington went on gravely.

"It's very difficult to incinerate a human body completely. In a crematorium, for instance, it takes an hour and a half at a temperature of 1800 degrees Fahrenheit. But the murderer did his best, though he slipped up badly. It seems he didn't realise that clothing under the weight of a body takes a long time to burn, when the fire isn't directly underneath. Parts of a garment which seem to have been a dressing-gown, as well as fragments of underwear, were still intact, though the front of the body was unrecognisable. And those bits of clothing reeked of paraffin. If the windows of the house hadn't been shuttered, the fire wouldn't have got such a hold before it was seen. Though, of course, it was started in the early hours of the morning when most people are in bed. The murderer couldn't have chosen a better time."

Peter raised the cigarette to his lips reflectively Grant, of course, had not wanted him to call at Pinewood that night, and, as a last resource, had drugged him to eliminate interference. Almost certainly he had been expecting another visitor, presumably the blackmailer. And though he had been so pitifully certain that he had got everything worked out, there had been a hitch in the final arrangements. Peter wondered if he would ever know what had actually occurred.

"Has Grant's step-daughter been told?" he asked presently, and Herrington frowned.

"Not yet. We haven't been able to find her. Perhaps you can tell us where she is?"

"She's staying with friends in Knightsbridge. Poor kid! This is going to be a great shock. You've no objection to my breaking the news to her, I suppose? I'm not anxious to take the job on—who would be?—but it's the least I can do. Better, I think, than a dispassionate official intimation."

"Yes, I'd like you to do that." He pursed his lips, eyed the bowl of his pipe reflectively for a few moments, then shrugged himself to his feet. "That's all for the present, Peter. I'm a busy man. If I want you in a hurry, I suppose I can get you at the Jermyn Street flat?"

"Yes, and I hope you'll keep me informed."

Herrington was striding to the door, but the significance of this remark was not lost on him.

"You mean if I don't I shall never hear all the finer details you've kept to yourself."

"Maybe there's something in that," said Peter coolly as he stubbed out his cigarette "You never know, I might be a great help to you. By the way, I suppose you still take a solitary meal round about seven at that little restaurant near here?"

Herrington merely looked at him.

II

Since he was still wearing the crushed and very discouraged-looking boiled shirt and tuxedo, he decided he must make himself presentable before calling on Sona Boyd. He took a taxi from Scotland Yard, and on the way to his flat considered his self-imposed and very delicate errand.

Sona thought of Grant as her own father. She was very

fond of him, and though Peter had no doubt that she would take the news bravely, he knew the sympathy he could extend would be very inadequate. Perhaps if he could enlist Marcia's assistance his task might be made easier. If she was at home he would call on her before he saw Sona.

He had not supposed that his absence or his bedraggled appearance would evoke any curiosity in Carver, for by this time that very matter of fact little man was accustomed to Peter Gayleigh's peculiar mode of life. Nowadays, nothing could surprise Carver. So that Peter took it as a matter of course when his manservant met him in the hall of his flat with the remark that it was a very fine morning.

" I take it you will be changing at once, sir," he added, eyeing Gayleigh's clothes with marked disfavour.

" Your deduction is correct, Carver," Peter told him gravely. " First the grey suit, and now this. I'm afraid I'm a little hard on my clothes. If this goes on I shall have to give you a rise."

" It has been going on for some considerable time, sir," the other reminded him sadly. " But I am quite satisfied with the remuneration I am receiving. I only hope, sir, that I shall continue to receive it."

" Oh? Is there any reason why you shouldn't?"

The little man shrugged.

" One day, sir, I fear you will depart on one of these excursions and never come back."

" Yes, I suppose there is that possibility. Though I can think of much more pleasant things to dwell on. You haven't been soaking yourself in Russian literature, by any chance?"

" No, sir," said Carver glumly. " I've been reading a humorous novel."

" It seems to have cheered you up no end ! I wonder what you'd have done without it? Jumped out of the window, probably."

" I'm not partial to lighthearted acrobatics of that sort, sir," was the reproachful reply.

" Anyway, I'm glad you didn't do it," said Peter kindly. " You'd have made an awful mess on the pavement. Er— I shan't be in to lunch."

He went into the lounge, looked up Marcia's telephone number, and a few moments later learnt that she was at home and would be delighted to see him. She sounded none the worse for her experience of the night before, and there was intrigued gratification in her voice, for although—thinking of the dead hoodlum—he told her there was no cause for alarm, he did not explain the reason for his visit.

He regaled himself with a cold shower, chose a pin-striped Savile Row suit, and a silk tie, with a care that said much for Marcia Lawson's sex appeal, and was on the point of leaving the flat when the telephone rang.

"Hullo? Is that Mr. Gayleigh?"

It was Dave Lyman.

"Speaking," said Peter. "How's tricks, Dave?"

"Maybe you've gotten a few," was the disgruntled response. "I'm right out, bud. I bin thinking maybe you could meet me some place, and wise me up to what's going on around here."

Peter thought quickly. He would gain nothing by seeing Lyman just now—nothing more than he could glean over the phone. And since this indefatigable private detective seemed to live for occasional glimpses of Merson . . .

"So you're weakening," he said provocatively. "I'm surprised at you, Dave. How about Merson? Aren't you afraid he might unload if you take time off?"

"I reckon he may have done that already. Seems he don't live here no longer. I'm speaking from a booth in the Four Hundred. And I'm not feeling so good. I bin up most of the night."

"You mean you've been following him?" His brows had come together sharply. "Where did he go last night. It wouldn't be Hampton Court?"

"Hampton Court? I dunno. After I left you and Miss Lawson, I went round the front as I told you. I gotten back in nice time to see Merson makin' a clean getaway in a car. Oh sure, I tried to follow him. But by the time I'd gotten myself a cab his rear light was nuth'n but a memory. What would he be doin' at Hampton Court?"

"I'll tell you later," said Peter evasively. "What time did he get back?"

"That's jest it. He hasn't come back. That's why I've bin hanging around—in case he did. So as I feel I'd like to catch up on some social life, how about you and me gettin' together?"

"Sorry, Dave. It'll have to be some other time. I've got an urgent date. I don't quite know when I'll be free."

"Yeah? Sounds like you was holding out on me."

"Make it tomorrow," said Peter. "Bye, Dave."

He hung up, stroking his chin. Lyman's information was disappointing. But if Merson had left the Four Hundred so quickly and had gone direct to Pinewood he would have arrived there first. And since he couldn't possibly know that Grant was expecting another visitor it was unlikely that he would remain lurking in the grounds. Why should he? He would have called on Grant at once. Yet he hadn't done so —unless this was something else Grant had kept to himself. No, if Merson had gone there it would seem that he had arrived later. But whatever his movements had been, he evidently knew a great deal about the murder, since he had been smart enough to make himself scarce.

Thank God Herrington was on the job. It shouldn't be long before the drag-net closed about Merson.

III

Marcia Lawson flourished a cocktail shaker, poured out two sparkling and frothy drinks, handed one to Peter, and said: "Well, it's nice seeing you. I never thought you'd condescend to visit me. I thought the only way I'd get you here would be to drag you along in chains."

"Sometimes I think you'd go that far," said Peter. "But, as you see, your appeal is irresistible."

He sipped his drink, and decided there were far less pleasant places than this airy drawing-room, with its French windows looking out on to a picturesque garden in St. John's Wood. And not the least of its attractions was Marcia Lawson. She was wearing a simple green dress with a white collar, yet she somehow contrived to look like a film star groomed to photogeneous allure. Perhaps it was the highlights in the crisp, natural curls, clinging so tightly to her head. Or perhaps the flawless skin, or the clean etching of her profile, the way she moved, the purely sensual desire she would arouse in most men. But to analyse her charm was like dissecting a beautiful picture. One should gaze at it from a distance.

As it was, he felt much too close to her for his peace of mind.

She said: "Did you want to see how I'd stood up to last night? Is that why you came?"

"Not entirely. Er—the fact is, I want you to help me."

"To help you!" She threw her head back and laughed deliciously. "I don't believe it. That's not Peter Gayleigh dialogue."

"No. But there are times when a man needs a woman."

"Hadn't you better explain quickly," she said eyeing him doubtfully. "I know the facts of life. I might get some wrong ideas."

Peter smiled.

"Don't let your hopes run away with you. And don't work yourself into a passion of virtue, my sweet. You'll be wasting your time. That isn't what I meant."

Marcia said coldly: "I'm trying to remember you're Peter Gayleigh. But, by gosh, you've got a nerve!"

"So I'm told. But the job I have to do needs something more than that. I have to break some bad news gently, and I thought if you'd rally round——"

"Really, Peter! What on earth are you talking about?"

She looked at him wonderingly, for this was not the forceful man she had come to know. Incredible though it seemed, he had spoken rather diffidently.

"Presently I'm going to talk about my friend, Jervis Grant. There was an epilogue, quite a lengthy one, after you left my place last night." He emptied his glass, and stared at it intently for a moment. "But I forgot to ask—your father arrived home in good order, I hope?"

"In good order? Oh, I see what you mean."

"I wonder if you do. What did your worthy papa say?"

She shrugged. "Nothing very much. I got back before he did. As a matter of fact he was very late. It seems the party broke up rather hurriedly after we left, so father went on to a night-club. You wouldn't think it, but he can be a gay old bird when he's seeking copy."

"Quite a man of parts, in fact. I suppose they heard us bouncing about on the floor above the roulette-room?"

"Yes." She smiled wryly. "They thought it might be the police. But Winniger stopped the panic. He said he was having some private trouble, and got them out as quickly as he could. Of course father wanted to know where you and I had gone, so I simply told him we'd left earlier. I can't have looked too bad, because he didn't ask any questions. But you were going to tell me about your friend Grant. Which reminds me," she went on as an afterthought, " father knows him, too. They belong to the same club in New York."

" You don't say. How did this come up?"

" You needn't look at me so suspiciously, Peter. I didn't say anything. It just happened that father took a phone call from Sona. She wants me to meet her this afternoon for tea. Father asked me who she was. I didn't see any harm in telling him that she was Jervis Grant's step-daughter. I'm surprised father knows him, though."

" Knew him, you mean."

" Why, Peter!" She had stiffened slightly as she saw the grim set of his mouth, the arctic coldness in his eyes. " You don't mean——?"

He nodded heavily.

" That's partly why I'm here."

He gave her a full account of what had occurred, while she listened with puzzled dismay, and with few interruptions.

" And you think it must have been Merson," she said, breaking a short silence after he finished.

" I don't know. Your guess is as good as mine. But what's worrying me is breaking this to Sona."

" Yes—Sona." She inclined her head slowly, and when she looked at him again there was a softness in her eyes, an enigmatic smile on her lips. " So this is what you've been leading up to."

" I'd be glad if you'd come along and hold my hand. Will you?"

" Of course. Need you ask." The douce smile lingered about her mouth. " You know, Peter, you're rather over-powering at times, and you say and do the most outrageous things. You're unscrupulous; you don't trust anybody; you've got immense faith in yourself and your lucky star; and you don't care a damn for most of the women who run after you. I don't think you really care a damn for me. And yet—well there's something very nice about you."

"Perhaps we'd better be going," he said rather abruptly. He got to his feet to find her confronting him. And she was very close and very lovely, and he knew from the light in those glorious eyes . . .

"Peter." It was a whispered caress, an invitation he did not want to resist.

Her lips were warm, and her body seemed to tingle with vitality as he pressed her to him. She gave a little sigh of contentment, then as he sought her lips again she pushed him gently back, looking at him with swimming eyes.

"You're right," she said breathlessly. "We'd better be going."

IV

Herrington had finished his dinner and was smoking a pipe over his coffee when Gayleigh entered the quiet little restaurant off Whitehall. He made his way immediately to the secluded alcove where the Chief Inspector was usually to be found at that hour, pulled out a chair and sat down, and in view of his parting remark at Scotland Yard, Herrington was not the least surprised to see him.

"I should have known better," he said. "I'd almost given you up."

"A white coffee, please," said Peter to the waitress. "And you might bring another for Mr. Herrington."

"Yes sir."

"Oh, and put the coffee and dinner on my check."

The girl went away and Herrington looked at him sadly.

"Such generosity! You'll have to watch yourself, Peter. You're becoming too obvious. You're going to tell me nothing. But at least it's good to know that you're prepared to pay for the information you expect to get from me."

"The trouble with you," said Peter unabashed, "is that you have a small, suspicious mind. You're so used to dealing with criminals that you don't know a gentleman when you see one."

"When have I seen one?" Herrington asked crushingly.

"That's just it. You wouldn't know. I see the evening papers are carrying a few paragraphs about Grant," he went

L

on more seriously. " ' Diamond-broker Burnt to Death. . . Terrible Accident.' "

The Yard man nodded.

" No use letting the real story break until we're ready. You've told Grant's step-daughter?"

" Yes." The waitress returned with the coffee, and retired. Peter helped himself to sugar, stirring it for a few seconds before going on : " That kid's all thoroughbred. She took it well. As it happened, Larry Becket the broadcasting correspondent was there. It helped. He met her on the boat coming over, and he's crazy about her. At his age I might be the same."

" H'm. You didn't tell her it wasn't an accident?"

" No, I pride myself I skipped rather skilfully over certain facts."

" That wouldn't require much effort. Your new girl friend, Marcia Lawson, seems pretty good at that sort of thing, too."

Peter did not reply at once. He kept his eyes from the other's face, and put more sugar very carefully into his cup. The silence grew. For he had made no mention of Marcia to Herrington, who was now staring at him sardonically.

" Good for you," he said presently. " I didn't know I was being tailed."

" You're not," was the satisfied reply. " But you're a notorious character. And Marcia Lawson is, or was, quite a good girl. But, of course, all fathers are apt to think that about their daughters."

" Go on," said Peter steadily.

" Surely you didn't think Lawson would let her go gadding about with you without doing something about it? When he saw you both at Winniger's gambling party last night he got a little worried. He doesn't actually dislike you, Peter, but despite his ineffectual appearance he's no fool."

" No—evidently not. When did you see him?"

" He spoke to me on the 'phone. Miles Lawson is a damn good criminologist. I've known him for years. He knew Jervis Grant, too, and all about Palmer. And when he saw that item in the papers he wanted to know more."

" Did he tell you I suspected him of very deep motives?" Herrington chuckled.

" He did. We got a great laugh out of that. If I had to

point out an honest man, I'd put my shirt on Miles Lawson."

Peter drew sustenance from his coffee.

"All right," he said philosophically. "You've had your fun. Still I consider it passing strange that he was at Winniger's party."

"Not at all. Under the pretence of getting material for his books he's put us wise to quite a few things. If you'd asked him, he could have told you that Mike Winniger is not Louie Palmer."

"Is that so. Maybe I'll get wise to myself soon. Ask me something. I know nothing."

"I wouldn't be too rash. I might take you up on that." He drank some of his coffee, and set the cup down very decisively. "I've seen Winniger. He's not talking much, but I've checked up on him, and he's been in this country for months. To listen to him you'd think he knew nothing about Merson. It seems they met in America, and, when Merson came over here, Winniger offered to put him up at the Four Hundred. I asked him if he'd seen you last night, and he said he had. He told me you'd been there for a meal, and that's all there was to it."

"Did you ask to see over the empty premises?"

"I did."

"And he didn't object?"

"No. And they *were* empty premises when I saw 'em. The roulette-table etcetera had gone. There was even some dust lying around. I threw out some hints about the rough and tumble on the floor above, and he said he wouldn't know anything about that. He asked me rather blandly if you were making any charge."

He was looking at Peter very dubiously, and Peter knew what he was thinking. He also knew what Winniger had thought, why he had been so smug. There was a dead man to be considered.

"I told him you weren't vindictive," Herrington pursued dryly. "But although you've only given me half the story, that man's on thin ice, and he knows it. And he's worried. I didn't need to be a psychologist to realise that. Something has gone wrong."

"You mean Merson has skedaddled."

The other's eyebrows lifted slightly.

"Your theories may not be worth much, but you still get around, it seems. Yes, unless I'm very much mistaken, Merson has run out on him. But he won't run very far. I've put out an all stations call."

"There are times," said Peter, "when the machinery of the law fills me with apprehension. You'll get him, of course. And he's the weak link in this chain. I fancy he'll break easily enough. Merson is just another small-time crook with ideas that got too big for him. By funking the issue like this he's putting the rope about his own neck. He's playing right into your hands."

Herrington nodded with grim satisfaction.

"Yes," he said. "I like to think so."

Yet information was forthcoming to prove that there was another far uglier picture on the other side of this jig-saw puzzle, and that the two were co-related much in the same way as Doctor Jekyll and Mr. Hyde. For as Peter had surmised, there were unplumbed depths in this conspiracy. Though that hadn't prevented him from thinking around faulty premises and building up an entirely wrong conception of the causes and effects—just as the murderer, who had manufactured these seemingly obvious facts, had intended he should do.

v

There was nothing further in the newspapers on the following morning, and as Peter had a luncheon engagement with an old friend, who has no part in this narrative, he decided to let matters rest where they were, and betook himself to the Carlton. In the afternoon he collected the Bentley from the lane in Hampton Court where the police had left it. There was a constable standing outside the gates at Pinewood, stolidly testifying to the official activities still going on there. But Peter did not wait in the hope of learning more. He returned to Jermyn Street, and was changing into evening clothes when the summons came, heralded by the ringing of the telephone.

"This is Herrington," he learned. Then very abruptly: "About the matter we discussed last night, Gayleigh. I'd like you to come to my office at once."

" You've got Merson? "

" That's one way of putting it."

He said this with a crisp cynicism that Peter had heard before. Very definitely the Chief Inspector was not pleased.

" You sound pretty grim, Herrington. Why the command performance? " And then a very unpleasant thought struck him, expressing itself in a seemingly casual quip. " Found another body or something? "

" I have," mordantly. " I'm sure you'll be interested."

" I'll be right over," said Peter, experiencing a feeling of intense nausea in the pit of his stomach. Presumably the dragnet had done its work. But what had Herrington meant by those few cryptic remarks? Had Merson ratted on Winniger? Had they both talked, disclosing the affair in the cul-de-sac? No, that was most improbable. But it looked as though the body had been found.

He lit a cigarette, puffing at it jerkily. What *had* happened? How much had Herrington discovered? Well, he reflected wryly, he would know that soon enough. Perhaps this was the opportunity Herrington had always been waiting for. And judging from the curtness of his summons he meant to take full advantage of it.

During the journey to Whitehall he felt that if he had been connected to an instrument capable of recording emotional stress, he would have been hailed as a phenomenon in psychoanalytical circles.

The impassive face of the constable who escorted him to the Chief Inspector's office conveyed nothing. He hadn't expected it would. And he certainly hadn't expected to find Larry Becket with Herrington. The broadcasting correspondent nodded to him gravely, and, it seemed, rather uncomfortably, as he was shown in.

Herrington's initial remark was equally ominous.

" Find yourself a chair, Gayleigh," he advised, barely looking up from some papers on his desk. " There's a very unpleasant surprise in store for you."

Peter glanced from one to the other, shrugged, and sat down. Both of them looked preternaturally grave, and—yes —sadly disillusioned. They might have been a couple of jurymen waiting for the judge to don the black cap. His own expression was mildly interrogative, though he felt like the felon in the dock.

"You must be wondering why Larry is here," Herrington pursued, leaning back in his chair. "His Chief of Staff decided he was the best man for the job. He doesn't like the idea very much, but he's prepared to go through with it."

"I've no choice," frowned Larry. "I'm scheduled to give a broadcast to America tonight, anyway."

The Chief Inspector nodded.

"Nevertheless, I'm very grateful for your co-operation." He turned to Gayleigh. "The B.B.C. have agreed to make a simultaneous broadcast. This is the script here." He held up a few typed sheets. "I've been vetting it. Of course I've given the story to the press, too."

Peter gave a little shrug of resignation.

"If there's one thing I like it's a good build-up," he said dryly. "Would it be too much to ask just what you are building up?"

"Fear," was the succinct and very weighty response.

"Did you say fear?" His expression was studiously polite.

"Yes—just that—fear."

"H'm, that's what I thought you said. You have me enthralled, Herrington. Go on."

The other picked up a pencil, tapping it reflectively on the desk. After a few seconds he said abruptly : "When did you last see Trevor Merson?"

"About eleven o'clock last night. He and his Yes-men were rather unkind to me. I didn't see him again after they trussed me up. I thought the statement I gave you made that quite clear."

"Up to a point. But it was midnight when you 'phoned me from your flat. In other words, some considerable time had elapsed."

"Er—yes."

He crossed his legs almost lazily, staring at the immaculate crease in his trousers as though he couldn't guess what was coming next. Herrington was going to ask him to account for every minute of the intervening period, of course. He would need all his wits to wriggle out of this, even though he had worked out a detailed and purely fictitious story on his way to Scotland Yard. He hoped it was an unbreakable story, but when it came to cross-examination he knew from past experience that Herrington was apt to spring some very unwelcome surprises.

"So that Merson had time to reach Pinewood before you got there?"

Peter inclined his head wonderingly. This wasn't the line he had expected.

"And you wouldn't see his car. He left it on the other side of the grounds." He tossed the pencil aside, and leaned forward slightly. "Now I want you to think very carefully. When you saw Grant did his manner strike you as peculiar?"

"Very peculiar. But then . . ."

"Yes, I realise that, of course. He was scared of Palmer. But did you notice anything else—anything that seemed strange in the circumstances?"

"Well, he refused to get into touch with you, as you know," said Peter, thankful that the conversation had taken a less dangerous turn. "Rather than do that, he was prepared to negotiate with whoever was blackmailing him. That seemed very odd to me, and when I last saw him he had an air of—perhaps I might describe it as expectant accomplishment. He thought he'd got an ace up his sleeve to trump Palmer's trick, though he wouldn't tell me what his plans were. Poor Jervis! He didn't know Merson."

"Didn't he!" was the sour reply. "He knew much more about him than you imagine. Judging from Grant's manner do you think Merson could have been in the house when you arrived?"

Peter pursed his lips.

"It's possible, of course, but I don't think so. I can't believe Grant would have deceived me to that extent. And, don't forget, I'd told him all about Merson; what sort of man he was. It isn't likely that Jervis would want to be left alone with him after I went. And if Merson was in the house, why did he lock the front door after me when I left? No, I'd say Merson couldn't have been there."

"As I see it, Grant locked the door because he didn't want any further interruptions," said Herrington grimly. The corners of his mouth tugged down. "Incidentally, I've put out certain inquiries. And you'll be interested to hear that some information has come in from a private detective agency in Victoria Street. Grant 'phoned this agency immediately after Merson made his first call at Pinewood. He wanted Merson tailed, and a detailed description of everyone he met. They had a man following him for a couple of days before Grant called the thing off."

"Is that so!" Peter's eyes had narrowed. "So he was lying when he told me he'd never heard of Winniger."

"Obviously."

"And he thought Merson was working with Palmer, I suppose. He must have thought that from the very beginning. Yet he said nothing to me."

"I'm not surprised. Jervis Grant kept quite a lot to himself. Take the sword Merson gave him, for instance. I'm pretty certain he knew all about that sword. And he understood the meaning of the verse that went with it. Because, you see, it was a poison sword. A very deadly weapon."

Recalling how he had handled it, as he believed, on the liner, Peter screwed up his forehead in disbelief. He said sceptically: "Are you trying to kid me?"

"No, I'm quite serious," Herrington resumed equably. "And its secret was meant to be discovered. That's why it was left in the flower-bed. I've got Doctor Winston's report on it. The blade is impregnated with a native poison, capable of entering the victim's body through minute abrasions in the skin. There you have the meaning of the verse. The warmth of the palms accelerates this devilish process. Winston has come across such weapons before, he tells me."

The cigarette drooped slackly from Gayleigh's lips. Were his ears deceiving him? He knew there was nothing unusual about the sword. Yet it was impossible to doubt what Herrington had just told him. Which could only mean—there was a replica, the weapon he had handled in Merson's cabin. That, of course, was the explanation. And, according to Herrington, Grant had known it was poisoned . . . An ugly picture began to form in his mind, a picture that refused to reveal itself clearly. It was blurred as though seen through dark, rippling water—the distortion of something which, he sensed, was incredibly evil.

"Grant wanted me to hold that sword," he muttered, speaking half to himself. "Then he snatched it away from me——"

"He did?" Herrington was looking at him keenly. "You didn't put that in your statement."

"I didn't think it worth mentioning."

"No? It means that Grant must have changed his mind —after he decided to kill you."

"What?" Peter's head jerked up in incredulous astonishment.

"Think, Peter, think," the other urged tensely. "What did you say just before he took it from you?"

He was frowning heavily as he replied: "He'd asked me a question. He wanted to know if I'd told anyone about his dealings with Merson or Palmer. I said I'd told Marcia Lawson."

"Ah! Did you tell her you were going to Pinewood?"

"No."

"But Grant didn't know you hadn't. That's why he changed his mind, that's why he decided to drug you so that you could tell me all you knew. You didn't suspect him, of course, and he knew you'd put me off the track. But with all his cleverness he made a big mistake. He thought the body would be burnt beyond any possibility of recognition. He reckoned without Winston and the very detailed post-mortem he carried out."

Peter gaped at him.

"My God, Herrington! What are you saying?"

But he knew the answer already, for the dark waters of comprehension had ceased rippling now. Only one interpretation could be put upon this grim accusation. So that he was dazed but no longer surprised when Herrington said:

"To the best of my belief Jervis Grant is still alive. It was Merson's body we found at Pinewood."

CHAPTER TEN

I

SNATCHES of past incidents and dialogues merged and jostled in Gayleigh's mind, like montage effects projected in rapid motion on to a screen. He was back at the telephone in his flat: "You've got Merson?" Herrington's reply: "That's one way of putting it." . . . His own voice again: "Found another body, or something?" The grim affirmative . . . Herrington again as the scene dissolved: "There's a big surprise in store for you." . . . Finally: "It was Merson's body we found at Pinewood."

The relief he might have felt was completely overshadowed by this staggering development. It conjured up a mass of detail, incidents that clamoured for attention all at once. His brain was numbed, yet in a turmoil. He felt he needed time to re-arrange his ideas.

Herrington waited for a few moments after delivering this broadside, then followed it up with a volley of small shot.

"Think of the onyx ring . . . The dead telephone line. Grant attended to that himself, of course . . . Think of the two shots. The first bullet must have killed Merson. The second was fired deliberately, in an attempt to shoot away the jaw bone, Grant's most pronounced facial characteristic. And, remember, the two men were about the same height. It was all premeditated. Grant had everything worked out to the last detail."

Each of these items, as Herrington enumerated them, provided a peg for Gayleigh's thoughts. Grant had always worn that onyx ring, but he had drawn fresh attention to it by the movement of his hand under the light in the study. As for the telephone, he could have fixed that when he went to get some more whisky. Almost certainly he had known the decanter was empty, and he had left it that way so that it would provide him with an excuse to leave his unsuspecting visitor, should that be necessary. While Grant was away he had scribbled the note, slipping it into the overcoat later, and after he had drugged the glass of whisky. He had played it all very cleverly. Diabolically. When he had killed Merson, and shot away part of his jaw, there was no danger of the shots being heard, for there was no one else in the house. He had been planning all this when he had got rid of the servants.

"There was no sign of the gun from which the shots were fired," Herrington went on. "But I got Winston's report early this morning, and since then I've had men examining the grounds, looking for patches of newly turned earth. They've done quite a lot of digging, and they haven't wasted their time."

"They found the gun?"

"Yes, and Merson's clothes. Grant evidently tried to burn them, then changed his mind. Perhaps your visit had something to do with that. In any case, he couldn't burn the metal parts of braces, suspenders, and the buttons, and perhaps he decided it would be quicker to bury the lot. We found a pair of shoes intact, a wristlet watch, some keys, and a signet-ring—all belonging to Merson. Winniger verified that, and he's a sadly disillusioned man to-day. I fancy Merson didn't tell him very much, and as he has a cast-iron alibi—he was in a Soho night club until four in the morning —he couldn't have been at Pinewood. So that lets Winniger out. He may have known that Grant was being blackmailed, but he couldn't have been involved in the murder.

"Grant laid his plans immediately after Merson's first call at Pinewood. Because on that day he purchased half a dozen tins of paraffin in Hampton Court. And he brought them back to the house in his car. The servants have been questioned and none of them knew anything about that. We found the empty tins in the cellar together with some empty petrol tins. Of course he thought the body would be burnt to a cinder : instead there were only fourth and fifth degree burns, that is destruction of some of the muscle. That's where he slipped up. He left the body on the floor. But even if he'd been smarter, I doubt whether he would have got away with it. Merson was a half-caste. The formation of the skull alone would have told Winston quite a lot, even if the rest of the skeleton had been reduced to ashes. The skull would have been the last part of the body to disintegrate.

" Thank God Sona isn't here !" muttered Larry, with a distasteful frown. " I guess her step-father was insane. He'd gotten to the end of his tether."

Herrington turned his head slowly towards him.

" Perhaps so," he said. " But if his idea had worked out, everyone, including Palmer, would have thought he was dead. The motive was logical enough."

Peter drew deeply at his cigarette, his brows puckered. For even now a piece of this jig-saw was missing. Why had Grant gone to such lengths to rid himself of these blackmailers? Why had he forfeited everything, his considerable fortune, his way of living, even his name when he might have——?

" What beats me," he said, " is why he didn't contact you at once after Merson called. Obviously he suspected him. Damn it, Herrington, there was no need for such drastic measures !"

" The guy was mad," Larry persisted. " Mad as a hatter."

But this Peter could not bring himself to believe. He had been the last person to see Jervis Grant and his manner, although overwrought, had not been that of a homicidal maniac. It was true that he had been devilishly cunning, but there had been a very logical reason for all he had done. Except for that one thing—his refusal to call in the police.

" I agree that, on the face of it, any sane man would have come to us," Herrington was saying. " Grant may not have done so because——" His voice trailed off as he drummed his fingers on the desk. " But, anyway," he went on without revealing his thoughts, " I think it is most unlikely that he's made any attempt to leave this country. Why should he ? So far as he knows, we think he's dead. Why should we look for him? But you can bet he's keeping an eye on the newspapers, and probably listening to the wireless reports of the case."

" I see," said Peter slowly. " That's why you've given this story to the Press, and that's why Larry is going to broadcast tonight."

" Exactly. When Grant realises things have gone wrong,

he may try to make a getaway. He'll have changed his name, of course, but if he stays where he is after his description has been circulated, he may be recognised. He might use a disguise. But if he does that, he becomes a stranger, even in a place where he may have establishd a second identity. And a stranger is naturally suspect. So I think we shall have him on the run."

Gayleigh would have been the first to admit that Herrington hadn't wasted any time. He was handling the case brilliantly. Sooner or later Grant would be apprehended. But even so, there was still the matter of the Van de Kramer diamonds to be considered. And Peter Gayleigh was very interested in those diamonds. What, he wondered, had become of them? It was unlikely that Merson had been carrying them about with him. And now that he was dead . . .

He put this to Herrington, who regarded him sardonically. "Your thoughts would run in that direction!" he said sourly. "But in case you come across the diamonds you'll be interested to hear that Van de Kramer is now offering a reward of £5,000 for their return."

"Five thousand pounds! Why that's probably more than a jewel fence would pay for them."

"Precisely. Your knowledge of these things makes it so much easier to explain! Van de Kramer is offering such a large sum for that very reason. He hopes the thief will return them. The reward will be paid, and no questions asked."

"Well, I wish him luck," said Peter. "I've a feeling the fish won't take that bait."

"Because you think Palmer has them."

"I do. And Palmer isn't a fool. He wouldn't take a chance like that, even if he thought it was on the level. And may I remind you there's a trifling matter that still puzzles me more than somewhat. *Who and where is Louie Palmer?*"

Herrington frowned. He, too, wished he could answer that.

II

Some three hours later. . . .

Larry Becket sat before the microphone in a small studio at Broadcasting House, his script lying before him on a table, his gaze fixed intently on the studio clock. His broadcast was timed to last for precisely three minutes, no more and no less, and he had rehearsed it again and again until he knew it would take just that long to deliver. One of the girl secretaries of the American network was also in the studio. She had been talking to New York on service matters concerning future schedules, but now she was looking at Larry wonderingly. For, accustomed as she was to the nervous tension of broadcasting correspondents, she had never seen him so nervous. Usually he was quite unruffled, very sure of himself, unlike some correspondents who occasionally spoke over this network and who were so overwrought, so fearful that something would go wrong that they made her life a misery. But tonight Larry Becket, one of the company's ace broadcasters, was behaving like a beginner. He was fidgeting about on the chair, as though unable to make himself comfortable, and while calling New York he had flipped over the pages of his script, pushed it away from him and pulled it towards him again. He had looked at his wristlet-watch, the studio clock, loosened his collar, fidgeted with his earphones, and had the height of the microphone adjusted. He had spoken more rapidly than usual, too, not in the easy way of broadcasting correspondents when attending to these preliminaries, but as though he was anxious to hurry the time on, as though he wished this particular broadcast was over.

"This is Larry Becket calling New York," the refrain ran. "In two minutes and thirty seconds from—now—I shall begin a three minute broadcast . . ."

He had repeated this with slight variations half a dozen times before a voice from New York came to him through the earphones.

"Okay, Larry. I guess that'll do. You gotten something special tonight, Gwenda tells us."

"Yeah, so hot it may roast someone, Joe—or maybe provide the guy with the noose they use over here. But your newspapers will have gotten most of my piece from the agencies, I guess."

"Sure. They're on the streets with it. Who you working for Larry? Scotland Yard, or the old firm?"

"Maybe you can tell me!" growled Larry.

"Okay, skip it. Charles has come through. He's sending

us something from Berlin. But we're taking yours. It better be good."

"It'll be good, Joe. Reception okay?"

"Yeah. We'll be taking you in fifty seconds from—now."

Larry stared at the clock, but though he watched the seconds tick away he was thinking of Sona. Why the hell had he been chosen, of all people, to give this broadcast with the B.B.C. hook-up? Another guy could have attended to that part of it, but it was no use arguing with the Chief. He was the Chief of Staff for all Europe. A big shot. He and Herrington had fixed this up between them. But it hadn't been easy to explain that to Sona. Gee, she was a swell kid. And here he was getting ready to rub salt into her wounds. True, her stepfather wasn't dead. But that didn't help. Better if he had been, since it now looked as though he was a murderer. Gee, how he hated this job!

Twenty seconds to go . . .

His eyes were on the red hand of the studio clock.

Ten seconds . . . Five . . . Three . . . One . . .

The green light flashed. He began:

"This is Larry Becket in London. I'm going to tell you tonight about a hideous crime perpetrated less than forty-eight hours ago in a country house near London—the home of a diamond-broker called Jervis Grant . . . "

A brief but colourful description of Pinewood was followed by word pictures of the blazing house, in which the unrecognisable body of a man had been found.

". . . the body of a man who had been shot twice through the head, before his murderer deliberately set the house on fire. Fragments of clothing on the body, and an onyx ring on one of the fingers, suggested that the victim of this cold-blooded killing was Jervis Grant himself. Only later was it discovered that—But first let me reconstruct this crime for you from the facts given to me by Scotland Yard. In the early hours of yesterday morning two men were alone at Pinewood—the murderer and his victim . . . "

He might not be feeling so good, but there was nothing wrong with the way in which he was putting over this broadcast, thought Gwenda. Larry Becket knew how to create suspense. She gave him the one minute signal, a downward sweep of her arm, and speeding up slightly he went on to the dramatic identification of the body, disclosed that Merson's clothes had been found buried in the grounds, and added that Jervis Grant had disappeared.

" . . . Officials at Scotland Yard believe that Mr. Grant is still alive, and since he may be able to assist them in solving this murder they are anxious to get in touch with him . . . "

No accusation, merely the usual official statement. Herrington had seen to that. But Jervis Grant would know quite well what that sentence meant.

There followed a very detailed description of Grant, before Larry concluded with a hint that Scotland Yard was already on the track of the murderer and that dramatic revelations might shortly be expected.

Herrington listened to the broadcast at Scotland Yard, and the tight set of his lips, the way in which he inclined his head slightly as Larry emphasised important points, indicated that he was well satisfied.

Marcia Lawson and her father heard it at their home in St. John's Wood. It was impossible to tell what Lawson was thinking, but Marcia's thoughts were with Sona. In her innocence perhaps she wouldn't realise that her step-father was suspect. The broadcast might have given her fresh hope, since it was clear that Grant was alive. But sooner or later she would have to know. Marcia sighed. She had become very fond of Sona, and decided to visit her at once.

But, as time was to show, the most important person who listened to that broadcast, discounting Jervis Grant himself, was Peter Gayleigh. He had returned to Jermyn Street, where the indefatigable Dave Lyman had eventually tracked him down. The broadcast had interrupted a discussion, which Peter had deliberately confined to Merson and Winniger, and it had come at a very suitable time. For though Peter tried to remember that this stolid detective had rescued him from the Four Hundred, he found Dave Lyman extremely boring. All the more so, as there was nothing new to be learnt from him.

" That boy Larry sure knows how to put it over," he commented as Peter switched off. " D'you reckon this guy Grant did it?"

Peter shrugged. " You know as much as I do," he said mendaciously. " You've stuck so close to Merson, you're going to miss him like a brother."

Lyman shook his head lugubriously.

"I'll say. If he hadn't made his getaway in that car. If I'd kept on his tail. If I'd trailed him to Pinewood——"

"Wishful thinking, Dave."

"Aw shucks. If I had, I'd be an important guy now . . . maybe bouquets from my firm, maybe even a fatter pay check. And jest when I might have gotten myself a medal I lose the guy. Yeah, I'm feeling kinda lost without Merson. That guy had no consideration for me. I hadn't figured he'd be such a dope as to get himself bumped off."

"Most unthoughtful," commiserated Peter. "Have some more whisky?"

"I don't mind if I do. Make it straight . . . I bin wonderin' if Winniger has the Van de Kramer diamonds. That's jest a hunch, and I'm not counting on it. But the boss in New York is askin' questions. He's beefing about my reports which, he say kinda sarcastic like, don't amount to much. Unless I get a lead soon, I'll be on my way back." He raised his glass, washed the whisky round inside his mouth, and swallowed it with a grimace. "Good liquor you gotten in this country," he observed, as though he could find nothing else good in it.

He reminded Peter of a stray dog that had found a comfortable resting place and was in no hurry to leave. He said nothing of any consequence, and kindly hints that he was overstaying his welcome failed to move him. So that Peter was glad of the interruption when the telephone rang almost an hour later. The call was from Marcia. She had seen Sona, and had learned something very important. Would he call at St. John's Wood as soon as he could.

"I'll come at once," he said, and for the other's benefit. "I've got Dave Lyman here, but he's just going."

He replaced the phone.

"Sorry, Dave. You see how it is."

"Oh sure." He levered himself reluctantly to his feet. "That dame knows sump'n. And maybe you know sump'n, too. Tell me straight, bud, because I'm right out of gags and smart talk—are you still holdin' out on me?"

So this was why he had prolonged his visit! Dave Lyman was dispensing with what he misguidedly thought was finesse. In the matter of the Van de Kramer diamonds he was a beaten man, and knew it.

M

"Listen, Dave," said Peter. "If I knew where those diamonds were I'd tell you. It would be worth it just to see you smile. But as I don't know where they are, all I can suggest is that you go and get drunk—on somebody else's whisky."

The other picked up his fedora and crammed it on his head.

"Yeah, I guess I'll do that. And afterwards maybe I'll dream they made me a lootenant or sump'n." He moved to the door, turning with his hand on the knob. "But I'll be around, and I'll be seein' you."

Peter stifled a sigh. He was afraid Lyman meant that.

III

The Bentley slid to a standstill outside the house in St. John's Wood, and Peter Gayleigh stepped out. He wondered if Miles Lawson was at home. If so, his reception might be somewhat lacking in cordiality. This was the second time he had called to see Marcia in less than two days, and it might seem as though it was becoming a habit.

He was approaching the front door when it was opened by the girl herself. She was wearing a black evening gown, which contrasted deliciously with the bare whiteness of her throat and arms : her lips were parted slightly, and her eyes glistened as she saw him. She looked svelte yet ethereal in the flood of light from the hall, and once again he found himself reacting like a callow youth to her enchantment, though a practical voice inside him whispered that he was a fool. Such a girl could have no part in the adventures that lay ahead of him, yet he was more than grateful that fate had brought them together, if only for a fragment of time.

"I heard your car," she said, beckoning him into the hall. "Sona's here, Peter. Er—you heard Larry's broadcast, of course?"

"Yes. How did Sona take it?"

"Like the grand little person she is. I called to see her immediately afterwards. Larry saw her before the broadcast, and explained how your detective friend had roped him in." Then glancing up at him quickly : "I suppose the police are looking for Grant because he killed Merson?"

He shrugged. "Does Sona realise that?"

"I don't know. She hasn't said anything to me. If the thought did cross her mind, she's the kind of loyal kid who wouldn't believe it. And, of course, she wouldn't breathe a word about it to anyone—except perhaps Larry. She's going to need him, Peter. Thank God for Larry Becket!"

"Love's sweet young dream," he was eyeing her ruminatively. "But why did you bring her here?"

There was a wealth of spurious innocence in those deep blue eyes as she looked up at him again.

"Because father's gone out. I thought you could talk to her without being interrupted."

"H'm." He smoothed his moustache with his forefinger. "You're a smart girl. Is there any particular reason why I should talk to her?"

She nodded in a conspiratorial way, twice.

"There is. About an hour before the broadcast Chief Inspector Herrington called to see her. He asked her a lot of questions about her step-father, and she gave him some information which I think you ought to hear. That is if you're interested in finding Grant before Herrington beats you to it."

"Lead me to Sona," he said very decisively.

He found her sitting quietly and disconsolately in the drawing-room, and she greeted him with a wan smile as he entered. The joyous girl he had seen on the boat was still as dainty as ever, but the glowing cheeks were now very pale, and the frank eyes were full of apprehension.

She asked him if he had heard the broadcast, and for a time they discussed its more superficial implications, and with a constraint that made conversation difficult. He felt she knew what people must be thinking about her step-father, though she spoke as though his disappearance would shortly be explained and without any discredit to himself.

"I hate to thrust myself upon you like this," he said presently. "I want you to know that I'm not here out of idle curiosity. Marcia told me——"

"Yes, I know. And I'm glad you came. You're one of father's oldest friends, and I'm sure he'd want me to tell you all I can."

Peter said nothing. Recalling how Grant had abused his

friendship, he decided there was nothing useful he could say.

"Marcia feels I ought to tell you what I told Chief Inspector Herrington when he came to see me this evening. He was very kind and very tactful, but—well, it was rather an ordeal."

Marcia looked significantly at Peter. She put her hand on Sona's shoulder, patting it sympathetically as the younger girl lowered her head.

"Of course, my dear, we understand. No one likes being cross-examined by the police."

"He asked me dozens of questions about father, all about his movements for years before—this happened. I'm afraid I can't remember everything I told him. It was all so disconnected. Because, of course, father travelled about such a lot. Sometimes I didn't see him for months."

"And sometimes you didn't know where he'd gone," put in Marcia promptingly. "There was the house in Argyllshire——"

"Yes." She looked past both of them, unseeingly, for a few moments before turning to Peter again. "You see, father spends quite a few holidays in Scotland. He's gone there ever since I was a little girl at school. I used to wonder why he never took me with him, but he said it was because he spent most of his time fishing and I should find it very dull. As far as I know—although he never said much when he got back—he went to various parts of Scotland, but any letters that came for him while he was away, were re-addressed to a friend in Argyllshire."

"That's very interesting," said Peter quietly, although he thought it was much more than that.

"Mr. Herrington seemed very interested, too. He wanted to know the name and address of the man to whom we forwarded the letters."

"Yes?" He leaned forward a little, avoiding Marcia's triumphant gaze.

"Malcolm Gourlay," she told him.

"And the address?"

"The House of Cladda. It's on the island of Seil, off the coast of Argyllshire. But, as I say, I've never been there and I've never seen Mr. Gourlay. He's nothing more than a name to me." She shook her head, puzzled. "I can't think why

Mr. Herrington was so interested—unless he thinks that father may have gone to Cladda to see Mr. Gourlay. But why should father do that? He has plenty of other friends, and he never went to Scotland at this time of the year."

"It does seem rather odd," Peter agreed, as casually as he could, for premonition had given place to certainty. He realised now why Marcia had sent for him, why Herrington had attached so much importance to this ingenious revelation. And by now, of course, he must have phoned the Argyllshire police. Perhaps he had received a reply to his inquiry. At last the threads were forming themselves into a definite pattern.

"May I use the phone?" he asked Marcia, and a few moments later put through a call to Scotland Yard. He was told that the Chief Inspector was not available, but from the delay that occurred before he was given this information, he was pretty certain that Herrington was, in fact, there. Which meant that he was going to keep what he knew to himself. He was forestalling any further interference.

Peter frowned. There was very little he could do on his own. For once it seemed that he was to be an also ran. Then he remembered that Miles Lawson was interested in this case, and that Herrington had a great opinion of Lawson . . .

He left the house in St. John's Wood soon afterwards—but not before he had extracted a promise from Marcia.

IV

When Peter Gayleigh phoned Scotland Yard, Miles Lawson was in Herrington's office. He had gone there immediately after the broadcast, for he had known the man who, it now seemed, was guilty of premeditated murder, and unless Grant had been insane—which he did not believe for one moment —it was obvious that his motive must have been much stronger than was apparent. Jervis Grant was a business man of international repute, presumably an honest citizen. Yet he had disposed of a blackmailer in this devilish fashion. On the face of it, such a crime was illogical, and as Miles Lawson saw it the explanation was to be found in the answer to one question : Why had Grant refused to call in the police? That, he felt, was the fulcrum of the balance on which causes and effects had been so carefully weighed.

He had put this question to Herrington, who had given him a very satisfactory answer. For this case had now resolved itself completely. A theory on which he had set to work earlier that day had been substantiated by detailed inquiries. All that remained to be done now was to effect Grant's arrest. And very shortly, perhaps in the next few minutes, that welcome news might come through.

He had given the novelist an account of the vital interview with Sona Boyd, and he had barely completed his recital before the 'phone rang. The call was from the main switchboard, and after muttering a few words in reply, he hung up with a thin smile.

"Our friend, Gayleigh," he explained, not without satisfaction. "Fishing for information as usual. But from now on he's not getting any. That man is dangerous."

"You mean he might interfere?"

"It has been known," said Herrington dryly. "In the past he's kept me in the dark when he's known quite a lot. Now it's my turn."

He began to fill his pipe, dismissing Gayleigh from his thoughts, and looking steadily at Lawson.

"You realise of course what Sona Boyd's evidence means?"

The other inclined his head weightily, as he considered this in conjunction with the latest information about Grant.

"I can guess—Jervis Grant and Malcolm Gourlay are one and the same person."

"Exactly. Grant bought this house in Seil, some years before he was involved in the Palmer case. And it's not difficult to understand why he bought it. He might have been obliged to make himself scarce at any time. So, after taking the name of Malcolm Gourlay, he set about establishing a second identity in Argyllshire. House of Cladda was to be the haven to which he could fly in case of emergency. You see, everything was in readiness. He had somewhere to go, and where his sudden appearance wouldn't arouse any suspicion. In short, he made use of the only really effective way in which a person can disappear."

Lawson nodded again.

"Which goes to prove that he's quite sane," he observed

ruminatively. "I gather you've already learned quite a lot from the Argyllshire Constabulary?"

"I 'phoned the Chief Constable at Lochgilphead as soon as I got back here. He put an inquiry through to the Oban division. It seems House of Cladda is near the coast of Seil, not far from the island of Easdale. I got this information, and more, only a few minutes after Becket went on the air. Malcolm Gourlay is well known in those parts, although nothing is known of Jervis Grant. I asked for a description of Gourlay, and it tallied in every particular with that of the man we're looking for. Moreover, Gourlay arrived at the house only this morning."

"He's there now?" Lawson asked quickly, and Herrington shrugged.

"I don't know yet. But if he heard that broadcast—— I wish now I hadn't been in such a confounded hurry to get him on the run. But even if he did hear it, he may still think he's quite safe. He may think that he's established himself so securely—being well known to the local police over a long period of years—that it won't occur to them that he is Jervis Grant."

"Probably it wouldn't have done if your inquiries hadn't been so specific. When do you expect to hear from them?"

"At any moment now. Once I was sure of my man I asked the Chief Constable up there to authorise Gourlay's arrest."

But it was fully an hour later before the call came through from Lochgilphead, and the news was very disappointing. Malcolm Gourlay had left Cladda secretly some time before the police arrived. As yet it was not known what baggage, if any, he had taken with him, though he apparently left in the car in which he had driven from London. The Argyllshire police had interviewed the woman who acted as his housekeeper, and they had got the number of his car, but it had not been located.

Nor was there any further news of him throughout the whole of the next day, although ceaseless inquiries were made.

Jervis Grant had disappeared completely.

V

Peter Gayleigh strolled into the " Salted Almond " cocktail bar at the Trocadero, and towards a vacant table suitably removed from the bar itself and as far as possible from a stout woman with two senile-looking terriers. A white-coated cocktail waiter came towards him, and he ordered a " Planter's Punch."

It was early afternoon on the day following the broadcast. Forsaken by Herrington, time had hung very heavily on Peter's hands. So far as he was concerned the Grant case was in cold storage, though he liked to think that he had friends who might provide him, and at any moment, with the impetus for useful action. Perhaps Larry Becket would have something interesting to tell him, or perhaps he had arranged this meeting to pour out his soul about Sona. A man in love was capable of anything, Peter reflected. Love was a terrible affliction. It hit its victims below the belt, making them cough up all kinds of banalities, under the misguided impression that the gift of transcendental thought had suddenly been bestowed upon them. Thank God that as yet Larry had shown no sign of that.

At the moment, Peter's philosophy was soured by the cool way in which Herrington had brushed him off.

He ordered another " Planter's Punch." It helped him to adopt a more tolerant attitude to life in general, and he was gazing, with nothing more than mild disapproval, at the two decrepit dogs, now wheezing saliva on to the carpet, when Larry Becket appeared.

" I was afraid you might be out when I 'phoned," he said as he sat down. " I guess I was lucky to find you in."

" I was brooding in solitude," Peter told him. " I am a man with a secret sorrow. Your friend Herrington has cut me to the quick."

" Oh?" His eyebrows lifted slightly.

" Yes, much as it pains me to admit it, Herrington has taken a leaf out of my own copybook. He won't see me. He won't speak to me on the 'phone. He's as elusive as I am, when I'm withholding information from him."

"Gee, that's tough," Larry commented solemnly, and, as Gayleigh caught the waiter's eye, decided that a "Bronx" would meet his requirements.

"All is well between you and Sona, I hope?" Peter asked. "I was rather afraid that broadcast might . . ."

"Sure. But I had another talk with Sona about it. She's a swell girl."

Peter smiled. "To which the correct reply is—they don't come any better. I suppose you've seen her this morning? Ah, yes—of course you have."

Larry nodded soberly.

"She's still carrying a torch for her step-father. She won't admit, even to me, that he may be guilty. That's partly why I wanted to see you. Because we both know that Grant's as guilty as hell. He may have been very fond of Sona, but I reckon that doesn't make him any less of a scoundrel. And I'll say he's a scoundrel. Some more info. has come in."

If the gods who controlled Peter Gayleigh's destiny had been visible he might have acknowledged this service with a grateful nod. He pushed his drink away and leaned across the table. Larry went on : "I wanted to talk to you before you saw Sona again. She said she'd seen you last night at Marcia's house after the broadcast, and I thought that since then Herrington might have told you . . ."

He broke off as the waiter returned with the drink. Peter hid his impatience. Then, as soon as the man had gone :

"You mean he's been arrested?"

"Grant?" He shook his head. "No, not yet. He's pulled a fast one all right. Seems to have vanished into thin air. He left his house in Seil before the police arrived. Oh yes, he'd been there, and you'd think he couldn't have gotten far. Yet nobody has seen a sign of him. It's mighty queer, since he was known pretty well in that part of the Highlands. You'd have thought some of the islanders would have seen him."

Peter digested this.

"Could any of them be concealing him?"

"The Argyllshire police don't seem to think so. They've been looking for the wreckage of his car in the sea. He didn't take any luggage, and they think maybe he committed suicide."

"But if that was his idea, why take the car at all? Is the house far from the sea?"

"Not more than a quarter of a mile. If there's a suicide angle it seems phoney to me. And even if they find the car I'll still say that. Grant is a pretty deep guy."

He was toying with the stem of his glass, his eyes screwed up slightly, as though he was thinking of something he hadn't mentioned yet.

"A very deep guy," he repeated slowly.

Peter didn't hurry him. He gave him a cigarette, and lit one himself, though his cool, level gaze hardly moved from the other's face. The sounds in the cocktail bar had faded into insignificance. He was conscious only of a keyed up feeling induced by the supersensory knowledge that he was to be given a part in the epilogue after all ; that Larry Becket had something to tell him which would change the whole aspect of this case.

He felt it was not Larry speaking but an ambassador of fate.

"I've just come from Scotland Yard," he went on slowly. "The Argyllshire police haven't gotten any forrarder, but Herrington's sure moving fast at this end."

"I hope he's grateful to Sona for giving him a lead?"

Larry looked at him quickly.

"Yeah, that's right. So you know that Grant used the name of Malcolm Gourlay."

"It occurred to me that he might," said Peter modestly. "And, of course, Herrington has been probing into Mr. Gourlay's private affairs."

"You bet. Grant used that name in London, too. There's a hell of a lot of dough standing to Gourlay's credit at one of the big banks here. I reckon Herrington himself doesn't know how much—banks are rather touchy about disclosing such things—and there are a lot of securities too, mostly bearer bonds. The bank didn't know that Gourlay had any connection with Grant until Herrington put them wise. Then, I guess, the high-ups got a bit jittery."

"So Grant had no intention of giving up everything," mused Peter, his eyes half closed. "When did he open this account?"

"About fifteen years ago, and it's been growing steadily

ever since. And I'm pretty certain there's no accounting for the money. Mind you, Herrington didn't say that, but judging from his manner I guess he's put through some tactful inquiries, and come to that conclusion. Incidentally, what I'm telling you is right off the record. None of this is being given out for publication, of course."

"No, I can appreciate that."

There was a short silence, while Larry emptied his glass.

"It makes you think, doesn't it?" he said, his eyes resting very significantly on Peter. "I wonder if Louie Palmer has gotten the Van de Kramer diamonds?"

Smoke dribbled slowly from Peter's nostrils as he returned the other's very direct stare. He knew why Larry had made this seemingly irrelevant comment, just as he could read the thought passing through the other's mind. But neither of them put it into words. Peter merely said : " Thanks a lot. This puts an entirely different complexion on the matter."

"Yep, I thought you'd get the hook-up. Maybe Palmer knew a darned sight more than he said when Grant gave evidence against him twelve years ago." He brightened the tip of his cigarette, exhaling the smoke slowly. " I've been wondering if Palmer *is* over here. Maybe we just think he is. Of course he gave the New York police the slip, but it doesn't follow . . ."

"Quite. I've been toying with that idea for days. But now I can't believe that Grant arranged all this elaborate set-up just to get rid of a small-time crook like Merson. No, I think Grant knew that Palmer had him by the short hairs, and that he had to do something about it pretty damned quick."

Larry Becket spread his hands helplessly.

"Then where is Palmer? Grant may have seen him, but I haven't, you haven't, and neither has Herrington."

"We haven't recognised him, you mean," Peter amended quietly. "If I knew where Palmer was I shouldn't be here. I shouldn't be here as it is," he added, disposing of his drink. " Excuse me, I must make a 'phone call."

The other eyed him in some surprise.

"Why the hurry?"

"Because there are other girls in the world besides Sona,"

he answered with an enigmatic smile. "Don't worry, I'll keep what you've told me very firmly under my hat."

He found a telephone-box, and rang through to his flat where, as he had hoped, Carver informed him that Miss Lawson had 'phoned.

"Only about a quarter of an hour ago, sir. She'd like you to ring her back."

"Thanks," said Peter, and severed the connection. He dialled Marcia's number, and a few moments later heard her voice.

"This is your secret lover," he said. "Sorry I was out when you 'phoned, my sweet."

"That doesn't say much for your faith in me, Peter darling. I thought you were going to hang over the telephone until I rang."

"That was my intention, it's true, and throughout the whole of this morning I abided by my good resolution. But the strain of waiting became too much for me. I nipped out for a quick one."

"So you really believed I'd pull it off?" There was gay raillery in her voice.

"Of course. Speaking from experience, I know you have a way with you. An elderly man like your doting parent should be easy meat."

"You underestimate father. He's pretty cute."

"Naturally—he's your father."

"How sweet! But seriously, Peter, I'd have 'phoned you before, only I couldn't get anything out of him."

"That's too bad. I thought he'd be difficult. But as I said last night he's very pally with Herrington, and he must have all the latest dope on Grant."

"Oh he has. I'm sure of that. And I've tried to pump him without being too obvious. I've worked really hard, but he hasn't let anything slip. I'm afraid he realises that if he tells me anything I shall pass it on to you."

"In other words, he's stonewalling."

"Up to a point. He hasn't told me how the case is progressing, but I'm sure Grant is still at large, otherwise father wouldn't be going to the island of Seil."

Peter's eyebrows came together quickly.

"You don't say! When is he leaving?"

" Tonight. He's going to Oban, which isn't very far from Seil, you know, and he asked me if I'd like to go with him. Perhaps he thinks he can keep an eye on me that way."

" H'm. Are you going?"

" Of course. Father's a pretty good sleuth. It might be fun. It might even be exciting if you were there, too."

" Curiously enough the same thought occurred to me."

" I hoped it would. We've booked a couple of sleepers on the night train to Glasgow. We shall go on to Oban in the morning. Last time we were there, years ago, we stayed at the Station Hotel."

" I'll remember that," said Peter.

" Then I'll be seeing you?"

" Pretty soon, I hope," he said, and rang off. He put through another call to Carver, asking him to pack a bag, then rejoined Larry to whom he explained that certain unspecified matters connected with his love life had now been satisfactorily settled. They had another drink, and parted soon afterwards.

Peter walked back to his flat to complete his travelling arrangements, and wondered if this adventure was going to pay a dividend. If he could recover the Van de Kramer diamonds he might collect five thousand pounds. And he thought that was not such a remote possibility as it had seemed an hour ago. Moreover, he didn't want to disappoint Dave Lyman, who probably hoped to share that reward with him, and whose faith in his capabilities was quite heartening. For Lyman had followed him from Jermyn Street, and was now following him back again. Peter caught occasional glimpses of him in the distant rear, and while he deplored Lyman's inability to make himself invisible he admired his tenacity.

Dave didn't trust him. Dave thought he knew something that he was keeping to himself. And, as it happened, Dave Lyman was right.

Peter smiled quietly to himself, eyeing the distant figure again out of the corner of his eye. He wondered how this stolid American would blend with the scenery on the island of Seil.

CHAPTER ELEVEN

IN WHICH MILES LAWSON SPRINGS A SURPRISE, AND DAVE LYMAN JOINS THE PARTY

I

IT was early afternoon on the following day when Peter Gayleigh reached Oban, having enjoyed a compartment to himself, and some of the finest scenery in Scotland, during the journey from Glasgow. He hoped Marcia and her father and the indefatigable Lyman had also had a comfortable journey, for he knew they were all on that train.

He was one of the last to step on to the platform, but not quite the last, as he noticed while surrendering his ticket. At the far end of the train a thick-set man was staring after him from one of the carriage windows. Sooner or later, Peter decided, he would point out to Lyman that he could save a lot of energy by stifling his suspicions and being a little more matey.

He crossed the road and without hesitation entered the Station Hotel, for he had no intention of hiding his own light under a bushel. He saw no sign of the couple for whom he was looking, but he had no sooner asked for a room, and given his name at the reception-desk, than the woman behind the counter smiled up at him brightly.

"You must be the gentleman Mr. Lawson is expecting?"

The effect of these words on Peter was as though he had suddenly been ducked under an icy shower, but he managed to look at her without blinking, which, he felt, was quite an achievement.

"Er—yes," he said, after an appreciable pause.

"Mr. Lawson hopes you'll be able to join him at lunch. It will be served in about ten minutes."

He muttered his thanks, and wondered if Marcia was responsible for this. Or had Lawson pulled the strings? The more he thought about it, the more he was certain that Lawson had been very astute. For he must have known that his daughter was fishing for information, and that she would pass this tit-bit on. Lawson had expected him to follow them to Oban. It was so obvious now that he wondered why he hadn't thought of it before. Miles Lawson was a man to be reckoned with.

The meeting promised to have its piquant moments, and after a wash and brush up, he strolled into the dining-room with an exhilarating feeling of expectancy. He had no difficulty in picking out Marcia and her father. They were sitting at a table near the spacious windows looking out on to the esplanade, and the girl glanced up at him dubiously as he approached.

"Hullo, Peter," she greeted him in a small voice. "I hope you don't think that I . . ."

"Mr. Gayleigh is not lacking in intelligence, my dear," her father put in equably. He extended his hand, his pale eyes twinkling. "Glad to see you, Gayleigh—although I can't say this is an unexpected pleasure. You'll join us, of course?"

Peter said : "I shall be delighted. It's good to see friends in this out of the way spot."

He sat down, and wondered what was coming next. Nothing of any consequence apparently, for Lawson kept the conversation to generalities, centring round the journey, and the amenities to be found in that part of the Highlands. Marcia said very little, but the novelist talked a great deal. One might have thought that he was there purely on holiday, and Peter helped to keep the conversation in these channels. It was very charming and insincere. He found it quite amusing.

Grilled whiting followed the soup, and he had ample opportunity to appreciate the excellence of the apple tart, served with cream, while the older man continued to expatiate with unabated goodwill. The waiter was placing coffee before them when Gayleigh noticed that Miles Lawson was staring very intently through the window. His face had gone rigid.

"Who's that man?" he asked tersely. "Out there in the street. He seems very interested in us."

Peter and Marcia glanced round, following the direction of his gaze, and just in time to observe a broad and very familiar figure receding into the near distance.

"Why it's Dave Lyman!" she exclaimed. "What on earth is he doing here?"

That crooked smile played about Peter's lips.

"He's keeping an eye on me. Our Dave has a very suspicious mind. You might say I brought him from London by remote control."

"He followed you?" This was Lawson, and very evidently he was not amused.

"Just that. He seems to think I shall lead him to the Van de Kramer diamonds."

"How perfectly delicious," smiled Marcia. "He's such an earnest and hardworking man. It's a pity he never seems to get anywhere." She turned to her father. "Peter and I met him on the *Cornelius*. He's a private detective employed by Lishman's of New York."

Lawson's face relaxed. He raised a thin smile.

"Is that so. I'm sorry I didn't meet him. You two must introduce me some time."

But despite this easy dismissal of the subject he said very little as he drank his coffee, and it devolved upon Peter to provide the generalities, which the novelist had been delivering with such unembarrassed smoothness.

"If you don't mind, my dear," he said, as they rose from the table, "I should like to have a few words alone with Mr. Gayleigh."

Marcia shot a quick glance at Peter, who caught the unmistakable flicker of her eyelid. Clearly she thought that Lawson was about to play the heavy father, but it didn't seem to bother her very much.

"Very well. But I hope you won't be very long. I'll wait in the lounge."

As soon as she left them, Lawson led the way up to his room, Peter feeling like a schoolboy being escorted to the headmaster's study. This was what came of yielding to the high-powered fascination of girls like Marcia, he thought.

He was not to know that when he left that room he would understand everything that had happened since he left New York. And he was to remember the next few hours, with their grim climax, as long as he lived.

II

The novelist closed the door of the room, produced a couple of cigars, and proffered one to Gayleigh. The bleached, almost non-existent eyebrows were drawn together as though with intense concentration, for he was not frowning at Gayleigh, but seemingly at his own thoughts. The ineffectual-looking, garrulous old gentleman had vanished, replaced by a man who spoke decisively and very much to the point.

"My daughter is a rather headstrong young person," he began, but as though he was still thinking of something else. "She is an impressionable girl, and as you must have noticed is somewhat prone to hero worship. But, of course, that is merely a phase. I shouldn't like to think that you are treating this infatuation seriously. But I have no qualms on that score, for I know you are not."

"I think I understand what you mean," said Peter.

"Yes, I realise that Marcia provides a means of keeping in touch with me—just another contact, as it were. And I admire your shrewdness, my boy. If I didn't, I shouldn't have let you follow me to Oban. I thought it possible that you might be of use in cleaning up this case. I know now that you can be."

This was scarcely the line Peter had expected him to take. Evidently he hadn't brought him there to talk about Marcia, for he had dealt with that aspect of the matter as though it were of no great concern. Peter might have resented the emphatic assumption that he could be of use to him if it had come from a younger man. In Miles Lawson he found it intriguing.

"Herrington didn't seem to think so," he said, commenting on the other's last remark.

"Herrington is a police official, bound by very clearly defined rules and regulations," was the reply. "You and I are not. You are an adventurer whilst I—well there are times when I have my own way of arranging things to the satisfaction of all concerned." He took the cigar out of his mouth and stared at it reflectively. "I'm thinking of Grant's step-

N

daughter Sona. A sweet young girl, so Marcia tells me. If Grant is arrested——"

He broke off, and Peter Gayleigh looked at him very steadily.

" I've got imagination, too," he said. " Maybe I can use it, if you tell me what you have in mind."

" That calls for something more than imagination. But I understand you're a man who will always take a risk."

Peter said : " What do you want me to do?" and there was a sardonic light in those cool, clear eyes. When someone handed him a bouquet, before outlining a proposition, he was sufficiently cynical to look for the wreath. Perhaps Lawson realised that. He seemed to be a very far-seeing man.

" I'll explain presently. If Grant is hiding in these parts, as I'm almost certain he is——"

Again he broke off, his eyes almost closed as a thin stream of smoke came from his pursed lips.

" I am a humanitarian, Gayleigh. I do not believe in causing unnecessary suffering. I do not believe that the police are the best people to tie up the loose ends of some criminal cases. In that, I think, we see eye to eye."

" Do we?" said Peter. " I wonder."

" Mind you, I can't be sure that this will work out to the conclusion I envisage. But with your assistance it might. Even if we forestall the police we shall have to play this game very carefully. Now listen . . . "

Half a minute later he had revealed something that struck Gayleigh like a blow in the eyes. And as Lawson plied him with questions, pieces in this jig-saw sprang into place with startling precision. Lawson went on talking, and Peter listened. Presently :

" Now you can appreciate the danger. Without you I can do nothing. The law must take its course. But I am pre-pared to withhold this information in the hope that we may find Grant before the police get him. I'm asking you to risk your life. But it is a proposition, I think, that will appeal to you. If it doesn't, now is the time to say so."

Peter said : " You can count on me. This might be quite exciting. Where do we go from here?"

" Good man. I hoped you'd take it that way. First I'm going to Oban police station to get the latest information.

I'm carrying a letter from the Assistant Commissioner, so there should be no difficulty about that. In the meantime——"

" I'll get busy hiring a car."

" Yes. And if you run up against your friend, Lyman, you might gather him into the fold. We must all stick together, eh, Gayleigh."

" It would be a pity to leave Dave out," said Peter. " He's tried so hard. Perhaps if he tags along with me I can help him to find what he's looking for."

III

He found Marcia smoking a cigarette rather impatiently in the lounge. She looked up quickly, and said : " So at last the lecture is over. I hope father didn't sling too many punches at you. His ideas about my boy friends are hopelessly out of date. Did you find him dreadfully old-fashioned?"

" Absolutely doddering," he told her. " He did his best, but you know what a poor old buffer he is."

He saw her eyes contract with resentment, and hid a smile. She might refer to her father disparagingly, but that didn't mean others could do so.

" He isn't old-fashioned, and he isn't an old buffer. As parents go, he's pretty good. But he never tells me anything."

" Perhaps he knows you too well," smiled Peter. " He and I have buried the hatchet. Your dad is like his daughter. He has a big heart."

Marcia eyed him severely.

" Now I *know* you two are up to something. What is it?"

" The first move, my sweet, is to hire a car. How'd you like to come along?"

" Very well. But why do you want a car?"

" Surely that's obvious—to drive to the House of Cladda."

He spent the next half hour in parrying further questions, and in acquiring a Ford of doubtful vintage but serviceable appearance. And when he suggested that she should drive it to the hotel herself, since he needed some cigarettes, she raised no objection.

He watched her drive out of the garage, waited a few

moments and timed his appearance in the street to a nicety. A few quick strides brought him up to the stolid American who was now walking away in the direction taken by the car.

Peter tapped him lightly on the shoulder.

"If you go that way you're liable to lose me, Dave," he said indulgently. Then as the other looked at him balefully : "Must you do this sort of thing?"

"When a guy holds out on me—" Lyman was beginning heavily, when Peter held up his hand.

"For heaven's sake don't give me that again! You may not realise it, but it's beginning to pall. And I'm more than hurt by your underhand behaviour, Dave. I thought you trusted me."

"Like hell I do," was the bitter response.

Peter gave a deep sigh.

"There seems no way to convince you that I've got nothing up my sleeve. But at least you might have the decency to keep your suspicions to yourself. You could do that if you came along with me, instead of hanging around like a hopeful bloodhound. What do you say? Perhaps you needn't say anything, because if you think it out, bud, you haven't much choice."

Lyman's capitulation took the form of a resigned shrug.

"Okay. I reckon you can slip it across me at close quarters same as at a distance. Though maybe it won't be so easy. What's the set-up?" He jerked his head towards the garage.

"The idea is to find Grant. If you're interested meet me outside the Station Hotel in half an hour.

"I'll do that," said Lyman, and watched him speculatively as he walked away.

The novelist returned soon after Peter got back, and again leaving Marcia to her own devices, despite her protestations, the two men went upstairs to the privacy of Lawson's room.

"The local police have found Grant's car," he said crisply, and without preamble. "Only a couple of hours ago. They've been dragging the lochs on the island of Seil. The car was found at the bottom of one of them, only about a mile from Grant's house."

"H'm. So it looks as though you may be right. Presumably he didn't go very far."

"No. But of course the police are working on that assumption, too. If we're going to beat them to it, we shall have to move fast."

Peter eyed him shrewdly. Lawson was a man of ideas, and evidently he hadn't revealed all of them yet. He pursed his lips, took a couple of paces about the room, then looked at Peter again.

"I know this coastline very well, Gayleigh. There are a number of small islands off Seil where a man could live for months without anyone being the wiser. And he wouldn't need to take any provisions—probably not even a fishing-rod. He could make one from wire taken from wooden bales which are sometimes washed up. He might even get butter, and lard, and other eatables in that way. Even if he didn't, he could live on fish from the pools and sea birds' eggs. He could make himself a fire from driftwood and peat. If he wanted, he could even build a beehive hut from the slate quarries. Slate quarrying used to be the principal industry in those parts."

"Maybe you've got something there," said Peter with considerable interest. "It's quite an idea."

"But an idea that must have occurred to the local police," Lawson pointed out. "Though before they found the car, they had no reason to believe that Grant was in the immediate vicinity. There wasn't sufficient evidence to warrant a search of the islands. They made inquiries, of course, but it seems he didn't take a boat. Nevertheless, I'm pretty certain he must have done. He had a boat of his own, but, of course, he wasn't foolish enough to take that."

"I see. You want me to make inquiries?"

"From boatmen along the coast. Er—you've talked to Lyman?"

"Yes."

He gave him a brief account of his meeting with the American, and the appointment he had made.

"Splendid," Lawson commented. "Take him along. I shall stay here with Marcia. Ring me at once if you discover anything."

IV

The water in Oban Bay, where sailing boats and a few larger craft lay peacefully at anchor, shimmered tranquilly in the afternoon sun. The vagaries of Highland weather, as Lawson well knew, might have interfered seriously with Peter Gayleigh's intentions, since, if the necessity arose, he would have found it impossible to reach any of the islands in a rough sea. But even the weather, it seemed, was favouring this dangerous project. The novelist's room overlooked the esplanade, and from the inconspicuous vantage point afforded by one of the windows, he saw Gayleigh exchange a few words with Lyman before they got into the car. He continued to watch it as Gayleigh backed out of the miniature car park and drove away, then, turning from the window, he bit the end off another cigar with slow and thoughtful deliberation. . . . . .

Peter found the Ford very easy to handle, and in reply to Lyman's questions, had explained the purpose of their trip before they passed Loch Feochan and came to the village of Kilninver. Lyman received the information stolidly, keeping his eyes on the road. The scenery did not interest him. Peter had not imagined it would. He would have been surprised if this stolid American had shown any æsthetic appreciation.

The road took them past Loch Seil, branching off a mile farther on towards the narrow stone bridge linking the island of Seil with the mainland.

"For your information, Dave," said Peter, "this is the only bridge across the Atlantic."

"Yeah?" muttered Lyman with scant interest. "It's kinda small, ain't it?"

"It's called Clachan Bridge, or sometimes Tigh-an-Truish."

"Tigh-an-Tru—" he scowled, boggling at the pronunciation. "Oh to hell with it. Seems they gotten adenoids in these parts."

"Inspired by your overwhelming interest," Peter rejoined dryly. "I should explain that Tigh-an-Truish means 'the house of the trousers'."

" Well what d'you know! It's a bridge, so they call it a house !"

" The name," said Peter with impish persistence, " really refers to that inn over there. It marks a famous spot in history."

" Oh yeah !"

" In less broad-minded days there was a time when Scotsmen were denied the privilege of wearing a kilt. The Seilmen defied the order, but were canny enough to change into trousers near this spot before crossing the bridge into ' Scotland '. Hence the name. Interesting don't you think? You should always try to improve your education, Dave."

" I get by," growled Lyman, glowering at him. " How far we gotta go now?"

" Only about two or three miles."

They continued along the road leading south-west across Seil, and five minutes later Peter swung the car west in the direction of Easdale. They were driving along the coast, where the broad sweep of the Atlantic embraced the distant islands of twisted rock veiled in bluish mist, when he pointed towards a solitary house away to their right. Built of unquarried stone, it was partly hidden by a belt of rowan and hazel trees.

" If my geography is correct, that must be the House of Cladda. Grant lived there under the name of Malcolm Gourlay."

" Until he heard Becket's broadcast maybe," muttered Lyman. " Then I guess he didn't lose much time making himself scarce."

" Correct," said Peter. " You've been hugging me so closely, Dave, I forgot you've still got to catch up on a few details. But they don't matter very much just now."

Lyman was staring at the gaunt house with much more interest than he had shown throughout the whole of the journey.

" You reckon it's worth while callin' there?"

" Hardly ! Since Grant left in a hurry, he's not likely to have come back. Try using your head, Dave. I'm told there's a hotel not far from Easdale—that's an island just off the coast. We'll park the car at the hotel and pursue our inquiries on foot. And, as we shall be lucky if we learn anything at all, we shall probably walk a long way."

A couple of hours later this prognostication had proved itself to be dishearteningly correct. Starting from a point about a mile north of Easdale they had worked their way steadily south along the coast, seeking out the multifarious inhabitants who possessed one or more small boats, and putting the same question again and again. Had they lost a boat two days before? None of them had, and most of them pointed out rather suspiciously that the police had been making similar inquiries. Eventually, Peter suggested a break. They trudged back to the hotel near Easdale for a meal, then resumed their inquiries, but without success.

" It's hardly likely that Grant would walk very far from the loch, where he ditched his car, before he took a boat," frowned Peter. " That is, if he did take a boat. It doesn't look very much like it. All we've discovered so far is that the sea was pretty choppy that night."

" And thet's a hell of a lot of use." He was mopping his heated brow with a capacious handkerchief. " But I ain't givin' up yet. We still gotta comb thet li'le island over there."

" You mean Easdale?"

" Yeah. Thet's where I'm goin' now," he added, fully establishing his reputation for dogged tenacity.

They found a boat, and since it seemed to be tied there for the convenience of anyone who wished to use it, rowed across the narrow strip of water. And they were surveying some of the small roofless cottages on the island—relics of a more prosperous age, when work on the slate beds was still a paying proposition—when a man wearing a blue jersey and waders came into view.

Peter stopped him as he approached, putting the question which was becoming monotonous by repetition. And again it transpired that the police, in this instance the constable on Easdale, had asked him the same thing. He knew Mr. Gourlay well, and added dourly that he might have disappeared but that: " He was na the man to rob a puir body of a boat."

" It was pretty rough that night, I believe?" Peter pursued conversationally, and the other cocked his head on one side.

" Och I wouldna say it was rough," he replied in the soft

Highland drawl to which they were becoming accustomed.
"There was a wee bit wind, but I hae seen it waur."

"So I suppose anyone could have rowed out to one of the
islands?"

"Aye. I canna think they'd hae onny deeficulty. Ma
laddie didna say it was sae bad."

"He was out that night?"

"Aye. At a party on yin o' the islands. The rascal didna
tie his boat up securely when he cam' back. It went adrift.
But what can ye expect from a laddie?"

"Boys will be boys," commiserated Peter, eyeing the man
keenly. "I hope you recovered it?"

The other shrugged.

"It's no' the first boat I've lost in that way. But, och, it
wasna worth much, whatever. Of sae leetle conseequence
I didna mention it to MacLeod."

MacLeod, as they had discovered earlier, was the constable
on Easdale. And he had not been told about this! Hardly
surprising, perhaps, since the loss of an old row-boat, carried
away by the tide, was considered to be a very ordinary
occurrence by the folk on this coast. But to Peter Gayleigh
it had definite news value. Grant could have taken that boat.
And if he had rowed out to one of the islands his task would
have been made easier since the tide was going out at the
time.

"I should imagine there's a very strong current in these
parts," he commented casually. "Could your boat have
drifted out to sea?"

"It's verra likely. The current would maybe tak' it past
Eilean Gorm, but we didna see onny sign o't next morning."

"Eilean Gorm?" frowned Peter.

"Aye, yon blue island." He extended a weather-beaten
hand towards a hump of twisted rock, wreathed in pale blue
mist, some four miles out to sea.

Though Lyman had said nothing, the significance of this
information was not lost on him. He glanced quickly at
Gayleigh, who deliberately avoided his eye. For a few
moments both of them stared silently at that distant island.
Then Peter dragged his eyes away, taking in the whole
panorama of the coast.

"You've got some grand scenery here," he observed, and

as he intended, this generality led to others. So that when they parted from the islander soon afterwards, he was still under the impression that he had told them nothing of any consequence.

Back on Seil they had no difficulty in hiring a small motor-boat, and while the tank was being filled with petrol and other preliminaries completed, Peter Gayleigh took the opportunity to return to the hotel nearby.

He phoned Miles Lawson.

CHAPTER TWELVE

IN WHICH THE SUN SETS AND JUSTICE IS DONE

I

Dusk was spreading over the placid sea, the crimson wash of the sun etching the islands in sharp relief. Soon they would be nothing more than stark silhouettes. But the sun was sinking slowly, and the bleak hulk of the rock that was Eilean Gorm was still clearly visible, superimposed on a backcloth of crimson. The sky to the east still retained some of its vivid blueness. The serenity was immense. Save for the chugging of the motor-boat there was an intense, brooding silence.

They had covered more than half the distance to the island, Lyman sitting hunched up in the stern while Peter attended to the controls. If Jervis Grant had come this way in a row-boat the journey must have taken him about an hour, even with the assistance of the tide. Gayleigh hoped to complete it in less than half that time. The sooner the better, for if Grant was on the island it was too much to hope that he wouldn't see them. Obviously he would keep a keen look-out towards the mainland, and it might be difficult to deal with him if he had time to make desperate preparations for their reception.

Eilean Gorm rose slowly to meet them. The motor-boat chugged on . . .

Soon the raised beach was visible, shelving up to the rock-girt fringe of a tiny, hidden valley, beyond which the rock soared again to hat-shaped cliffs. The island appeared to be about a quarter of a mile in length, but considerably less in width.

They reached the shore. There was no indication that any-one was watching them. A few gulls rose screeching, disturbed by the beaching of the boat. But if Jervis Grant was there, he had either not seen them, or was biding his time.

There was no need to discuss the next move, for their plan of action had already been decided. Gayleigh had suggested that they should proceed in opposite directions, circumscribing the whole island if necessary.

"Okay," muttered Lyman. "I'll be seeing you."

His hand was in the pocket of his jacket. His gun made a noticeable bulge. Gayleigh watched him as he began to pick his way with grim determination over the smaller rocks, then set off himself and with equal determination, his fingers wrapped about his own gun.

His conversation with Lawson was fresh in his mind. He knew full well what was expected of him, though the novelist hadn't actually put it into words. And he was going to do his utmost to bring it about. The debonair Peter Gayleigh was gone; his mouth was like iron as he climbed the shelving rock to gaze down into the valley beyond. He saw a half-completed hut, built in bee-hive fashion from pieces of slate, and the hastily extinguished remnants of a peat-fire. But the man he sought was not there. Perhaps Grant was peering at him from behind one of the rocks at that very moment, for Gayleigh had no doubt now that his quarry was on the island.

The discovery did not come as a surprise, and the thin smile that twisted his lips was as inscrutable as fate. All along he had felt that he had been guided to this island, that he was the instrument of destiny, a puppet with a duty to perform. It just had to be. Grant had an appointment with the hangman. But he was not going to keep that appointment if Gayleigh could prevent it. A bullet would ensure a much more satisfactory finish.

From where he was standing he could see Lyman nosing, like a hound on the scent, into every rocky opening large enough to afford concealment, and the smile still lingered on Peter Gayleigh's lips as he moved away along the uneven, rocky ground flanking the tiny valley.

Perhaps Lyman would find Grant first. The thought did not dismay him. On the contrary it tugged down the corners of his mouth into a gesture of supreme cynicism.

He had progressed less than a hundred yards, darting from rock to rock, and varying his direction slightly according to the cover available, when he found the row-boat. It had been hauled from the beach into a gulley, where it now lay invisible to anyone more than ten yards away. Beyond the gully was an out-thrust of solid rock, which looked as though it might yield something larger than the rudimentary caves he had seen from the beach. He began to climb down, and in his eagerness to satisfy his curiosity dislodged some small stones which went rattling down to the shore, shattering the intense silence. Gayleigh cursed softly, waited a few seconds, then as nothing happened, went on. He reached a broad ledge running under the out-thrust of rock, and saw immediately that his surmise had been correct. There was a cave, and the wide mouth suggested that it was a large one. He edged silently towards it, until he was in a position to peer cautiously inside. He saw someone move in the deep gloom. Then, since it had to be played this way, he forsook all caution, took his hand from the gun in his pocket, and stepped into the cave.

It was Jervis Grant who halted him, backed by a levelled automatic.

"Stay where you are, Gayleigh, or by heavens I'll finish you now!"

II

His voice had the huskiness of desperation. In the gloom, the barrel of his gun resembled the evil black head of a snake. Gayleigh stayed where he was. He knew when a man meant business, and he had no wish to be blasted into eternity.

He said : " What's the use, Jervis? You're all washed up. Why not call it a day?"

The other came slowly towards him. He saw that the strong face had shrunk. The jutting chin seemed to have become even more pronounced. Jervis Grant had aged ten years since he had left Pinewood. But every wrinkle welding itself into his hard, implacable expression, indicated that he was prepared to deal with this situation.

" Put up your hands."

Gayleigh obeyed. He had walked into this trap with his eyes open, although he had known that he was taking a gigantic risk, and an icy coldness clamped itself about his chest as the other relieved him of his gun. Grant thrust it away into his pocket, then stepped back out of reach.

"I daresay you're wondering why I haven't put a bullet through you already?"

Gayleigh shrugged. He thought he knew, for Grant must have seen two men in the motor-boat.

"Could it be for old time's sake?" he hazarded cynically. "But no, of course not. You never regarded me as anything more than a dangerous busybody who had to be propitiated. Twelve years of quiet laughter at my expense and Herrington's. How you must have enjoyed it!"

The man's tense, watchful expression did not change. Gayleigh went on bitingly: "The only fly in your lucrative ointment was Louie Palmer. The man you ratted on twelve years ago. Remember? It wasn't difficult—because you were a jewel-fence. You still are a jewel-fence, which accounts for the nice little nest egg you have in the name of Malcolm Gourlay. You thought it might come in very useful if things became a little too hot for that uprighteous, law-abiding business man, Jervis Grant."

Still the other made no comment, though the lines about the thin, merciless lips seemed to bite even deeper into the gaunt face.

"As a diamond-broker it was comparatively simple for you to dispose of the stones that came into your possession. It was a sweet racket, wasn't it, Grant! And your reputation as an honest citizen was so good you weren't afraid to squeal on Palmer when he became too dangerous, as, I suppose he must have done. You see, I haven't got all the facts, because we haven't got Palmer. But I'm much wiser than I was when I sympathised with you at Pinewood. You remember the look Palmer gave you when he left the dock? No wonder he was sore. You must have covered yourself so well that nobody would have believed him if he'd denounced you in Court. So he bided his time . . ."

"It's no use, Gayleigh," Grant snapped coldly. "You'll not talk yourself out of this. I always knew you were smart. But you won't be smart much longer."

"I'm not trying to talk myself out of it. In fact I'm asking for trouble. I know that, but it's worth it to get a few things off my chest. Up to a point, you fooled all of us. But the only man you fooled completely was Palmer. It now rests with Herrington. He knows everything. He'll get you in the end."

"He knows I'm here?"

Peter stared at him disdainfully.

"What do you think?"

"I think," he said steadily, "that you've worked on your own once too often, Gayleigh. This is the last time you'll interfere in my business." His voice took on a more peremptory note. "But don't imagine I'm blind. Two of you came here in the motor-boat. Who is the other man?"

"Suppose *you* tell *me*."

"He might be the islander from whom you hired the boat."

"Very possibly."

"In which case he will be unarmed. But, of course, your friend may not be the boatman. He may have a gun. Either way, he'll realise I'm here when I squeeze this trigger. Call him, Gayleigh."

Peter's eyebrows shot up.

"Did you say—call him?"

"I did. I'm going to get both of you. This way will give me an advantage. When he comes he won't be expecting a bullet."

"But aren't you afraid that . . .?"

" . . . you'll warn him?" He shook his head very slowly. "I saw him leave the boat, so there's no danger that he'll slip away from the island immediately, even if you try any tricks. If you do, this gun will go off. I shall be obliged to deal with him later."

"That would be a pity," drawled Peter. "All right, have it your own way."

He was given no opportunity to dart out of the cave. Grant watched him like a cat. But as he cupped his hands about his mouth he thought this was going to be good. Very good indeed. Lyman might be unprepared, but he had a gun—and looked like the kind of man who could hit a dime at twenty paces.

"Hul-lo" he called, his voice sounding inordinately loud in the silence broken only by the suspiration of the sea. "Hul-lo."

"Tell him where you are," snapped Grant.

Peter shouted again: "Ov-er here . . . There's a cave."

"That's enough. Now come back out of sight. And move to the right, unless you want to get my first bullet."

"You always were a good organiser," Peter conceded, as he obeyed. "While we're waiting perhaps you'd enlighten me a little. Was Merson working with Palmer?"

It was several seconds before he received a reply. Then Grant said curtly: "Yes."

"And Merson had the Van de Kramer diamonds, of course. Palmer had told him you were a fence. But when Merson called at Pinewood you didn't know he was associated with Palmer. Correct?"

There was no response, but the silence was answer enough.

"As I see it, Merson brought the diamonds to you. And you bought them, as you'd probably arranged to do before you left America. But you didn't realise that the sum you handed over was a mere fleabite—that Palmer was behind Merson, and that their idea was blackmail. All right. But what I don't understand is why Merson gave you that sword, since, obviously he didn't want you to kill yourself accidentally. That would have spoilt everything. Perhaps he told you it was poisoned. But even if he did, I still don't get it."

"Your thirst for knowledge is remarkable," Grant retorted acidly, his wary gaze darting to the mouth of the cave. "You haven't long to live, Gayleigh. But as your friend is keeping us waiting——. Merson hid the diamonds aboard *S.S. Cornelius* in a harmless replica of the sword. He brought the original to me, explaining its properties, since in the circumstances he thought I might be interested. That was what he said. Ostensibly his visit had nothing to do with Palmer. At the time I didn't know they were working together. And Merson knew I should see possibilities in that sword. He guessed I might like to keep it for a time."

"In other words it suggested a good way to get rid of Palmer if he came that close. Accidental death. Yes, you might have got away with it."

"I might. Merson didn't give me the sword. I asked him to lend it to me, just as he knew I should. But Palmer had no intention of calling. He knew all about the sword. That cunning rat Merson merely left it so that he could collect it later. It provided him with an excuse for a second visit."

"But in the meantime you got a private detective-agency to check up on him."

Grant nodded grimly.

"I'm a difficult man to deceive, Gayleigh. When he came again I was ready for him. As a matter of fact, I was completing my preparations when you rang. And as I couldn't put you off, as you were determined to call on me that night, I knew I had to work fast. Merson arrived less than half an hour before you did. He meant to put on the screw. He was going to explain, of course, that he'd come from Palmer, and that their racket was blackmail in a big way. He thought he was quite safe, since if I pulled out a gun, or did anything foolish I should still have Palmer to reckon with. Poor fool, he little knew!"

He paused for a few seconds, listening as he stared expectantly past Gayleigh.

"But I didn't let him get as far as that. When he arrived I waited just long enough to lock the front door behind him. Then, as he was standing in the hall, I shot him through the back of the head."

Peter made a grimace.

"How very, very brave," he said interestedly. "When did you complete this target practice? You shot part of his jaw away, I believe."

"Yes—I did that after you left."

"So the body was in the house when I called?"

The other inclined his head.

"In the cellar."

"It must have been rather cluttered up—what with the body, and the paraffin and petrol tins. It must have been a hell of a job picking your way to that bottle of whisky. Then, of course, you fixed the telephone, and wrote that note for me. That was after you'd decided I'd be of more use to you alive than dead. The story I told Herrington was just what you wanted him to know. But it's a pity you didn't make a more careful study of forensic medicine. If you had, you'd have known how difficult it is to char a body completely, and you wouldn't have . . ."

"Quiet!"

The interpolation was like the crack of a whip. Grant had heard the faint, the very faint sound of Lyman's approach, and because Gayleigh had heard it, too, he had gone on talking. If Lyman had heard those last few words he would guess what was in store for him.

There was absolute silence now, a silence pregnant with doom. And as the seconds passed, with the timelessness of eternity, Gayleigh knew that Lyman was waiting out there, calculating his chances, bracing himself to strike. Peter could do nothing to help him. The initiative rested entirely with the other two. He felt curiously detached, as though he had no part in this drama, but the thumping of his heart was like a hammer-beat.

The stillness stretched itself to a point at which it induced a physical ache. It was tearing at his nerves, as though it were a sub-human entity born of the waves and the rocks; an all pervading presence that could not be banished. It seemed that it would go on for ever.

Then, suddenly, several things happened almost at once. Lyman's gun appeared round the mouth of the cave. There was an ear-splitting explosion as Grant fired. Lyman's head and shoulders darted into view. Two further spurts of flame. Two reports like crashes of thunder. Then Jervis Grant toppled to the weathered rock, a bullet through his brain, and there was silence again, and a thin pall of smoke spreading the acrid smell of cordite.

Dave Lyman stepped into the cave. He stared at the dead man for quite a time.

"I shot him in self-defence," he said. "You saw that."

Gayleigh nodded grimly.

"I reckon we can't leave him 'ere. Maybe we'd better take him back with us."

"Maybe we had," said Peter.

Lyman thrust his gun away, and went towards the body. Grant's sightless eyes gazed up at him. He spat contemptuously. He bent down. He began to go through the dead man's pockets.

"That's my gun," Gayleigh told him as it came to light, and stepping forward gathered it into his grasp with an easy movement of his arm. "What are you looking for? The Van de Kramer diamonds?"

"Yeah. I figure he was carryin' 'em."

"I figure that, too," said Peter.

Lyman found them at last, after ripping the lining of the jacket. He scooped them avidly into his palm, then transferred them very carefully to his pocket. He was getting to his feet when he saw that Gayleigh's face had all the impassivity of carved granite, and that his eyes were like chips of ice. He saw more. The barrel of a gun was levelled very ominously only a few inches from his back.

"This is as far as we go, bud," said Peter Gayleigh. "You've had your fun. Now I'll have mine. I'm going to make the world a little cleaner. I feel the real Dave Lyman would have enjoyed this. But that's only one of the reasons why I'm going to kill you, Louie Palmer."

III

There was silence again. Neither of them moved. They might have been wax figures in a dramatic tableau. For a fraction of time it seemed as though some eccentric sculptor had set them there, far from the eyes of an audience, fifty feet above the desolate gloomy beach and sullen seas of Eilean Gorm.

The day was dying fast, and after those few moments of frozen inactivity the man whom Gayleigh had unmasked sought an alliance with the gloom. His hand streaked to his pocket, but by Peter Gayleigh's standards he was slow. The barrel of the gun smashed down on to his groping fingers, and as he lifted them like maimed claws, sucking in his breath, Gayleigh's other hand moved with lightning rapidity. When he stepped back he had Palmer's automatic. Very deliberately he tossed it out of the cave, waiting until he heard it strike the rocks below.

"That should prevent any further interruptions," he said equably. "I'm not going to ring down the curtain just yet. I'm in a reminiscent mood. And as minor details worry the hell out of me, I'm going to get a few things straight. You're going to help me, Palmer, because you'll live a little longer that way."

Silence again. The other was staring at him calculatingly. Then gradually his heavy face screwed itself into that earnest and baffled expression that Gayleigh knew so well.

"Say, what the hell's gotten into you?" he muttered aggrievedly. "You gone nuts?"

"You can stop acting, Palmer." His cold, merciless eyes contracted slightly. "What do you think I am—a dope? I'll admit I've given a pretty good imitation of one. But all that's over. You've given your last performance as Lyman. It's a bit late to stage a come-back."

"Aw now listen, bud, you're all off the beam. You've gotten . . ."

"You lost your public after you peered at me through the window of the Station Hotel in Oban," Gayleigh interrupted curtly. "That was an unfortunate move on your part, because the man I was with recognised you at once. Miles Lawson was in court when you were sent down for that last stretch at Sing Sing. And that, Palmer, was after the operation on your face. It's too bad, but it's just one of those things."

A gathering scowl was ousting the other's injured expression, as Gayleigh went on :

"He'd have recognised you before, of course, but, as it happened, you two had never come face to face after we left New York. Lawson was on *Cornelius,* but he kept to his stateroom, and although you saw his daughter on board, and after we landed, you didn't meet Lawson. I had a talk with him this afternoon, Palmer. We arranged this very neat finale."

"You worked it so's I'd get Grant?"

Peter shrugged. "I hoped you would, though it didn't matter much if he got you. In that case I should have shot Grant. You see, with both of you out of the way Grant's stepdaughter need never know what a scoundrel he was. Neither of you will come up for trial. The case will fizzle out. I'm very fond of Sona, and I think it will be much better for her this way, don't you?"

He spoke mildly, as though he were carrying on a very amiable conversation, but the look in his eyes suggested very forcibly that he was not.

Palmer's mouth twitched.

"You're not God Almighty. You can't get away with it."

"On this island I can," said Peter. "Think it over.

You've been out to get Grant for twelve years. And now you've got him. But during the gunfight he got you, too. How could he miss at such short range?"

"I'm still here, ain't I?"

"True. But not for long. You see the way it is. There'll be no one to disprove my story. I'm expecting Lawson at any moment, and he'll back it up. The world will be rid of a couple of blackguards, and everyone will be happy."

He felt no compunction at what he had to do, and he meant every word he said. When the time came he was going to kill Palmer. The thought was satisfying, for he was merely anticipating legal justice. Fate had given him the opportunity to end it this way.

"Now we'll get down to cases," he resumed firmly. "And I mean that literally. There was a cabin-trunk that Merson dumped overboard. You remember that, of course?"

Palmer scowled. "I dunno what you're talking about."

"I'm talking about the man you murdered. The real Dave Lyman was in that trunk. He must have been hot on your tail after you and Merson got away with the Van de Kramer diamonds. Whether you murdered him on the boat or not I don't know, but afterwards you had a brain-wave. You took his clothes, his papers, and his identity. And you and Merson were working together all along. I figure you planned the robbery, but as you were out on parole and had to watch your step, Merson carried it out. He'd make a very good waiter, and the Van de Kramers engaged quite a few that night."

"So what?" snarled Palmer.

"So you and Merson got on board with the diamonds. And after you'd disposed of Lyman it looked like a cinch. But the diamonds were just chicken-feed. With Merson's help, you saw how you could settle your score with Grant, and wring a fortune out of him. Yes, it was quite a smart set-up. I particularly like the way you fooled us with that scrap of paper, showing that Lyman was a representative of Lishman's Incorporated. You didn't drop it accidentally, of course, and you knew someone would find it. When Sona Boyd happened to be the one, you put on a great act, didn't you. That strengthened your position tremendously. Once we thought you were Dave Lyman you could keep pretty

close to Merson. More, you could enlist my help without
arousing my suspicions, and you could keep an eye on me.
Any private detective might have been expected to do just
that. I fancy Merson must have been a great trial to you.
He couldn't help being a small-time crook. If he hadn't
cheated me after that game of bridge, I should never have
got wise to all this. And I realise now why you hung about
outside Merson's cabin while I was searching it, just as I
realise why you didn't tip off the Customs when we docked.
You weren't the real Dave Lyman : someone might have
checked up on your authority. And, of course, it was you
who left that warning note on my mat."

"You gotten a good imagination ! I'm learnin' sump'n.
Keep on talking."

Peter smiled thinly.

"I thought you'd like me to do that. But the sands are
running out. Another couple of minutes, and you won't
be interested any more." He took a deep breath. "How
I misjudged you, Palmer ! I thought you were just another
flatfoot with a one track mind. You had to be close to
Merson, so you let me think you were trailing him, though
it never seemed to get you anywhere. I'll say it didn't !
You always managed to lose him at convenient times—
when he went to Pinewood, for instance. But you did
your very earnest best, didn't you, Louie. You tried so
hard !"

His voice dripped irony. He felt it was a pity he couldn't
see Palmer's expression, but the darkness was stealing about
them like a wraith. The bulky figure, only a few feet away,
was becoming indistinct, so that any slight movement might
pass unnoticed. Gayleigh realised this, that every passing
second fought for the man under sentence of death, but
the thought did not deter him. He had a little more to say,
and nothing was going to stop him, for, as always, he was
supremely sure of himself. It was a conceit for which he
had paid heavily, though no misfortune could eradicate it,
and as he collected his thoughts and went on, he did not
realise that the other was now crouching slightly.

"You did your best at the Four Hundred too. Your
appearance was beautifully timed. I had——"

And then he was gasping for breath, for Palmer had taken

a lightning step forward, kicking him full in the stomach. Almost at the same moment a powerful forearm swept his gun aside. Belatedly, he squeezed the trigger, but the bullet bit harmlessly into the wall of the cave. Then he was knocked backwards by the impact of the American's fist as it smashed under his jaw. The thought flashed through his mind that he deserved this. He had been a self-satisfied fool. He had taken far too much for granted.

Palmer hit him again, leaping upon him like a madman and bearing him down by sheer weight on to the rock near the mouth of the cave. Five seconds before he had been master of the situation. Now his head was reeling, his vision blurred, and he was struggling for his life, flattened to the rock by the immovable weight on top of him. Palmer had gripped the gun, attempting to wrench it from him, but dazed as he was he kept his fingers clasped about it like bands of steel. Then his knuckles were smashed down on to the rock. Stabs of agony darted up his arm, but he kept his grip. And now he had his left arm free. From the position in which he was placed, it would have been impossible to deliver a punch with any weight behind it, but he got the heel of his palm under the man's chin, and flexing magnificent shoulder muscles, tried to heave him sideways. The manœuvre wasn't very successful, but it gave him a moment's respite before Palmer struck the arm away. The gun was slipping from Gayleigh's numbed fingers. He knew he couldn't hold it much longer, and with a gigantic effort, he jerked his wrist beyond the mouth of the cave, opened his hand and let go. He heard the gun drop on to the rocks below, but by then it seemed certain that he would follow it. For Palmer's intention was only too clear. He was gradually forcing him over the edge of the cave, regardless of the blows which Peter jabbed into his ribs. They were rather feeble blows for the dead weight above him restricted the movement of his arm. He brought his legs up and tried to squirm round, but it was useless. His head was now hanging over the rock, and inch by inch his shoulders were being pushed after it. Palmer shifted his own weight with devilish calculation, heaving and bearing down again before Gayleigh could escape.

The end seemed inevitable. In the twilight he could see the rocks stretching up as though waiting to receive him. If he was not dashed to death at once he would be knocked unconscious, or crippled. It would be simple for Palmer to climb down to him and administer the *coup de grâce,* perhaps with Grant's gun. That gun was of no use to either of them at the moment, but if Palmer tried to get it, Peter felt he would have a chance. Not that Palmer was likely to do that. His quickness had given him the advantage. He didn't need that gun.

Gayleigh's shoulders were beyond the edge of the cave. Away in the distance, over a sea of grey velvet slashed with crimson and gold, he glimpsed a pinpoint of moving light. A small boat. Lawson would be in that boat with the police. But they would be too late. And Palmer would be waiting for them when they beached.

There was very little Gayleigh could do, though the increasing precariousness of his position enabled him to reach the other's face again with his left hand. He hit the heavy jaw twice with all his remaining strength, and as the man shifted slightly, jerking his head away like an angry bull, Peter drove his fist into the massive chest.

The result was astonishing. Palmer had given the impression that he could take a score of such blows with nothing more than a grunt of annoyance. But now he pressed a hand over his heart, and toppled sideways with a groan. Gayleigh squirmed free, drove home another couple of punches, then staggered to his feet. He tottered to the gun which Grant still held and almost fell on it. He wrenched it from the limp fingers and swung round, levelling it at the man who was lying in a cowering heap near the mouth of the cave.

"'Don't move, Palmer," he panted. " You've got about one minute more. And then, by heaven, I'm going to let you have it!" He paused, blinking the mist from his brain, and sucking in his breath. " I don't like being interrupted, bud. You're going to hear me out before the end."

Afterwards he realised that stubbornness prompted his words as he stood there, gasping, determined to have his own way. But he spoke coherently and with cold emphasis, and at the time it was sheer bliss, for he was conscious cf nothing but blind anger at the ease with which he had so nearly been thwarted.

"Too bad, Palmer. You almost pulled it off. Though not with the cunning you showed when you rescued me from that room in Soho. That was smart. Damned smart. Because you didn't show up until I had a gun—until it was obvious I was going to make use of it. But that would have meant shooting, an uproar on the premises. You didn't want that, of course. So you unlocked the door with your own key, and helped us to get clear of the place. But not entirely clear. Oh no! You'd organised that ambush in the cul-de-sac. That's why you left us so hurriedly. Not to return to the Four Hundred, but so that you could follow behind and join in the slaughter. Those gunmen were Winniger's hoodlums, which means he's a lot to answer for. Was he wise to your blackmailing racket too?"

There was no reply. All the fight seemed to have gone out of Palmer. He was crouching there quite motionless.

"Probably he wasn't. Maybe you hired his men for the occasion. Anyway, Winniger doesn't count very much. He's going to be lucky, because when I fix you there'll be nobody to give evidence against him. Now get ready, Palmer, here it comes."

He gripped the gun a little tighter, adjusting his aim slightly and with remorseless determination, and he was actually squeezing the trigger when he suddenly realised that Palmer had neither moved nor spoken during this indictment. And it was more than strange that he had made no attempt to get the gun himself.

Peter hesitated, frowning heavily as he moved forward a couple of paces. He paused warily, and held his breath. There was no sound of heavy breathing, no sound at all except the cry of gulls mingling with the gentle plashing of the waves. He reached for his torch and thumbed it on.

Louie Palmer's eyes were wide open. His face was an expressionless mask.

The light revealed something more. His jacket was unbuttoned, and the shirt covering the broad chest was stained with blood. Gayleigh bent over the corpse and examined the wound. He had been shot just above the heart. Which

accounted for his sudden collapse after that frantic exertion.
Jervis Grant had not missed, though for a time it had
seemed otherwise. Palmer had killed him, but Grant had
cheated him even at the end.

Peter Gayleigh straightened himself, and gazed towards
the tiny beacon coming to him across the sea. Then,
turning, he stared at both men, his eyes hard and cynical.

Two must die!

He didn't trouble to collect the diamonds. They could
wait. He stepped out of the cave, filled his lungs with the
pure air, and went slowly down to the beach. Standing
there waiting, his feet set firmly apart, he presented a
stalwart impressive figure in the sunset, now painting rain-
bow colours on a glass-like sea. But its splendour did not
impress him. His mind was full of more vital beauty.

He was thinking of Sona Boyd.

"I DON'T know where this leads," said Marcia. "But let's go this way."

She indicated a leafy path meandering round the hills above Oban, and neither of them realised that her words crystallised Peter Gayleigh's philosophy. They were thinking of more tangible things, for he was leaving very shortly, and she knew in her heart what that implied. But she was loath to admit it, and so, as they strolled up the winding path to a hill overlooking the bay and the long green slopes of Kerrara, she talked about things that didn't really matter.

"I'm glad you got the diamonds, Peter," she said presently. "But then I always knew you would. After the risk you took, you deserve the reward."

"Perhaps—I can think of other rewards."

She glanced at him quickly, then turned away so that he couldn't see the wistfulness in her eyes. After a few moments she said with valiant inconsequence : "Isn't the view marvellous from here?"

"Delightful." And he was still looking at her.

"That building over there, like an amphitheatre, is called 'McCaig's Folly'. I always think it seems to be wearing a crown."

Her profile was fascinating. Once he had thought her just another hero-worshipper. It was strange. She was much more than that. And some day she would meet a man . . .

"Do you?" he said, interrupting his own thoughts very abruptly. "You must have your father's imagination. He's got some very fine ideas."

"Yes—I know."

There was much that hadn't been explained to her, but the tone of her voice told him she wasn't concerned with these unimportant details.

"In future I shall read all his books," he continued with an attempt at lightness.

But it was no use. Her tense expression did not change. She continued to stare into the distance for some time before she turned round, lifting her eyes to his.

"It's got to be faced," she said. "I understand, Peter. But—but I've become rather fond of you."

And then she was in his arms, her lips seeking his desperately, despairingly. Other women must have experienced this desolation, this fierce reluctance to let him go. And there would be many others, as he strode onward fulfilling his fate, that quizzical smile on his lips, and recklessness in his very being.

"You'll come back?" she whispered. "You'll look me up in London?"

But as he nodded silently she knew that Destiny was laughing at them; that he would be swept on to further achievements in which she could have no part. She was studying him very intently. She wanted to remember every line in that strong face. Then, meeting his eyes again she smiled wryly.

"I'm sorry. It's just—that I'm damnably human. Must you go?"

He shrugged. There was nothing he could say.

"I shan't forget you, Peter. I've been a pretty good apprentice, haven't I."

"None better."

"My only fault was that I learned a little too quickly."

There was no answer to that either, and he knew she expected none.

Half an hour later he was on the train. He arrived in London next morning. He went to his flat, and told himself it was good to be back. It had been a great adventure. He had tucked in all the loose ends. And yet—and yet there was a thread which persisted in twining itself into the face of a girl with crisp blonde curls, deep blue eyes, and . . .

And he was Peter Gayleigh—all that name implied. He mustn't forget it. He sighed philosophically. He mixed himself a drink.

THE END

NOVELS BY WINSTON GRAHAM

WINSTON GRAHAM is such a vivid and brisk writer, and makes his characters so real and his backgrounds so effective, that it is always a delight to settle down to one of his novels, no matter what the theme. He is one of the few authors who bring a nice subtle touch into the treatment of plot and characters.

The House with the Stained Glass Windows

Into the Fog

The Riddle of John Rowe

Without Motive

The Dangerous Pawn

The Giant's Chair

Keys of Chance

Strangers Meeting

No Exit

Night Journey

My Turn Next

The Merciless Ladies

The Forgotten Story

Ross Poldark

WARD, LOCK & CO., LTD., LONDON AND MELBOURNE